About the author

The writer has been, at various times, a GP, a surgeon, a playwright, a professional actor, and a published novelist, as well as running a street theatre. This is a first and only foray into erotica, and that because the novel started off as a serious look into the 'who's exploiting whom?' in the world of the sex worker, and the erotica just crept in. Rather fun, really…

The Velvet Band

A. J. Mcqueen

The Velvet Band

Chimera

CHIMERA PAPERBACK

A CIP catalogue record for this title is
available from the British Library.

ISBN 978 1 90313 682 9

Chimera is an imprint of
Pegasus Elliot MacKenzie Publishers Ltd.
www.pegasuspublishers.com

First Published in 2021

Chimera
Sheraton House Castle Park
Cambridge England

Printed & Bound in Great Britain

Death is simply another form of life but experienced in
a different place.

Chapter One

Widowhood is not without its consolations. The untimely death of my second husband provoked an outpouring of emotion that took me by surprise. Not grief — how could it be? No, more relief, a sense of freedom, happiness at the legacy that Howard had left me, and an unfamiliar tingle of excitement that had its roots between my legs.

I opened the French windows and stood on the balcony to breathe in the salty morning air. Below me, carriages made their way along the promenade, and even occasionally, one of the new motor cars ostentatiously but noisily hooted at the strollers to get out of the way. Beyond, small waves lapped the Brighton sands like a thousand small tongues. Already, couples were strolling along the front, self-consciously fashionable in their long dresses and casual suits. The breeze played with a few loose tendrils of my hair, making me feel restless, and aroused. I had been through the prescribed period of respectable mourning; now it was time to embrace the greater world outside and taste the many pleasures it offered. This was all new to me. I had been in Brighton a few days only, merely time to unpack and have my seafront rooms arranged to my taste. I hadn't yet ventured out more than a few steps along the promenade.

I rang for my maid. Janet duly appeared.

"Mrs. Edwards?"

She was a trim little thing. I'd hired her when I moved to Brighton and out of that dreary London flat after Howard's death. I'd had to dismiss the equally dreary Mrs Pike who suspected the truth about my husband's accident. She couldn't prove anything, though. Nevertheless, I was thankful to leave the desiccated, bible-addicted, tight-mouthed old crone behind. Janet, a local girl, on the other hand, had been a find. Somewhere in her twenties, perfectly good at her job, and unfailingly polite, she nevertheless had a young confidence amounting to an unspoken challenge that I found fascinating. The perpetual half mocking smile on her wide, sensuous mouth seemed to challenge the world around her, and her violet eyes, for all their innocence, delivered a perpetual invitation. Black tresses framed her oval face. She was delicious.

"Choose me something to wear, would you, Janet?"

"You're already dressed, madam."

"I'm sick of this charade of widowhood. Time for a change. Pick me something." I paused. "Something… suitable."

Her smile widened a little, and I watched her as she rifled through the wardrobe, her neat figure expertly flicking through the clothes. Her black hair was braided and tightly coiled up on the back of her head. Idly, I wondered what it would look like unpinned and unbraided. She turned, a bottle-green dress in watered silk held aloft. She helped me out of the purple and black dress that had been my prison for the past year, her hands lingering a fraction too long as they touched the skin on my back and then peeled the dress off my breasts. I stepped out of the dress and she pulled on the fresh one. Her hands absently strayed over my breasts as she helped me into it. She led me over to the mirror when she had done.

The dress was in the latest fashion, and felt so much looser and freer than the stuffy garment I'd been wearing. Now that King Edward had taken the throne, fashion had changed. He was a well-known libertine, and the fashionable world was quick to design clothes that suited the new air of freedom that the new reign promised, although the suffocating corsets were even more constricting. The fashion emphasised all the attributes of our sex: narrow waist, prominent *derrière* and a forthright bust. Manners and class distinctions were as rigid as ever, but there was a frisson in the air. I looked at my reflection in the mirror. Fashionably full chested and narrow waisted, with an intricate mass of straw-coloured hair piled elaborately on my head, I was quite a beauty, even at thirty-three. I clasped my hands behind my head, pushing my breasts forward. Standing behind me, Janet placed a green velvet band around my neck, and then moved her hands on my hips, stroking them down onto my thighs then back onto my buttocks, pretending to smooth out the creases in the silky material. A shudder of pleasure passed through me and I felt an unaccustomed dampness in my undergarments.

"Where am I to go, Janet? What delights can this town offer a young widow?"

"Well, m'am, the promenade's right in front of you. That's where you go to be seen and show off, Then there's the pavilion. That's a beautiful building, and you should see inside! You never saw anything quite so grand."

I assured her that I probably had, being well acquainted with the delights of London.

"All right then, there's the Lanes, if you want to do some shopping. I love wandering round, not that I can afford anything there. No? Well, you might care to try the pleasure pier, it's one of the marvels of the age. And there's all manner of delights around and on the pier. Though you might find it a bit cheap for your tastes. Although..."

"Although...?"

"You might try the photographer opposite the entrance who..." Her voice trailed off and she gave a slight shrug. She knew, bless her.

I pulled on my white lace gloves, as Janet pinned a fashionable, wide-brimmed hat to crown my hair. A glance in the mirror, a nod of satisfaction, a little smile. I picked up my lace parasol.

I walked out of the door of this Georgian terrace, down the three steps, and onto the promenade. It was eleven o'clock on a warm cloudless day. I opened my parasol and walked the quarter mile towards the pier, taking pleasure in the stares of men who hadn't noticed the mourning widow before. A shuttlecock hit me on the hip. I startled, then saw a young man sporting a fine moustache and wearing a striped beach tunic vault over the railings between promenade and beach to retrieve it.

"I say, I'm most awfully sorry," he said, scooping it up. "Bit of a wild shot, eh?"

He had been in the water, and his costume was still wet, his manliness apparent. He knew this, but made no move to hide it, nor the fact that it was swelling as he faced me.

I tried not to look, but failed.

"No harm done. It's quite all right." I smiled. He leered at me, aware of the effect he was having. Too obvious, I thought, too obvious. I pursed my lips, shook my head and moved on, satisfied just knowing I could arouse a man in so short a time.

At the entrance to the pier, I stopped to lean on the railings and gaze out over the beach and the sea. So many people on the beach, each with their own stories and secrets, and out there, vast oceans of experience. I'd tried to live a closed and cosy life, and failed, twice. I'd grown bored so quickly as my husbands had performed their duties in the English style and with horror at any other sexual diversions I had attempted to devise. Sensing their inadequacy, their members wilted before my demands, forcing me to use my fingers night after night to satisfy myself, stirring my honeypot and tasting the sweet fluid that I conjured out of my hungry cunny. I would not be trapped like that again: there was an ocean of possibilities and experiences out there, and wanted to try them all. How empty a life where experience is hedged by convention!

The photographer's studio was easy to find among the stalls and shops that lined the front. It stood out from the other attractions. It was larger, for a start, but unlike the other gaslit and gaudy stalls vying for business, the studio seemed reticent, secretive almost. A wooden structure, painted black, with shuttered windows and it had a most curiously carved doorway. Black painted like the rest of the building, the doorframe was elaborately carved with intertwined snakes and crescent moons, although the door itself was painted dark blue with a single large eye painted in cream. Above the door was a painted sign, again, in blue and cream that read 'Peregrine Pollitt — Photographer'. Beside the door was a glass fronted case in which were pinned examples of his work: rather unremarkable pictures of depressingly formal family portraits and artificially posed portraits of ladies with parasols and forced smiles. The whole place seemed designed to deter, and I felt an urge to turn away and seek pleasure elsewhere. But Janet's knowing smile came to mind. I knocked on the door.

A small peephole in the centre of the painted eye slid open and a human eye peered out, swivelling upwards to look up at my face. The peephole shut, and the door swung open. Inside, it seemed as dark as pitch. Nevertheless, I walked in.

While my eyes became accustomed to the darkness, I smelt the musky incensed air. It was a surprisingly large room with an area against one wall with a large comfortable settee and a low table in front of it. The whole place was lined with black velvet drapes. The low gaslight revealed a dimly lit space with a large wooden camera mounted on a similarly robust mahogany tripod beyond this, and further beyond, a painted Arcadian backdrop, a white pillar with a luxuriant fern spilling down it, and a *chaise-longue* taking centre stage: the usual studio setting. A door led off to the right. But where was the photographer?

"Madam?" A voice came from the dark shadows behind the door; a figure appeared in front of me. Too short to be a normal man, too big to be a dwarf, he was a strange sight, and reminded me of that French artist: the one who painted those fashionable posters — monsieur Toulouse Lautrec, that was it. He sported a similar beard, and oiled-down hair, parted in the middle.

I assumed he cultivated the similarity. His lips were too full and his nose too sharp to call him good-looking. I half expected him to speak with a French accent; instead he spoke in the most cultured tones.

"Can I be of service?" he asked.

I was momentarily caught off guard. What had I come for? Not a photograph, certainly. I fear he sensed my hesitation, for he raised his eyebrows and smiled.

"A portrait perhaps? Or one of my framed prints of the sea front? Others? I have many highly artistic images."

"Oh?"

His glittering eyes with their green irises met mine and held my gaze. He was reading me like a book, I thought, feeling, for all my elaborate layers, naked under his gaze. The musky atmosphere and dim light lent the whole situation an air of unspoken danger.

"Come, see if there is anything of interest. Come."

He beckoned me to a small, stifling room which smelt of cigar smoke behind his studio backdrop. Framed sepia photographs of Brighton beach adorned the walls, which were lined with crimson velvet. I made some bland compliments about them, but again, he gave that all-knowing, half smile.

"I also have a fine collection of figure studies — artistic renditions of the human form, if madam pleases?"

"I have no small interest in aesthetics, and the human form in particular. May I see them?"

"With pleasure, madam"

Delicious! He wanted to show me some lewd photographs, and I wanted to see them. We understood each other, but still hid carnal desire under the wrappings of art. He unlocked and opened the top draw of a wooden cabinet, and brought out a sheaf of sepia prints.

The models, men and women, were tastefully draped in gauzy materials that hid the most coveted parts of their anatomy, but suggested much to the imaginative observer. He had posed his models in classical guises — nymphs and naiads, Hercules, Bacchus, Tarquin and Lucrecia. As I thumbed through them, I felt that exhilarating sense of being unchained once again.

"These are very beautiful," I told him, truthfully. "You have an eye for composition and beauty."

"Madam is most gracious. It is my profession and my talent. I observe," he replied, inclining his head slightly.

I was curious. "Where do you get your models from? An agency?" I asked.

"Pfff! I don't need agencies! People queue up to pose for me. As long as they can call it art, they are keen to reveal themselves to my camera. The social rules say we must behave with decorum and cover up our bodies to a ridiculous degree, when underneath there is still a bit of the savage in us all. In the confines of this room, the savage can escape. I ask them if they want to buy their photographs, but they say no; they are frightened that they would be discovered. They are just happy that they have released the savage, and that their secret is locked away in this cabinet. They go away happy."

This so accorded with my own feelings that my question came out unbidden. "Would you care to take such an image of me?"

His green eyes glistened in the dim light. "I would care to very much, madam. For my usual fee, of course. I have an hour tomorrow afternoon, if that would suit?"

It would.

"And what is the name?"

"Mrs Edwards, Mrs Cordelia Edwards," I replied.

"Ah, and your husband, would he be…?"

"My husband is dead, Mr Pollitt," I replied and added, "Sadly."

"I am sorry to hear that, Mrs Edwards."

I could almost hear him recalculate his fee: a well-to-do frustrated widow… We fixed upon a time, and I left to explore any diversions that the pier might offer. The sea breeze was a welcome relief from the heat of the day. The new pier was an impressive structure; the longest in Britain, I'd heard. Only nine years old, it was already amassing a collection of stalls and cheap entertainments. They were places that belied the glossy veneer of Edwardian society, exposing its tawdry side. It was where the classes met on equal terms.

After taking a light lunch, I wandered into the penny arcade, to be greatly engrossed by a few mutoscope machines. The flickering, faded images revealed no more than a bit of leg, titivating by suggestion rather than display, but they made me think of my photographic tryst the next day. How much would he ask me to reveal? How much did I want to reveal? Who would see the photographs? I had no doubt that Mr Pollitt made a very good living out of them, collecting a fee from the sitter and then selling them on, but where? There would be too many repercussions if he sold them locally. There were quite a few questions I wanted to ask the man: after all, one has a social position to maintain.

Except I didn't. I was newly arrived in this place, my slate was clean. I had cut off all but a few of my London contacts as, after my second husband's death, I was no longer welcome in most social circles. Giles had been the popular one: urbane, witty and cultured, he was the darling of so many *soirées,* while I never bothered to hide my boredom with the chattering company. Offstage, at home, he had been a spoilt brat, a womaniser, and a complete failure in bed, shocked into detumescence by my demands. I was well rid of him. Now I was free to become whoever I wanted to be. I was, as yet, unknown in this town, and for the time being relishing my anonymity.

As I sat on one of the benches looking out over the sea, I thought about the opportunities that afforded. Who did I want to be? To be truthful, I didn't know. A more than strict upbringing had made me into a creature who only knew what she didn't want, and that was most things. I had hated my puritanical father, who it seemed to me, could only communicate with me by beatings and fearful threats when he wasn't touching me between my legs and pushing his finger or swollen member painfully into my tight, dry quim. I hated my mother for her obsequious silence. She knew damn well what he was doing to me, but he was a man of God, and God moves in mysterious ways, doesn't he? My hate would later take on many forms: world weariness, sarcasm, *ennui*, ruthlessness, cunning… the list could stretch far longer. I belonged nowhere. My father had died some years ago, having had his genitals roughly hacked off in his own church after his throat had been cut. All the carefully rigged evidence pointed to my mother, who had hung for it.

But that was all in the past. Forget it: move on. I decided, as I had no idea of what I really wanted, and that I was in the fortunate position of being able to choose, that I would, paradoxically, let fate decide. The unconscious mind knows far more than our consciousness believes. Life is a series of choices. I would let my "heart", that is, my subconscious, rule my rational mind.

For merely a penny, one can animate so many ingenious models in the penny arcade. I watched 'The Launching of the Lifeboat' but then saw 'The Condemned Man'. I was fascinated: encased in the glass case was a skilfully built model of a prison frontage with a balcony. In front of this, a scaffold. Painted people looked out of windows. Inserting a penny caused a whirring of hidden machinery, then a doorway opened and a bound prisoner with a crudely painted horrified expression and hair standing on end glided onto the scaffold with a noose around his neck. A clergyman appeared with arm upraised in valedictory blessing as a tearful angel passed above the scene. A prison governor shot from a window with a flag, and a masked executioner pulled a lever. The prisoner dropped and swung from the rope until a coffin scooped him up and pulled him back through doors which opened to draw him to his mechanical rest while the other figures disappeared and the machinery stopped its whirring.

I pushed in another penny, and stared at the scene again, then another penny, and another. The grisly enactment mesmerised and excited me. Pressing myself against the machine, I pushed my hand down to my crotch and teased myself as I watched the unfolding execution yet again. I was aroused and needed relief.

I walked briskly back home, and was glad to reach the front door and enter my sitting room. I fanned myself, glad to be out of the heat. Janet put her head around the door.

"Would you like your afternoon tea now, Mrs Edwards?"

"Not now, Janet, I would prefer a rest first. It's such a hot day."

"Are you happy here, or would you rather retire to bed for an hour?"

"Bed, please. It has been an eventful day."

She escorted me to my bedroom, and undressed me with the same sensual dexterity with which she had dressed me earlier. The dress came off, then my chemise, my corset cover, my corset, petticoats, bustle, finally my camisole and drawers. I dismissed a proffered nightgown, protesting at the heat. and asked that she strip off the top layers of the bed, leaving only a sheet to cover my nakedness. I settled myself under the sheet, and Janet turned to go.

"No!" I heard myself crying out. "Don't go. Come and stroke my hair."

Janet smiled and sat down on the chair beside my bed with a hairbrush. I lay on my side, as she brushed gently. It fanned my already inflamed senses. Soon, she abandoned the brush and stroked my hair, then my cheeks, then my face. I rolled over onto my back. Still sitting on the chair, her hands moved to my neck, then my shoulders, while I made little sounds of pleasure. At last, her hands moved to my breasts and stroked them, lightly at first, then kneading them and teasing my erect nipples. I reached out and grasped her thigh, moving my hand upwards until it found her buttocks. She pulled away, but only to take off her pinafore, and peel her black dress over her head. Unlike her social superiors, she had no corsets or petticoats, just a camisole and drawers. She ran her hands over her body, cupping her beautiful breasts at me as she stood beside me, teasing me. I put my hand over my secret parts, feeling the wetness. Finally, she pulled back the sheet and straddled me. She unpinned her hair, letting it fall over my chest and swaying her head so that it stroked my breasts. I reached out to grasp one of her breasts under her camisole, but she pushed my hand away. Here, in my bed, she was the mistress, and I had become her servant. She pulled off the thin upper garment, and leant forward, so that her generous breasts brushed my face. I sucked and bit lightly on her nipples, while she reached behind and, pushing my hand aside, kneaded my quim, while all I could do was moan, then shout as I climbed through mounting degrees of ecstasy as her fingers pushed deep inside me. After the most intense orgasm I have ever known, I lay back panting. I tried to repay the compliment, but she just pushed her juice-soaked fingers into my mouth to let me let me suck them clean like a baby at the breast, before climbing off me and dressing herself again. She bent over, then kissed me on the lips like a mother would a child. I pulled her face towards me and returned her kiss with passion. She responded, and our tongues slithered around each other's until she pulled away, tucked me in like a baby, and left.

I'd never made love to another woman before. It was unbelievably good...

I fell asleep before I could relish the sensations or worry about what this meant for future relations with Janet. When I woke, it was dusk; I must have slept for hours. I rose and looked out of the window. The sunset was magnificent. Below me, a couple walked by. The man looked up to see my upper torso leaning out of the window and stared. His companion glanced and cuffed him round the head and walked on. I put on a dressing gown and wandered downstairs.

To tell you the truth, I was a little apprehensive about seeing Janet. Our glorious lovemaking had rather altered things. I entered the kitchen. Strange, I'd never been in there before. Janet was bent over the sink washing some pots, but turned round when she heard me. She grinned, wiped her hands on a towel, and walked up to me.

"You slept well. I've kept supper warm for you: a few nice morsels and some trimmings."

"Janet, I need to know... I mean, I'm not sure where..."

She responded by kissing me firmly on the lips, while her right hand darted inside the opening of my dressing gown and landed on my left buttock.

"Don't concern yourself. The way I see it is that you pay me my wages, so during the day, you are my mistress and I am your maid, and I'll be a good and polite one. But you want for companionship, so I'll be your companion when you want for one, and, in your bedroom, I'll be your mistress and you will be my slave, because that's how I like it and I think you like it. Happy with that?"

She said it so matter-of-factly. Yes, of course that was what I wanted! No, how dare she! I tore myself away just as her finger was heading for my anus. I walked out into the hall to think, confused and cross. I was her social superior, but what had I just decided? I was not going to fit into the social norms, I was a free spirit, yet here was my servant girl, dictating terms. But yet, hadn't I just answered my own objections…

I walked back into the kitchen.

"All right, I'm happy with that."

She kissed me on the cheek. "You won't regret it, I promise. Right, then, my pet, as it's getting dark, that's my time. Go and sit down at the dining table."

Almost like one of the figures in the penny arcade machines, I obeyed. The dining room was laid out to perfection. The polished walnut table was set with the usual silver cutlery and fine porcelain plates, but instead of my single place setting, there were two. The gaslights were unlit, but the room shone with a myriad of candles. A single rose lay on my side plate. Janet appeared, now dressed in a simple peignoir, and laid two plates of *consommé* before us.

We talked in the candlelight as she served up more delicious courses. We talked as old friends, although I'd known her barely a week. She was well read, and conversant in the arts, which we discussed at length. I thought of my husbands' rich friends, those boorish, ignorant men and women who could never raise their nose out of their balance sheets. As we approached the dessert course, a syllabub, I well remember, we were touching on how we'd both got to where we were, and were both relaxed by the food and a few bottles of fine Chablis.

My dressing gown had worked itself open, as had Janet's kimono. We both regarded the other's breasts, my head getting increasingly fuddled by the wine. Janet took a handful of syllabub from the crystal bowl and walked over to me, smearing it over her chest, then cupping her breasts, proffering them. Like an obedient dog, I slavishly licked the sweet concoction off her skin, feeling hopelessly aroused. Then I took a handful of the syllabub and spread it over my bushy privates. Janet knelt in front of me and licked it very slowly off, holding the lips of my tunnel of love wide apart. I was swooning with pleasure and soon reached a noisy climax.

We never reached the cheese course.

I woke up in my bed the next morning. The sun lit up the room and made rippling patterns on the wall. I lay there, half content and half anxious. Janet and I had been so uninhibited in our intimacy last night, I had no idea where our relationship stood. But she was true to her word.

"Madam?" She came into the room after I'd rung, dressed in her maid's uniform and the picture of formality.

"Janet, I don't know—"

"What will you wear today? I've prepared breakfast."

She dressed me in a rather showy dress of powder blue with white lace trimmings. There were none of yesterday's teasing touches. I was relieved and disappointed in equal measure. Having breakfasted, I retired to my room to read the newspapers and a rather tiresome novel that was failing to engage me. My thoughts kept straying to the afternoon's appointment with a mixture of anticipation mingled with doubt. Why was I subjecting myself to the camera's (and Mr Pollitt's) gaze? Idle titillation, I told myself, but I knew that to be wrong. The real reasons lay deeper, much deeper than that. My body was desirable, with the power to tempt men like the glittering lures on the fishing lines that dangled from the pier. I wanted control, not love.

At the appointed time, I knocked on Mr Pollitt's door. He ushered me in, complimenting me on my dress and appearance. I started talking, too quickly, about nothing, showing my nervousness. Mr Pollitt — "Call me Peregrine" — obviously used to this initial anxiety in his subjects, chatted nothings back in a low hypnotic tone which, though obviously practised, both soothed and excited at the same time.

He suggested a few preliminary images just as I was, fully dressed. He had removed the floral pedestal from the set and replaced it with a rather threadbare stuffed lion caught in full roar with a front paw raised aggressively, and showing its claws. I began to think that Peregrine might have a talent for reading his subjects. He took a few pictures, me standing with my hands clasped behind my back, thrusting my chest forward, then sitting in a demure pose, though with a hand up to my face, head tilted to one side and staring into the camera with a coquettish expression. After each exposure, he would remove the glass plate with a flourish, and place it in a black bag.

He suggested we try more poses, this time without the expensive photographic plates, as a practice for our more suggestive images. He allowed me free rein to pose, as he exclaimed "Pouff!" on each pretend exposure. I grew bolder in my poses, and more provocative, and he repeatedly cried "Yes, yes!" with each pose. I was emboldened, excited and ready.

Sensing this, he ushered me behind a screen to disrobe. I had already come with a few less layers than was usual. He had left a blanket-sized piece of muslin to drape myself in: it smelt of other women, a vaguely musky, fishy smell. I inhaled the scent then draped the flimsy material modestly over my beasts and pudenda. I walked onto the studio set. No nervousness now; I felt in control. I heard Peregrine's low whistle. He set about posing me, but I waved him away, confident about my powers to excite. We went through a series of dummy exposures until he emerged from under the dark cloth that covered his head.

"Mrs Edwards, may I say, you have a natural proclivity? I have been in this business for many years, and never come across a model with such a natural talent before. Unleash yourself, Mrs Edwards, pose!"

I saw the bulge of his erection in his pinstriped trousers. Astonishingly, it nearly reached his knees, and, stunted as he was, it was impressive. I was exciting him, and this spurred me on.

Poses and exposures followed, each getting a bit more provocative, while he would cry out instructions: "Tuck that arm in a little further!" and "Lift your leg a little more and pull the drape up just a little." I was enjoying myself immensely, aroused beyond measure, using the stuffed lion as a very suggestive prop. I longed to dispense with the muslin altogether, but, when I tried, he cried, "No! No! Not yet!" Eventually, after about twenty exposures, he announced himself satisfied with the results. Our one-hour appointment had stretched to two, but the results, I hoped, would be worth it. The poses, all too obviously, had satisfied Peregrine and for a moment I wondered if I should satisfy him in another way to relieve him of his all-too-obvious erection. But no, let him dangle on my bait. He could be the key to further excitements.

I dressed while he attended to his photographic plates, then emerged, the picture of a respectable Edwardian lady in a powder blue dress.

"I have captured some wonderful images!" he exclaimed. "Are you comfortable with today's session?"

I was pleased, very, but comfortable? No. My body was a fiery flush and my undergarments were damp with excitement. I was aroused beyond words. I was to return in two days to view the photographs, and flattered that he declared that there would be no fee on this occasion. We bade courteous goodbyes, and I walked briskly back to my house.

Janet opened the door, and smiled her knowing smile.

"Enjoyed your day then, madam?"

I was trembling, standing there in my own hallway. "You can leave out the 'madam' just now, Janet? We have an arrangement, do we not?

"An arrangement? Perhaps, perhaps not. You'd better ask me nicely." The little bitch ran her finger over the swell of my breasts, teasing me.

"Please, mistress, you know what I want," I murmured.

There had to be limits to our arrangement, and I was not going to be taken for a fool, but she was to be my mistress and so entitled to some roleplay, but get on with it, for God's sake! I was desperate. She held my hand, intertwining her fingers with mine and circling my palm with her thumb. She led me upstairs to my bedroom, then pushed me roughly onto my bed. I watched as she took off her apron and dress, her shift and then her underwear. She stood naked before me, and began to stroke her bushy slit as she cupped an inviting breast. As her circular strokes grew more intense, she moved towards me and offered her crotch to my waiting mouth. It was an order, not an offer. I pulled apart the petals of her rose flower, then sucked and licked voraciously at her juices, wanting my own release but savouring the scent of her, like a *sommelier* with a glass of vintage burgundy. She tasted of sweat, pomegranate and tin. My fingers burrowed into her and she gasped. I pushed a third finger inside her, then a fourth. Her wet slit opened like a ripe fruit. As my tongue worked on her clitoris and my fingers furrowed her tunnel, she gyrated and squealed. You might be playing my mistress, I thought, but this moment you're at my mercy. I withdrew my lips and fingers before she reached a climax, thinking to tease her and prolong her pleasure but she pushed me roughly backwards onto the bed and pinning my legs down with two strong arms, knelt above my prostrate face, pushing her vulva onto my tongue. I grasped her buttocks, kneading them with my fingers as I pulled them apart as I resumed my tongue's delving into her slit. Finally, she shuddered and screamed in her fierce orgasm. She rolled over and collapsed beside me, shuddering and panting, her body glistening with sweat. As she lay there, I ran my hand over the soaked sateen of my dress, and stood up, peeling off my damp garments and feeling unbelievably excited. I lay back on the bed, naked.

"My turn now."

She repaid my favours generously, pushing her fingers and tongue into every secret place they could find. Then it was my turn to shout out and spasm uncontrollably, and when the shaking stopped, she lay beside me like a lamb. We kissed each other tenderly holding each other close, until sleep came.

Janet stuck to our rules even when, feeling an urge, I would caress her breast while she was working away in the kitchen, she would calmly pull my hand away, and continue with her task. I had to respect that, although I was troubled that she could switch her passion on and off with such facility. What was she thinking? Did she harbour any genuine feelings towards me? Did I feel any great tenderness towards her? No, I had to admit, I didn't. I really didn't know her; we were just the receptacles for each other's lusts.

Our exertions should have been enough to satisfy me, but these last few days had woken a dormant monster. I strolled the seafront and I bathed, nodding politely at other strollers and bathers, but all the while covertly glancing and flirting with my eyes, my mind conjuring delicious little scenarios. I took my tedious book to read on the seats, but my mind was elsewhere.

Eventually, it was time for my appointment with Mr Pollitt. He greeted me enthusiastically.

"Ah, my dear Mrs Edwards! Come in, come in! I have been anticipating this moment all day." He sat me down, fussing and talking animatedly. He pushed a glass of wine into my hand, while he went into his back room, and produced a cardboard package, like a conjuror with a rabbit. He sat beside me as he undid the string around the parcel.

"You and I, Mrs Edwards, have surpassed ourselves. I hope very much you approve of them, for I may say with sincerity that these are my finest works, and all thanks to your natural attributes and my artistry. Behold!"

The pictures were rich sepia prints, each mounted on black card with a line of gold around the picture. They were superb. He handed them to me one by one, commenting on each, tracing a long finger over my curves like an artist's brush, pointing out the harmonies in the composition. They were extraordinarily erotic, the muslin revealing more than it hid.

"These are quite magnificent, Mr Pollitt."

"I'm so glad you agree. We have excelled ourselves, I think."

I asked the question that had been puzzling me while I was examining them. "WHAT happens to these prints now?"

"Ah, dear lady, anything you want! You can purchase one of them or all of them; the price is a guinea each. If you do not wish to keep them, my fee is five shillings and they are locked away safely or destroyed, as you wish. On the other hand…" He paused.

"Yes, Mr Pollittt?"

"On the other hand, I have clients who are keen collectors of the photographic arts. They would pay handsomely for exceptional images such as these."

"They pay *you* handsomely, you mean."

"No, Mrs Edwards, they pay *us*. I would pay you a generous proportion."

A warning bell sounded. "But I would be recognised, and…" The prospect of these being passed around would ruin any hope of social advancement.

"Ah, my dear Cordelia, have another glass of hock, and do not concern yourself with that. My clients are not local. They are mostly London gentlemen. *Connoisseurs*. Besides which — *voila!*" He handed me another duplicate image of the final pose. I gasped. The face was not mine.

"I am more of an artist than anyone realises. I can make tiny changes to the plates and your face is altered beyond your best friend's recognition."

This man was extraordinary. We sipped the wine in silence for a while. The close, perfumed air hung about us. The idea of rich and powerful men leering and lusting after my body with all its suggested promises was irresistible.

"I'll take this one" I said, "and this and… this. But I have no objections to your selling the altered pictures. The prospect has a certain appeal, I admit."

"Ah, delightful! My clients will be clamouring for these, I'm certain. Please take the ones you've selected with my compliments, and shall we say, a quarter share of the proceeds?"

"The money is not material, Mr Pollitt. It is the exercise of any talent for modelling I might have that gives me pleasure." That wasn't the entire truth. The money was a material factor. You see, Howard had left me with more than the gonorrhoea that had taken several courses of mercurials, to eradicate, I had also inherited his mountain of gambling debts, of which I had known nothing, which had all but eaten up his estate. In reality, I could scarcely afford this house, but one must keep up appearances.

"Then we understand one another, I think, my dear Cordelia." A small pause while he wrapped the photographs in thick brown paper and secured it with a length of narrow red ribbon. "I can offer you many more such chances for you to display your obvious talents."

"That would please me immensely, Mr Pollitt. I hope I may trust to your complete discretion. I am new to the town, and hope to cultivate the acquaintance of the right people."

"Not only can you trust my discretion, but I am in a position to introduce you to the cream of Brighton society. Please, write down your address. I will be in touch."

I held the package close to me as I stepped out into the dazzlingly bright dance of the sun and the sea. The sun was lower in the sky, but the day was still warm. Much of the beach crowd had drifted away to rest before changing for dinner. I could have lingered there, watching the remaining figures on the sand form an ever-changing pattern of long shadows. But I was aware that I had to get the pictures back into the house as quickly as I could. Besides, I wanted to show them to Janet.

Disappointingly, she didn't wish to look at them immediately, insisting that the pleasure was deferred until after dinner. We worked our way through oysters, a slice of terrine, some roast cod, good mutton, and a fine pink rhubarb tart. Janet was in an expansive mood, talking frankly about her family and their squabbles and her past. Her father was a sailor, she told me, and had spent long periods at sea, and eventually failed to return at all. They didn't know whether he was dead or living in a far-off port with another woman. Her mother had been a seamstress but had taken in lodgers to supplement the family's income, but realised that the greater the number of lodgers passing through, the greater her profit, until the 'lodgers' were taken in by the hour, and Janet was left to fend for herself and had chosen to move out into service. I was intrigued.

"So your mother is a lady of—"

"My ma's a prostitute, that's what you mean, and that's what she is. It's not that shocking, really. There's loads around here have had to turn to it. Know what I heard? That one percent of the British population, own seventy percent of the wealth. That's not very fair, is it? Then it's the rich that look horrified when they hear the word 'prostitute' and turn away, though the rich ain't averse to calling on their services when they want. I'd like to see how they got on if they were starving. See what happens to their morals then."

Janet was remarkable in so many ways. She was self-educated to a degree that put my expensive schooling to shame. I think that, like me, her passion was one born of anger. I knew that her bible was *Das Kapital*. It had occurred to me that I might represent the very classes she railed against so strongly, and I asked her as much. She screwed up her face as though she'd bitten into a lemon, and thought.

"I don't know. I hadn't thought about it like that. Of course I don't dislike you, I like you very much, you know I do, Cordelia. I take each person as I find them. There's a lot of my class I don't like one bit, and a lot of yours I do. It's not people, it's the system. It's all wrong. Don't suppose it'll ever change, though. Look at all the revolutions — you get rid of the rich then the new leaders get corrupted by power and they just become the rich. It'll take more than a revolution."

I decided to steer the conversation onto quieter waters.

"Have you got a young man? Are you walking out with anyone?"

"Nah, none I fancy round here. Besides," she added, "I haven't got the energy left over."

I imagined she was referring to more than her housekeeping duties.

"Talking of which," she said, "let's go upstairs and look at your pictures."

I went upstairs, while she disappeared into the kitchen. I was half undressed when she appeared, with two plump sticks of pink rhubarb and a wicked grin. As was our arrangement, I submitted to her instructions.

"Take off my dress. Now take off my camisole. No, slowly! Now kneel and take off my drawers."

Soon we were lying on our stomachs on my bed, both naked like two overexcited schoolgirls, giggling, for it was a warm night, and I unwrapped my pictures. One by one, I passed them to Janet, who gazed at them while her hand ran absently up and down my spine and buttocks. She was impressed and excited by them, I could see, her hand coming to rest between my legs, her fingers busy. I extricated myself and put the pictures on my dressing table. She reached beside her and grasped the rhubarb stems. We rolled back onto the bed together and clasped each other tightly, while her lips found my long nipples.

She was so inventive when it came to the rhubarb.

Afterwards, we lay on our backs, stroking each other's private parts. I smoked a cigarette, my eyes closed. Janet, drowsy and sated, stared up at the ceiling.

"Do you think we could do some pictures together?" she asked, apparently casually.

I opened my eyes and looked at her.

"Would you want to?"

"Why not? It would be a giggle. No one locally, need know. Might be some money in it, too."

The notion excited me, and I told her so. We moved under the sheets, I kissed her tenderly, and we slept.

The next few days were a little tedious. I relished my anonymity in some ways, but I was aware that I needed to form the right social connections. Money, I was finding, ultimately buys you little but boredom. I almost envied Janet her round of shopping, chatting, housework and cooking. It kept her busy, useful, engaged. I, on the other hand, had a prospect of aimless existence between Janet's bountiful meals. There would be breakfast: porridge, kippers and kedgeree with toast and boiled eggs. It would take an hour to get through and suffice before a three-course lunch, afternoon tea at three, with scones and jam, some dainty sandwiches and pastry fancies. Then a four-course dinner in the evening. In between, we were supposed to write letters, but who did I know?

Painting? Laughable. Read improving books? I really can't get past the first few pages of anything. Embroidery? I draw the line at that. I felt like some useless grub being force fed by nimble worker ants just to be used as food for their colony. My routine consisted of my strolls to the pier, and a shilling or two spent on the machines on the pier.

It was while I was watching the 'Condemned Prisoner' machine play out its grim scenario yet again that a voice behind me spoke.

"You're very fond of that, aren't you?"

I turned round. A young, smartly dressed man was standing behind me, his hands in his white trouser pockets. He sported a thin moustache and was very thin.

"One can't but help admire the ingenuity of these machines," I said, momentarily on the back foot.

"Obviously this one in particular," he replied. "Personally, I prefer 'The Haunted Mansion'. Far more going on. Have you seen it?"

"Yes, of course. Each to his own."

"Oh, absolutely. Tell you what, can I fritter away a few more pennies and buy you a cup of tea?"

"Why not? That would be nice, thank you." He was rather attractive, after all, and he was trying to pick me up.

So we sat at a table in the Crow's Nest Tea Rooms, and a pasty-faced waitress delivered our teas with a plate of fairy cakes without even glancing at us. Nicholas — that was his name, Nicholas Fairburn — had a ready wit, and between his gentle mocking of the other customers around us, fairly quickly drew my circumstances and history from me. I rather liked him. He was some years younger than I, with a nice lean body and a handsome, slightly angular face, which still radiated that idealistic optimism which so quickly vanishes as life is revealed to be more complex than the young can grasp. It transpired that he was a painter. I have no abilities as an artist, but I do take an interest in art, being particularly attracted to the new impressionist movement and the symbolists. There is something sensual about their sweeping, chaotic brushstrokes and the play of light they evoked. But Nicholas labelled himself rather confusingly as a post-pre-Raphaelite painter. His eyes flashed with passion, as he spoke of the transcendent nature of colour and the harmonies of form.

As he talked, I thought about having sex with him. It had been all too long since my field had been ploughed. Rhubarb might have its uses, but it was no substitute for an erect and willing phallus. I might pursue our relationship a little further.

We shook hands, and parted, after he'd told me that he was in the habit of frequenting the Pleasure Palace most days at two as a break from his work. I nodded, and smiled at him.

Returning home, Janet presented me with a white envelope, addressed to me. I took it upstairs and opened it. Good old Peregrine! He'd been as good as his word, for the letter contained an invitation to attend a musical recital at the home of Sir and Lady Padgett, and a brief message from Peregrine, which said, 'Don't worry, I shall be attending, too!' The invitation was for a week's time. I sat on the bed and smiled to myself. Things were beginning to look favourable.

I lay back on the bed and thought about Nicholas as the evening sun lit the room with a drowsy golden glow. I imagined him dressed in nothing but a painter's smock, his member swelling as he watched me undress, teasing him into a full erection. My hand strayed between my legs as I thought of taking his hard cock into my mouth and performing the act of fellatio on him. My hand burrowed through my clothes to my quim as I thought of his body over mine, pushing his rigid staff into me, and as my fingers worked up a creamy wetness, I neared my climax. I could almost feel the spasms of his ejaculation bringing about my own release as the delicious fluttering's of my vagina, like a trapped bird, spread through me until my whole body was convulsing with pleasure. I lay there in a delightful torpor until Janet called me to dinner.

The next day, after Janet had left my bed, I thought about what I should do today. The fine weather had turned cloudy, and the road was shiny after a night's rain. I determined on a visit to the art gallery. I would arm myself with a few names and opinions before I met Nicholas again. But I wouldn't see him today. Let him wait a little longer; let delay sharpen his appetite. I rang for Janet, and asked her to pick me a suitable dress. She pulled out the purple sateen thing I'd bought on an impulse. Its lace frills scraped the ground and its high, boned collar nearly choked me. The wide, constricting belt dug into my waist. I argued with her, but she was adamant; if I wanted to be noticed at the art gallery, this was the right dress. The colour was sensuous, but the cut was forbidding, implying academic leanings. I could only agree with her, but resolved to take her with me the next day to buy some new dresses, if this provincial town could supply any as good as my London creations.

I had to loosen the wretched collar to eat the boiled pork and sausages she'd prepared. I finished off with some tasty pastries, before letting her button it up again. Although it was only a few hundred yards away, I felt it would not be right to visit on foot. Janet secured a cab, which was just as well, for the rain had set in again.

The art gallery was next to the pavilion, and I had to marvel at its extravagant architecture. London buildings are built to impress with their *gravitas,* the pavilion was built to be a monument to frivolity. I would explore it soon. Perhaps Nicolas would escort me: we would talk of style and decadence. We would talk of the free rein of the senses, then retire to my rooms, where the conversation would stop as our own decadence overcame us.

The gallery was not what I was used to in London. The art was worthy, but dull, dull, dull. The few other visitors were as uninspiring. I felt ridiculously overdressed, and I would tell Janet so. Then, entering another room, my eye was immediately drawn to a canvas. It was not overly large, and on the face of it, was simply a portrait of a woman in a red hat. Her eyes though! They were knowing, sensual and drew you towards her. The pose was subtly suggestive: she seemed to mirror my own sexual longings. I stared fascinated, and was irritated by the appearance of a well-dressed elderly lady who entered the room with a younger companion, an equally well attired, attractive woman of around thirty years. The elder talked in the loud tones of someone who was used to being heard and obeyed as she commented on the paintings. We nodded stiffly to each other and, my concentration broken, I left the gallery.

After lunch, my resolved weakened and I decided to stroll to the pier to meet Nicholas. I changed into a more alluring dress. As I passed Peregrine's studio, the thought occurred to me that I might indicate a willingness to model for the young artist, and a number of suggestive poses ran through my mind. I could become his Lizzy Siddal! While I waited among the amusement machines my mind idly sketched a vision. He would be dressed in his smock and tight trousers, glancing at me as I lay reclined on a couch, draped in thin silk, my legs slightly apart and one breast exposed. He would hurl his brush across the room, completely inflamed with lust. Then, kneeling beside me, he would suck at my breasts, rolling my erect nipples between his fingers and teasing my luxuriant bush before my hand guided his head down to the swollen lips between my legs…

It was half past two. He hadn't appeared. I felt a flush of annoyance as I roughly jabbed a penny into 'The Condemned Prisoner' and frowned as the grisly scene played out once again. I took a cup of tea in the tea rooms and went home.

Janet was working in the kitchen, preparing our evening meal. I seized her wrist and dragged her upstairs to my bedroom. It was breaking our rule, she protested, but I told her I needed her that very moment. She looked at me, gave me a little smile, then pushed me back on the bed. I watched as she undressed then lay back as she straddled me. She understood what I needed and treated me accordingly, roughly removing my clothes, slapping me and nipping me with her teeth. We bucked and thrashed, spat and clawed our way to a simultaneous orgasm, her fingers inside me and mine inside her.

We dined rather later than usual, dressed in nothing but our peignoirs. Our exertions had melted my frustration, and I watched her as she ate, her robe gaping open to reveal the sway of her full breasts. We slept separately that night; I was quite exhausted.

Janet took me shopping the next day in order to find something suitable for the Padgetts' *soirée*. First, we decided to call on Peregrine, if he was free, to find out a little about them. Were they ostentatious or plain? Young or old? Frivolous or serious? We knocked at his door. The peephole opened, then shut, and he opened the door a fraction.

"Five minutes," he whispered. "Just give me five minutes." We waited at a distance, and a few minutes passed, when an elderly man walked out with a large parcel. Peregrine saw him off, then waved to us to enter.

As Janet looked around in awe, I saw Peregrine looking hungrily at her, a glint in his eye. I could tell what he was thinking. He greeted me as an old friend, and I stooped to receive a kiss on both cheeks in the French style. I introduced him to Janet; he took her hand and kissed the back of it, like a courtier would a queen, and she gave a small giggle and winked at me. He had charm, I must say. We told him the nature of our visit, and he laughed.

"Be as frivolous as you may, my dear Cordelia! Would I lead you into dull company? Sir Philip and Lady Margaret are not young in years, but they are both as bright as buttons, and hold rather progressive views. You will find they hold wit and intelligence above titles and privilege. I would say wear something bright. Nothing too *outré,* mind you; not on your first introduction. Not that you will find much of that in the shops around here, but I'm sure your charming maid knows the right establishments."

We thanked him, and left. As we stepped out of the darkness, he beckoned me back. "If you're free, come and see me tomorrow morning. I have some good news." I opened my mouth to ask what it might be, but he put a finger to his lips. "Tomorrow…"

Janet led me into the Lanes, the old heart of the town, and a warren of expensive emporia. We treated ourselves to a coffee at one of the many mahogany-panelled establishments, served by obsequious waiters with oiled hair and long aprons. Janet had borrowed one of my dresses; we looked like two friends — it would hardly be proper for me to be seen with a servant. Janet fell into the role very naturally. We clung on to each other's arms, giggling like the best of companions, as I suppose we were. Ours was not the usual relationship, and that was the way I liked it.

We scoured the shops, and I was pleasantly surprised by the quality of the fashion on offer. Although I was starting to have a few anxieties about my financial situation, I was only too aware of the importance of presenting oneself as best one may, and prices here compared very favourably with London's. I have no idea how many dresses I tried on. Each time, Janet would join me in the dressing room, stealing kisses and running her hands over my body at every opportunity. I ended up with three new dresses: two evening gowns which at least allowed a show of shoulders and a hint of cleavage, and a gorgeous day dress, which although it covered me up to the neck, as was required, at least did so with the upper panels in chiffon, showing the skin beneath.

I bought us a substantial lunch in an extravagant restaurant. It was rather amusing to watch Janet's reactions: she had obviously never dined like this before. Her delight pleased me, in fact, in retrospect, that day was the happiest of all the days that were to follow. We drank a bottle of Chateauneuf du Pape with the beef, then another, and a Sauterne to accompany the rich trifle we indulged in for dessert.

I had planned to visit the pier that afternoon in case Nicholas should be there, but we had drunk too much, and anyway, it was too late. We walked home with my purchases, and, as soon as we reached the hallway and we had shut the front door, Janet pinned me to the wall and kissed me passionately, rubbing her body against mine. We went upstairs, and Janet hung up my purchases, and took off her borrowed clothes as provocatively as she could. She was a little unsteady from the wine, which spoilt the effect a little, but I, too was slightly tipsy, and struggled to remove my clothes. We tumbled naked into bed, fumbling clumsily at each other before we both fell asleep in the warmth of the afternoon.

Chapter Two

Next morning, I called on Peregrine as he had asked. He chatted about this and that while he made a pot of tea. As we sat side by side and drank, I asked him what his good news was.

"Ah! Of course, dear Cordelia. I talk too much, I'm afraid. Too much time working here alone. My thoughts all pile up, then come out in a load of senseless chatter. I merely wanted to tell you that our images have been received with enthusiasm. Already we have ample payment for our efforts."

He handed me an envelope. There were ten pounds in it.

"There will be more to come. Much more. You have something about you that feeds their fantasies, and that is the business we are in. It is a pleasant notion, is it not? My clients are rich and powerful men, yet you and I are more powerful still, are we not? We have power over them, feeding their lusts as we do."

I agreed. He had hit the nail on the head. Having the power to arouse men, to toy with their desires, to get into their minds and control them, that was my ultimate satisfaction.

"I have discovered a great demand for similar artwork." He leaned a little closer to me and lowered his voice. "But a little more specialist, a little more unusual. Perhaps — but no, it is unfair of me to even suggest it."

"Peregrine, if these things are done anonymously, then what harm can be done? I like the thought of driving big men mad."

"Which you do with great facility, my dear."

"Do I, Peregrine? All men?"

"Oh yes."

"Including you?"

"Especially me. Remember, I am a connoisseur in such matters."

I laid my hand on his leg, and leant closer. I was excited by the prospect of posing for some truly intimate photographs. He ran his hand over the swell of my breast, his eyes fixing me like a snake. We kissed long and hard, our hands exploring each other's bodies. My hand found his astonishing erection. We pulled apart and undressed. He was short, yes, but stockily built and muscular, and his huge phallus reached most of the way to his knees. Or it would have, had it not risen, extending rigidly out in front of him as he watched me squeeze my breasts and push my pelvis towards him. I stroked his member, then clasped it and led him to the *chaise longue*. I sat on it while he stood in front of me. I took his erection in my mouth, or as much of it as I could. I spat on his shaft and milked the drops of precum into my mouth. I cupped his sack, massaging his balls, while he teased my breasts lightly and expertly.

After a while, he withdrew and dropped to his knees. I parted my legs for him and sat back, my fingers pulling my lips apart, offering him my pink honeypot. He pushed his head between my thighs as his tongue flicked over my little button of pleasure and thrust itself inside me. I could hear myself moaning with delight as he lapped my juices. He teased me, pulling back and kissing my white thighs when I was nearing a climax, then working me up again. Eventually, he lay on his back on the floor, his erection like the leaning tower of Pisa. He stroked it as I straddled him, then lowered myself onto him, letting my quim slide up and down his shaft, lubricating it with my copious juices. I raised myself a little, grasping him, then lowering myself onto him. We both gasped as he entered me, each thrust taking him deeper until I had managed to accommodate his full length. The slow strokes grew faster, and my breasts swayed wildly as I leant over him. All too soon I climaxed with great shudders, panting, collapsing so that my hair brushed his face. But he wasn't spent yet. He took one of my breasts in his hand and guided the nipple to his mouth, teasing it, while he started to move slowly inside me again. Aroused again, I helped him by raising and lowering myself on him, and soon, as I felt the waves of orgasm wash over me again, I felt his prick start to spasm as he grunted with one ejaculation after another. We lay together, sticky with sweat until, at last, I raised myself off him, his sperm dripping out of me onto his belly. I reached down and gathered some of our mingled juices onto my fingers, and licked it up.

After we had tidied ourselves up and dressed, we took tea.

"Thank you," I told him. "I haven't been with a man for some time."

"A waste," he replied. "There are few that can make love with such expertise."

"Oh, I have many more things I can show you. I have a very fertile imagination."

He lifted his index finger to interrupt me.

"Believe me, I would like nothing better, but it must be this once, and no more."

"Peregrine! How can you say that?"

"Not for any lack of desire, I assure you, but remember our task. I am the artist, and you are my model. We will do our best work when we are lusting after each other. To make love once just serves to inflame that lust. Repetition dulls the edge."

"You disappoint me, Peregrine. Members like yours are very rare."

"And bodies like yours are even rarer, my dear. It is very hard for me to deny myself the pleasures it can afford, but tell me you understand. It is not for lack of desire, believe me, but because that desire needs to be honed to the point of pain, like a surgeon's scalpel."

"Dear Peregrine, I believe I do. Of course, we must be professional about this. There may be some money at stake, I think?"

"Some? Cordelia, I do not wish to entangle you in my business interests, but there is more to our joint venture than you can dream of. We can both become very rich, and you can indulge your natural proclivities at the same time."

"You talk of powerful men as your clients. May I ask who?"

"No, you may not," he said with a smile. "The whole enterprise depends on utter discretion. I am the only one who knows who they are, and they know that. I am trusted not to reveal anything. Nor will I, but I will just say it's a very extensive and exalted list. You wouldn't even believe me if I told you."

I had to be satisfied with this. We arranged another posing session for a few days' time. The day before the *soirée,* in fact. I left him with a small kiss on his cheek and a feeling of both exhilaration after the sexual act, and anticipation of progressing our artistic ventures further. I would visit the pier that afternoon, I decided.

To Janet's ill-concealed annoyance, I only picked at my lunch. I was in a hurry to get to the pier to see if Nicholas might be there. I mollified her by asking her to save it, and we would share it that night, so she might be spared cooking anything else and take the afternoon off. That cheered her up. She tentatively asked my if she might borrow one of my day dresses to walk out in. I agreed readily, anxious to mollify her. She hugged me and kissed me.

I was a little late getting to the pier, but felt a little *frisson* when I saw Nicholas leaning over the pier railings staring at the sea. I walked up behind him.

"Hello, Mr Fairburn."

He spun round, then smiled and gave a small bow. "Mrs Edwards! I hoped I'd see you here. How are you?"

"I'm well, thank you. Shall we take tea? My turn to pay, I think."

To tell the truth, I was rather missing lunch, and feeling hungry. We found a quiet table, and I ordered two special afternoon teas. They arrived on a doilied three-tiered cake stand. He was an artist: he was bound to be hungry. I certainly was. I helped myself to a salmon and cucumber sandwich, and one of fish paste. I gestured for him to help himself. He took one. After a few of the usual conversational niceties, I spoke with my mouth full of an egg mayonnaise sandwich, a few strands of watercress poking out of my mouth.

"Now, Nicholas, I want to hear all about your art. Now, looking at you, I would say you were one for the *art nouveau* style, something sensuous, yes?"

"Well, not really," he replied. "That's what I wanted to talk to you about. You looked like the sort of lady that would understand what I'm about. Forgive me, but you are a lover of fine art, I think?"

I swallowed the egg mayonnaise and lined up another. "I would say so, yes."

"And I would go further and suggest that you have a visceral, emotional response to art."

Cleverly put, I thought.

"You are very perceptive, Nicholas. Or may I call you Nick?"

"I prefer Nicholas. You see, I've been very much affected by the pre-Raphaelites. They got so close to the Universal Truth, don't you think?"

He was still toying with his first sandwich. I finished the last two.

"They've certainly had something. Is there such a thing as Universal Truth?"

"Oh yes! And I believe I have seen it! They came so close, but I believe I have taken their art a step closer to the divine."

I put my hand on his arm. "How exciting, Nicholas. I'm dying to see some of your work. Do you have a studio?"

"Oh yes. It's not far, in White Street. I would be honoured to show you my work one day. There are so few round here that understand my work. But I saw some of that divine light in your eyes. That's why I had to speak to you."

"How very flattering. But why delay? I've nothing pressing today; why don't we go and have a look at them now?"

"Would you? I should be so pleased."

"Let me just finish the *petit-fours*. Want one?"

"No, thanks."

We walked to his studio, about half a mile away. He walked with rapid strides and I struggled to keep up with him. We entered a rather run-down brick house, with a small front garden overrun with weeds. A drab, draughty hallway led to a dark flight of stairs. We climbed to a door leading to an attic room; I was out of breath but curious to see an artist's studio and excited by what might ensue. The room was a shock: dirty and smelling overpoweringly of stale sweat, it contained a bed, a table, a chair and a small cooking ring. I couldn't take in much else, it was so crowded and chaotic. I felt nauseated and wanted to run away, but I wanted to see his paintings first. He flung aside a pile of crumpled clothes revealing a number of canvasses propped against the wall. He was talking rapidly and incoherently about God and punishment. He was scaring me.

He pulled out a canvas and propped it up on a broken easel. It was, well, appalling: a mess of muddy browns which suggested a cross.

"It's very striking," was the best I could say. He hauled that one off, and replaced it with another. It was virtually identical. So were they all. The man was plainly mad. I glanced toward the door; I had to escape. He was standing in front of the last canvas.

"Behold, the doorway to the divine! I have captured what others never have. The purity of suffering, the glittering pathway of pain which leads us to the ultimate being. To see these works is to know suffering."

I had to agree with him on that. He had flung his jacket into a corner, and was taking of his shirt. He turned and stood before me, stripped to the waist. His skinny torso was covered in livid stripes.

"I must go," I said, my voice shaking. "Thank you, for showing them to me." I turned to the door, but he grabbed my wrist and I saw that he was clutching a short whip with leather thongs.

"No!" he shouted. "You must help me towards the light!"

"I can't. Please stop this. I must go—"

But he turned the key in the lock and grasped it tightly in his fist. I couldn't escape. There was nothing for it... He thrust the whip into my hand, quickly removed his trousers and laid on his back on the bed, naked. I brought the whip down onto his chest as gently as I could.

"No, harder! Hurt me!" He cried. I hit him harder. He urged me on, and, teeth clenched, I whipped him hard, then harder still. His penis became erect as I worked on him, and he squealed with the pain. I realised that I was enjoying this, revelling in his whimpering as I shouted insults and profanities at him. At last, with a drawn-out cry, he ejaculated, his prick twitching as it spat out the semen. His whole body went limp as he curled up, crying like a baby. I prised open his fist, took the key, threw the whip at him and escaped. I walked quickly down the street with a curious mixture of revulsion and exhilaration swirling inside my head.

That evening, Janet and I dined on the heated remains of lunch. She was still wearing the dress I'd lent her that afternoon. She looked rather desirable in it, I must say, the orange material almost glowed in the sunset light. I told her about my adventures that afternoon, but not about the episode with Peregrine, which was best left unspoken. As I recounted the tale, she looked astonished, putting her hand to her mouth, then smiled and giggled. That set me off, and we ended up laughing out loud as we drank the wine. Janet stood up, came over to me, lifted her dress and straddled me. She gave me a little kiss on the lips, then stroked my cheek, with a quiet smile on her face.

I avoided the pier for the next few days. I really didn't want to see that awful man again, although I supposed he'd be avoiding it too. Instead, as the weather had turned warm again, I spent most of the days on the beach with a book. I politely discouraged any social advances and just allowed myself to daydream, closing my eyes and letting the voices around me drift into a pleasant blur.

When the morning came for my posing session with Peregrine, I dressed in the minimum of undergarments, hoping people on the promenade would not notice my rather deflated silhouette. I hurried along to the studio. Peregrine was the epitome of politeness, giving no sign or reference to our coupling a few days previously. He poured me a small glass of port, presumably meant to embolden me, although I needed no such stimulus. He asked if I was still happy to undertake "the more advanced poses", as he put it. I was more than ready, so he bade me undress. I noticed the *chaise-longue* had been replaced by a day bed, covered in a richly embroidered Indian fabric. The backdrop had been replaced by another well-executed one showing a rather indistinct orgy, with shadowy couples locked together. To each side of the setting, were bulky metal contraptions which Peregrine explained were the very latest in studio electric lighting. He would have to use flash lighting for the main light, as he had in our previous session. He warned me as I disrobed behind the screen (which struck me as ironic) that he would be rather closer this time, and warned me not to breathe in the fumes from it. He busied himself with his camera and switched on the electric lighting. I sat on the bed, naked, waiting.

Peregrine stood in front of me, head on one side, looking at me thoughtfully. Then he nodded and told me to kneel on the bed, my feet under my buttocks and my legs slightly apart. One hand he placed behind my neck, the other playing with the opposite nipple. As he scuttled behind the camera I looked into the lens with an expression of desire. I imagined a tall muscular man, naked and ready, walking towards me… The flashlight went off, momentarily blinding me and I felt the sting as some of the hot powder sparks hit my skin.

"Good, good!" cried Peregrine. "Now hands and knees facing me, please. Let your breasts hang down. No, don't sway them, they must be absolutely still for the exposure."

Exposure. What an appropriate word, I thought. The poses became more intimate, each time Peregrine coming forward and making tiny, fussy adjustments to my pose. I thrust out my breasts towards to my imaginary lover; I opened my legs for him, I thrust my buttocks towards him, I cupped my breasts for him. I pushed my fingers deep into my moist honeypot to excite us both. Peregrine moved closer until the final shots showed my private parts in close up, my fingers holding the inner petals wide apart. The sparks from this last shot were painfully hot, and I couldn't help but breathe in the horrid fumes.

We were done for the day. Our session had tired us both. I dressed as Peregrine wrapped his plates in his darkroom. We shared a bottle of wine as Peregrine expressed himself highly pleased with our day's work as we sat there like polite social friends. How quickly an experience gets wrapped up and put in our treasure box of memories! Our strenuous lovemaking and this photographic session were already something in the past, as we talked like old acquaintances. I suppose the same holds true for my relationship with Janet: we were able to put our daytime relationship in another box from the wildly different roles we assumed as the sun set. Both equally real, both so natural.

Peregrine was talking in confident terms of our arrangement. The images were unprecedented, he said. Yes, he assured me, my facial features would be retouched to preserve my anonymity, except my eyes, of course. It was my genius to entice whoever saw the images with my eyes.

"I could get any number of attractive whores in this town, and have done, but I cannot get them to express anything except boredom and detachment. But you, my dear, flatter them with your eyes. Our circle of clients is expanding in a very satisfying manner."

A thought struck me. "But where could we go from here? One cannot conceive of anything beyond what we have accomplished today."

"Ah, but I can! The human form is capable of an infinite number of poses, and a subtle seduction is often more erotic than the merely anatomical. Besides which…"

He paused, for once waiting for the right words to come.

"Besides which…?" I queried.

"I was intrigued by your maid. Janet, isn't it? You seemed more intimate with each other than your respective stations would normally admit."

"We are in some ways more like friends than servant and employer. I know so few people here as yet, and she is entertaining company."

"I am glad to hear it. I think she may be even more than that, perhaps."

"What do you mean?"

"Dear Cordelia, I have told you: my genius lies in observation. I see things which might be hidden to others. I think she possesses the same sensual qualities and inclinations that you do, and forgive me, but I think you share these inclinations?"

"Peregrine! What a thing to suggest! We are more friendly than our respective situations would normally allow, but to suggest anything more…"

"Ah, then forgive me. I have overstepped the mark."

We sipped at the claret in silence, his eyes on me. I gave in.

"Peregrine, you have quite frightening powers of perception. There are sapphic elements to our relationship, I admit."

"Then perhaps she might like to share some poses with you? Merely a suggestion."

The idea had occurred to me, I must admit, but I hardly dared broach it with Janet. The labouring classes tended to have rather simpler morals than the more nuanced ones of their superiors. However, Janet was hardly typical of her species. I could find an opportunity to mention it, perhaps.

The next day was largely taken up with preparations for the evening's gathering. I admit to having been slightly nervous: first impressions count, and I was determined to make a good one. I was getting a little bored with my solitary status, floating like a dandelion seed. I wanted to get established and put down some roots. Janet fussed around, preparing me like a new bride. She bathed me, she washed my hair, she rubbed cream into my skin. I felt like a queen bee being attended to by her drones, and the more she fussed, the more nervous I felt. At least Peregrine would be there, but would people wonder how I knew him? I appraised myself in the long mirror. Janet had done a good job. I looked rather fine.

The time came, and Janet arranged a cab to take me to the Padgetts' house, a rather grand affair set in large grounds in Hove, on the seafront. The cab took me up a short front drive, in a line of other cabs, lined up to disgorge their guests. We smiled to each other. Many of them knew each other well, I could see. We lined up to be announced by their butler. There was a distinct pause and a turning of heads at the announcement of a new name. "Here goes…" I thought, and lifted my chin to greet the hostess.

I recognised her immediately: she was the elderly lady I had seen at the art gallery a week ago, and much to my surprise, she recognised me.

"Why, Mrs Edwards, we meet again! I was rather struck by your beauty when I saw you in the gallery last week. How good of you to come tonight. Now make yourself at home. Dear Mr Pollitt is here already, no doubt he will introduce you to some of our friends. We will talk in a short while and you must tell me all about yourself."

She must have been about sixty, I surmised, but sprightly and with a handsome face which twinkled with a sense of mischief. I replied with a bright smile and a few complimentary phrases, then moved into the room. I felt somewhat surprised to find it compared favourably with the fashionable London houses. There was little of the capital's stuffiness here. There, there was an underlying tension as important men constantly tried to outmanoeuvre their peers and the women discreetly and politely savaged one another mercilessly. Here, they seemed to enjoy each other's company, and there was a welcome intermingling of the sexes.

I was pleased to observe a number of male heads turning as I entered, and turning back to their companions with raised eyebrows and the flickers of smiles. Peregrine was there, talking to a small group. He excused himself and hurried over to me.

"Ah, my dear Mrs Edwards! I'm so glad you could come. Let me get you a glass of wine. I'm in need of a refill myself." Bless him, not a hint of anything other than an acquaintanceship. He introduced me to his group. I need not repeat the names, but they included two artists of some repute, a young banker and his pretty wife, a glassblower and a jovial, chubby woman who was the matron of the local hospital. I made an effort to remember their names.

Lady Padgett came up to us, chatted a little, then took me by the arm and drew me aside.

"It is so nice to welcome you to our society, my dear. I'm told you have come down here from London. I hope we're not too provincial and dull for you."

"On the contrary, Lady Padgett, there is such life here. I am so grateful to you for including me. It is always a little daunting, breaking into new social circles."

"Please, call me Margaret, if I may call you Cordelia? Such a lovely name."

"I should be so pleased if you would."

She asked, and I told her, a little about my background, and my sad loss, and my recent emergence from mourning. She was sympathetic, but then tapped me conspiratorially on the arm with her fan.

"New beginnings, Cordelia. Come, let me introduce you to dear Tristan, but first, promise me you will take afternoon tea with me on Monday. The Fitzroy Tea Rooms: do you know it?"

I did, and we arranged to meet at three. She led me over to the said Tristan. He was standing by the buffet, talking to a distinguished looking man with an unruly mop of grey hair.

"Phillip, dear, stop hogging Tristan, and let me introduce Mrs Cordelia Edwards, our new arrival. Cordelia, this is Philip, my husband, and this is Tristan Hartley. I don't know whether you've heard of him, but he's making quite stir in musical circles. He will be giving the entertainment tonight."

I shook both men's hands and made some small talk before Margaret led Sir Philip away. I was left to amuse this Tristan. This, it turned out, was a bit of a chore. He was tall and handsome. No, really. I am five feet ten inches, he must have been six feet two inches, which would have been enough to attract attention, but he had a strikingly large head which could have been lopped off a bust of Beethoven. I assumed the similarity was intentional.

I searched for something to say. "Do you live in Brighton?" I asked.

He looked rather surprised, as though everybody should know the answer. "Yes, do you?"

I explained my circumstances, and he listened politely, helping himself to some *vol-au-vents* and glancing around the room as if seeking more engaging company. I asked about his musical career, he reeled off a number of positions he'd held, and some recitals he'd given. I asked him if he knew Fanny Davies, a frequent guest at our London *soirées,* he sniffed and smiled rather condescendingly and said he had. Now Fanny was an old friend of mine and was at the time one of the best-known pianists in Europe. I adored her playing, and rather disliked his insinuation.

Time to move on, I thought, before I start to show my teeth. Just at that moment, however, two rather strange ladies came hurrying up to him. One was a tall, willowy thing with a pale face and chestnut hair which had been inexpertly piled up unto her head. Her slash of bright scarlet lipstick was a mistake, but I could see she might have been the first choice of a model of most of the Pre-Raphaelite painters. The other was shorter, perhaps an inch or so shorter than I. She had a pleasing face, by no means beautiful, but strikingly framed by a mass of red hair which fell in unfashionable ringlets around her face. Both were rather alarmingly dressed. They each grabbed one of his arms.

"Now then, Tris," said the willow, "they are ready for your recital! Oh, I see you've found a new friend!"

Tristan introduced me to them: Lavinia Borwick-Fellowes, the willow, and Izzy Fallon, the redhead. They must have been in their twenties and rather engagingly enthusiastic. They fluttered and giggled and said they were part of 'Tris's set'.

At that moment, Sir Philip banged a gong and asked if we might all move into the music room as we were about to be treated to Tristan's recital. Without asking, the girls took my arms and propelled me to a chair and sat either side of me. They waved at people, explaining who they were to me whispers. Their innocent enjoyment was quite infectious.

The recital was not outstanding, to my way of thinking. Sir Philip announced Tristan, probably quite unnecessarily, but the niceties have to be observed. Tristan made a theatrical entrance, seating himself at the piano with a flourish, then closing his eyes and lifting his face to the heavens like a spiritualist medium, presumably drawing down his God-given muse, before ploughing into a Chopin *Prelude*. Although already resenting him for slighting my friend, the foremost concert pianist of the day, I use the word 'ploughing' advisedly. He played well, I admit, but with theatrical trills and flourishes that completely undermined the piece. His playing was about him, not the music. And so it was with a new piece by Debussy, and the Mendelssohn, although that was better suited to his style. He should have stuck to Wagner.

Afterwards he came up to and asked if I'd enjoyed it. I lied and said, "Yes." After all, this was no time for making enemies.

He still looked slightly taken aback, as though he'd expected a rather more enthusiastic accolade. "So kind," he said, and moved on to find more enthusiastic fodder for his vanity.

After that I mingled and drank until my cab arrived at ten-thirty. I said goodbye to my hosts, and winked at Peregrine. Lavinia and Izzy hugged me like an old friend, and I hugged them back. We exchanged addresses.

Back at my house, I shut the door behind me with a sigh of relief. I called softly to Janet to see if she was still up. She appeared in a peignoir, clutching a bottle and two glasses. Bless the girl! She knew me.

We retired to bed with the wine, and we drank while I told her of the evening's encounters and stroked each other, lightly teasing one another's bushes. I poured a little of the claret over her privates then dived down to lick it from her. She licked some off my breasts and that way we finished the bottle before turning to each other in a drowsy embrace.

After our next night's sexual adventure and while we smoked cigarettes, I put Peregrine's proposal to Janet after telling her what I'd been up to in his studio.

"Anonymous, you say?" she asked, after a moment's thought while she picked a shred of tobacco from her lips. She took a mouthful of wine — we had taken to the habit of taking a bottle to bed with us — and smiled. "Then yes, why not? We could certainly give the gents something to goggle at. There'd be money in it?"

"Quite a lot, I'd say."

"Say that again."

I turned onto my side to look at her. "A lot of money. Heaps of it. Money. Mo-ney. Moneymoneymoneymoney." I tickled her and buried my head between her breasts. She squealed with delight, spilling her wine. We put down our glasses, she parted my legs and we were at it again.

The next afternoon, I sent a message to Peregrine which simply said 'J willing (and able). When? C.' Half an hour later, the messenger reappeared with a note: 'Excellent! 2.00pm Tuesday? P.P.'

I dashed off a reply, paid the messenger and went to tell Janet. She hadn't changed her mind, although she was concerned that it might disrupt her routine. She had the meal to prepare.

"Tush! Never mind that, I'll treat you to dinner on the town, afterwards. You can help yourself to one of my dresses."

The same messenger appeared an hour later. Another note! Not from Peregrine this time, but from Izzy Fallon. I tore open the envelope:

'Dear Cordelia, We did so enjoy meeting you. It would be splendid to get to know you better! Would a picnic, weather permitting, be agreeable? We thought Wednesday, pick you up at 11.00am. Just the five of us — do say yes! Yours affectionately, Izzy (Fallon).'

I smiled. My social diary was filling nicely. I sat at my writing desk and wrote a response:

'Dear Izzy, What a kind thought! I was so glad to make your acquaintance at the Padgetts'. I would be delighted to join your picnic and will furnish some wine and some picnic food. I shall be ready at eleven! Yours in anticipation, Cordelia (Edwards).'

I dispatched the messenger with the note and paid him. He appeared a little later with Izzy's reply:

'Dear Cordelia, we are all so pleased! Please note that this is a bucolic country picnic — we shall be wearing our roughest and flimsiest rags — do you likewise! Our little group does not hold with convention, and as we gather, neither do you! See you 11, Wednesday. Izzy xx'

I waved the messenger away. What did they mean, I don't hold with convention? I thought I was putting up a remarkably good show as the respectable widow. Had Peregrine said anything? I'm sure he wouldn't; he wouldn't risk killing a golden calf or goose or whatever it was. There would have bound to have been comments on the New Girl after my departure from the Padgetts', but what had I done? Ah! I'd taken my maid out for a meal. Or had I been spotted fleeing from that ghastly man's house? I was beginning to realise that Brighton was a small town, with few places to hide and a veneer of gentility to maintain. I decided this was said on the basis of our brief conversation alone, and forgot about it.

The weekend was spent writing letters to some London friends, and a letter of thanks to the Padgetts. Then a tentative stroll along the pier. After all, I couldn't stay away forever. I loved the mingle of the crowds. The pier was a great leveller. It was open to all: lords and ladies, the new middle classes, the artisans and the workers. The criminal underclass was here, too. One had to take a little care. Oh, and there was Nicholas! He was talking to another wide-eyed lady who was being taken in by his earnest nonsense. He saw me and looked away quickly. I couldn't very well warn his new companion. Who knows, she might enjoy giving him a good thrashing as much as I had.

Otherwise, I sat in the kitchen with Janet, talking, and watching her prepare the meat, fish, vegetables and dessert for our meals. I was fascinated, for I had not been privy to the secrets of the kitchen. She had obtained an ox heart and was going to stuff it for our evening meal. I was questioning her about it when she turned, perhaps exasperated by my constant questions, said, "Do you want to have a try? You want to know what I'm doing? Well, the best way is for you to do it."

"Oh, I couldn't!"

"Fair enough."

I watched her take the heart from its wrappings and place it on the marble slab. I could sense the sneer on her face, although her back was turned to me.

"No, wait! Go on, show me, I want to know. I'll prepare it!"

She pulled me off my chair at the kitchen table and kissed me. "That's the sort of mistress I could respect. All right, all yours."

I approached the heart gingerly. It was larger than I expected, and heavier. It was repulsively cold to the touch. Janet handed me a long knife. She instructed me to cut off the great blood vessels attached to it. I did so with trepidation, and sliced them off. Janet seized the knife from me and cut them off at the root in a few deft strokes. She handed the knife back.

"Now the deaf ears," she ordered. "Them bits of fatty stuff, there and there. Go on. That's right."

My repulsion soon gave way to a sensuous, almost loving, feeling, as I sliced at the heart. I had a momentary recollection of slicing off my dead father's genitalia. I sliced the heart in two, between the ventricles, watching the flesh open up under the blade, like a red rosebud flowering. It was an extraordinary sensation. I removed the clotted blood from inside the heart, then under Janet's instruction, removed the 'strings' — the valves and cords inside the great organ which a day or so ago had beaten the relentless drum of life through a living being. She handed me a plate of forcemeat, which I placed inside the cavity, before binding the two halves together with string. I looked at my hands — they were covered in blood, yet I felt nothing but satisfaction. Janet placed my work on a tray, and into the oven.

That evening, we ate it by candlelight.

Later still, I reached over to Janet, wanting her. She shied away, and I noticed the towel protecting her.

"No," she said, "I can't. Not now."

I thought of my hands that afternoon, covered in blood.

"All the better," I told her.

"Try the tradesman's entrance," she replied. So I did, with the handle of my hairbrush.

Chapter 3

Monday came, and my rendezvous with Margaret. I'd spent the morning with a sketchpad, trying to draw some flowers. I was quite hopeless, but it was listed as one of the accomplishments a single lady should cultivate, and I was damned if I was going to do any embroidery.

I met lady Margaret at the appointed hour. The Fitzroy Tea Rooms was the place to be seen, the prices deterring most people, including me. It had a sunny aspect overlooking the sea and inside was richly decorated with impressionist murals and samite drapes. She greeted me like an old friend, giving me a light kiss on the cheek. We ordered tea, while I thanked her again for a splendid evening.

"It was rather fun, wasn't it," she laughed, "and we hold them fairly often, so I shall see to it that you're on the list again. You are such a ray of sunshine, and I'm sure you noticed a few male heads turning. I do hope you met some interesting people."

"Oh, yes, I did," I replied. "I'm sure I'm going to make some good friends here. People seem so natural and open after London."

"Oh, they are, they are! Phillip and I came down here from London some ten years ago when he retired from the diplomatic service. I was sure I'd miss London, but not a bit of it. You can breathe more easily here, and I'm not just talking about the sea air. You can be yourself; none of that awful pretence that you need to keep up in London."

I replied that had been my impression at her party. We chatted about this and that and our past lives. She really was a delight. She was obviously well cultured, but didn't flaunt it. She gossiped, but not in a malicious way, and all the time her eyes twinkled with the same mischievous look I'd seen before. She obviously relished life. She enquired about my parents. I told her they had died of tuberculosis. To have to admit to my story that my mother had hung for my father's murder would not have been at all politic. I had to tell her about my late husband and his 'accident'. I did not mention the first one. She tutted sympathetically, with exclamations of, "Oh, how terrible for you!" and "My poor dear, how you have suffered."

"And now what?" she suddenly asked, "What are your plans?"

"I've no idea," I said truthfully. "I'm in no hurry to be wed again."

"No? Very sensible. Husbands are all very well, but we women seem to manage very well without them. I was on my own for many years while Philip was trotting round the world to so many ghastly places. I went with him to India for a six-month tour, and that was quite enough, I can tell you."

"So what did you do while he was away?"

"Oh everything, my dear! I played the cello in an orchestra, I painted — rather well, though I say it myself, and Good Works, lots and lots of Good Works. Terrible thing to say, but it makes one feel rather good about oneself on the back of the suffering wretches you're trying to help. If you wanted, I could get you onto one of my committees?"

"Thank you, but not at the moment."

"No, of course not! Silly me, you're far too young and beautiful for that. You really are remarkably handsome, my dear. Make sure my Philip doesn't start making overtures to you."

"Oh, I'm quite sure he wouldn't—"

"And I'm quite sure he would. He never got a chance to talk to you properly at the gathering, but I could see he was itching to."

"I'm most terribly sorry if—"

"Cordelia, darling, let me tell you a little secret that's not a secret. Philip and I have a wonderful marriage, we are the best of friends. But as long as I have known him, he has kept mistresses all over the damn place."

"Oh, gosh, how awful for you."

"Not at all. The arrangement works very well. I was never hugely interested in that side of things, so what could the poor man do but find satisfaction elsewhere? His career took him all over the world, and I've no doubt he was rogering everything in sight. He still does. I mean, you saw him; he's still a very attractive man, isn't he?"

"Er, yes…"

"But, bless him, he never gets romantically involved with any of his conquests. We still have a very good marriage."

I didn't know what to say, but I didn't have to.

"While we're talking of handsome men, what did you make of our Tristan? I see you made quite an impression on his companions."

"Well…"

"What did you think of his playing?"

"Well…"

"Ha! I see you have a good ear. He thumps that poor instrument around like a prize boxer, doesn't he?"

We both laughed, and I told her my thoughts about his playing for his glory, not the music's. She clapped and said, "Oh, well put!" then she put her hand over mine. "Tread carefully with that set, my dear. They will want you in their circle, I'm sure. You will find them a very entertaining bunch, but, well, you saw Tristan and his monstrous self-adoration. They're all a bit like that: all cultivated mannerisms with little substance. Now,

I'm as keen on Bohemian circles as anyone — wish I'd been one myself, really. But the essence of the true Bohemian life is honesty, the total lack of hypocrisy, and Tristan's circle are anything but honest with themselves. I think they exist to serve Tristan's somewhat eclectic sexual tastes. But these are strange times. Society has been liberated from the constraints of Victorian times, and you yourself have been liberated from the constraints of your marriage. But new found freedoms come with new opportunities to stray into danger. Be wary, my dear, that's all." I wasn't sure what to say, but she just broke into a laugh. "Listen to me, gabbling on! Forgive me, you must do as you please. You are intelligent, you can make up your own mind."

"Ah. That's interesting. I have been invited to a picnic with Tristan and his set on Wednesday."

"I know, my dear. That's why I mentioned it. Brighton is a very liberal place, and God knows, people take advantage of that, which is fine, but it's so important that we maintain the veneer of decent society. Don't you agree?"

Margaret was obviously not one to let anything past her. I wondered how much she did know about me. We changed the subject, and chatted away happily for a long time as the waiters glided to and fro, and we demolished two cake stands of dainties and drank our teas. Other pairs of ladies were at the other tables, whispering, nodding and smiling smugly with tight lips. There were few secrets here. The murmured gossip hung over the tables and sunk into the rich drapes. Reputations were being undone in the nod of a head. I really have to be extraordinarily discreet, I thought. This is a tight community where everyone knows everyone and everyone watches everyone. I wondered whether anyone knew what Peregrine got up to behind his successful portrait business. I must make sure that Janet and I went in separately tomorrow. Margaret was still talking about various town notables. She obviously had great affection for them, but her descriptions were sharp and most amusing. I hadn't smiled so naturally for a long time. We discovered that we had many tastes in common. We were both keen on art, and made a date to visit another gallery the following week. We parted good friends, I think.

Arriving home, the hallway smelt of mutton. I walked into the kitchen to find Janet busy preparing dinner. She seemed a little fidgety, I thought. I asked if everything was all right.

"Oh, yes, ma'am," She replied, for it was not yet the hour of our time as equals. "It's just… Well, me ma's ill, I heard, and I wondered if I could take the evening off to see how she is. She hasn't got anyone else. I've sorted your dinner out, and all you have to do"

"I'm sure I can manage to serve my own dinner. Of course you may. I'll take over here, so you can leave me to it. Where does she live, your mother?"

"Up by Albion Hill way. Not far, I can walk it, no problem. You are an angel, ma'am, thank you."

"Off you go, and give my regards to your mother, er—? Betty. Look and take that bunch of fresh flowers from the drawing room in some newspaper."

She broke the rule and kissed my tenderly on the lips. I had a thought.

"Oh, Janet, we have an appointment tomorrow, and last night you were, ah…"

"Oh, yes. Don't worry, nearly done. Be all shipshape tomorrow."

It was odd, dining on my own. I mulled over the day, and drank a liberal quantity of wine. I had thoroughly enjoyed my time with Margaret, but, looking back, I realised her pleasantries had a warning buried in them. What did she know? What might she be hinting at? I decided she was only giving me some general advice as a young and single lady. She was right; this town accepted liberal behaviour, boasted about it even, as long as it remained hidden, well, half-hidden. There was a subtlety to it, and it boiled down to class. The lower classes were expected to be morally degenerate, and so were the upper classes. It was the crossing over of the two which was forbidden, and perhaps my easy attitude towards my maid had been noted and disapproved. Careful, Cordelia, I thought, careful.

I was in bed and asleep when I became aware of Janet creeping into my bed and curling up against my back. She smelt of drink and cheap perfume. Sick mother, indeed! I wanted to quiz her about her activities, but I was too drowsy, and I think she was too drunk, to talk. We drifted off to sleep.

In the morning, the sun was relentlessly worming its way through the curtains. Janet still lay beside me. I looked at the clock. Nine o'clock! I shook Janet. She startled awake and leapt from my bed in a panic. I reached out and grabbed her arm, dragging her back into bed. I rolled above her and pinioned her down, my hands holding my arms, and my legs locking hers in a spreadeagled position.

"Sick mother, eh? You little liar!" I tugged at her hair. I was genuinely angry. I wasn't going to be taken for a soft touch. She was my maid, and I was her mistress. I'd thought her something more, but trust the lower classes to take advantage of any goodwill from their betters. All right, I felt betrayed. She'd cheapened herself, and me into the bargain.

"It's true, honestly! Me ma isn't well and I did go and see her!"

"Go on…"

"She's been right sick. It's the truth! And she cried when I gave her the flowers. I did everything I could, then I left her and I was on my way back here when I thought I'd have a quick one in the Ship Inn. I only meant to have one, I promise!"

"And…?"

"You're hurting me!"

"I don't care. What then?"

"Well, there was this bloke who fancied me. I mean, he was a bit tiddly when I met him, but he was rather good looking, with a moustache and all, and buying me double brandies, so we got chatting, that's all."

"No, it isn't. Come on."

"Honest."

"I want to know. I want to know what happened after."

"Nothing!"

I spread her legs as wide apart as they would go.

"Please! Nothing much, honest!"

"Just tell me, then I let you go, all right?"

"All right!" I slackened my hold. "We went outside. There was this mucky little passageway outside. He did it to me, that's all."

"No, that's not all. I want to know! I want to hear your pretty little mouth telling me exactly all the dirty little things you did."

Janet pulled herself free. She looked at me with a look on her face I couldn't decipher.

"All right, I'll tell you. He was called Albert. Traveller in ladies fashion, he said. Said he could get me a load of stuff, good stuff, real cheap. Anyways, we went outside, then he starts kissing me, pinning me against the wall. I'd got a load of brandy that he'd bought inside me, so it would be rude to shove him off. Anyway, I wanted him to. His tongue — well, you could tell he'd had a lot of practice. Then he starts groping away at my bum, so I start kneading his. Then he's fumbling at my teats while I'm stroking his manhood, which ain't up to much, to be honest."

I was beginning to realise she was telling me what I wanted to hear.

"Keep going…"

"Then he pulls my breasts out and starts licking and sucking at them. I enjoyed that, and then he tries to pull up my skirt but he's making a mess of it so I pull it up for him, petticoats and all, showing him what I've got on offer, so that there's just my draws but they're open at my crotch, so he starts rubbing away and I've got his trousers down and rubbing him back. Then he's got my legs up round his waist and me shoved against the wall while he tries to get his thing inside me, but he can't, it's not hard enough, so I push myself against him and guide his shaft into me. Then he's inside me…"

I slid two fingers inside her as deep as I could and stirred them around her tunnel.

"…and starting to shaft me and he's like grunting and holding on to my buttocks and staring straight into my breasts and going red in the face, then he gives a yell and when he does, I pull him out quick and there's his spunk all over my bush and his little prick withers away as he pulls up his trousers. No 'thank yous' or anything. He just disappears into the dark."

I worked my fingers harder, and Janet forgot her tale and abandoned herself to her pleasure as my lips worked on her breasts. Eventually, she cried out, shuddered and collapsed limply beneath me. I wondered if my fingers had been churning around where Albert's prick had been, but there was no crusted semen on her pudenda. I think that was a story for my benefit, but it excited me nevertheless. Janet rubbed and fingered me until my own satisfaction came in those waves of ecstasy which started as small flutters inside me, then engulfed me, causing my juices to flow over her fingers and onto the bedsheets.

I rolled over and slept until eleven o'clock. Janet brought breakfast to my bedroom. We talked of what the afternoon with Peregrine might hold in store. I did broach the subject of keeping up appearances with Janet: that she should dress in her maid's clothes and stop borrowing mine, and that we should arrive separately. She was ahead of me, agreeing willingly to both, for she knew Brighton and its whisperings better than I.

I arrived at Peregrine's studio at the appointed hour and went in after a glance around to see who might be watching. I told him that Janet would be along in a short while. He nodded approvingly, and busied himself with finishing off the set, which this time consisted of the same day bed, but covered in white satin, in front of a backdrop depicting a luxurious *boudoir*.

"What are you planning to do this afternoon?" I asked him. He shrugged.

"I have no idea, my dear. I have to sense the chemistry of the moment, but I will take a few poses with Janet alone first, to try her out, if you are agreeable?"

"Of course! I'll enjoy watching."

Janet appeared after a few minutes. She seemed flustered, but Peregrine welcomed her and tried to put her at her ease. I could see she was struggling to know how she should conduct herself: was she the shameless libertine of our bedroom, or a maid in the presence of her betters. Peregrine sensed this, and chatted with us over a glass of *eau de vie*. She started to relax. Peregrine told her that she need do nothing that she wasn't comfortable with, and suggested a few poses fully clothed to start with and suggested I join her for these. We stood on the little stage together and tried a few poses, but Janet seemed stiff and lifeless. I wondered if Peregrine might give her up as a bad job, but I think he was used to camera-shy subjects.

He asked her to look as though she was really shy, a stroke of genius on his part, as, in trying to convey that, she adopted a waif-like look of utter vulnerability.

He caught the moment, praising her. Encouraged, she slipped more easily into depictions of sadness, reading a letter, then, with me, saying farewell and so on. I don't think Peregrine actually took any exposures. He announced himself satisfied, and asked her if she would like to stop at that. Janet, by now a lot happier, shook her head and said she'd try a few 'art poses'. She went behind the screen to disrobe and emerged, clutching the length of muslin that Peregrine had given her. I heard him give a low hum of appreciation.

Janet certainly possessed a magnificent body. At twenty-four, she was at the peak of perfection: fully matured but before her skin lost its juvenile tone. She had shiny bible black hair which was now unpinned and tumbled to her chest in loose curls. Her breasts were full, but so taut that they seemed to defy gravity, her nipples pointing upwards. Her face had a slightly androgynous look; I couldn't look at her without being reminded of the flower-bedecked figure of spring in Botticelli's *Primavera*. She had that same half mocking look on her features, too. Peregrine took her through a few demure poses, but again, she became wooden.

"Look at Mrs Edwards," Peregrine said. "Pretend it's just for her."

"I can't!" She was close to tears. "Not while she's sat there with all her clothes on."

There was an answer to that, so I took off my clothes without bothering to retire behind the screen, and sat, naked, in front of her. It seemed to work nicely. Instead of being the lady, I was now her lover, and she was mine. She started to taunt and tease me; Peregrine could scarcely keep up, and didn't have to direct her poses. "Yes, yes!" he kept crying. She was certainly having an effect on me: I had to start rubbing myself, discreetly at first, then parting my legs and pushing my crotch toward her, as she dispensed with the wispy cloth and reciprocated my arousal.

Peregrine didn't have to ask me. I stood up and joined Janet on the dais. We embraced and started to play with each other. We became oblivious of the camera as we stroked, kissed, cupped, licked, probed, fondled and penetrated each other, tumbling onto the white satin, oblivious, although I noticed that Peregrine had dropped his trousers to his ankles and sported an erection of legendary proportions.

Finally, with a loud cry which was probably heard by any passer-by outside, Janet reached the climax of her pleasure, and we lay there, panting in the heat of the studio. Despite being dazzled by by the lights, I could see in the darkness that Peregrine was stroking himself to his own orgasm.

I think we were all a little overawed by what had just taken place. We dressed, then sat and drank more *eau de vie* in silence. Eventually,

"We have achieved perfection today," Peregrine said. "We have made history. My dears, I have to tell you, we are already creating a big stir amongst the connoisseurs, and what I have captured today breaks new boundaries. The plates will naturally be altered to protect your identities, and I have so many priceless images. I will release them in small batches, so I shall be absent in London for a week or two. I have a lot of work to do. There will be quite a sum of money coming your way, I think."

We drank a lot more *eau de vie,* and talked, and drank a bottle of his claret. I mentioned tomorrow's picnic with Tristan and his followers. He raised his eyebrows.

"Well, enjoy yourself, but a word to the wise. Keep them at arm's length."

"Oh? Why?"

"Let's just say they have earned a certain notoriety. They possess some talents between them, I admit, but they flaunt their self-styled genius and think and act as though it places them on a different plane from the rest of society. That is all, and of course, what you do is entirely your own business…"

He tailed off, but I was curious to know more. His words were an echo of Margaret's warning. I pressed him further.

He showed us some of his previous 'art poses' and I could see why he had been lucky to stumble upon me, well us, now. And perhaps this afternoon we could draw a line under it and I could join Brighton society with a clear conscience. Janet had been drinking more than she was used to, and it was beginning to show. I thanked Peregrine, and he thanked us, and I took Janet home.

I had to support her on the way back, and worried that this would not look good by anyone's standards. I was by no means sober myself. We hurried along the Promenade, and happily the sun had been obscured by clouds and a chill wind had got up, so the crowds had gone. We stumbled up the steps and into the house. Janet had a small bedroom off the kitchen, so I took her there. She fell on it, and took me with her. We lay there, clutched together on her small bed, and fell asleep.

I woke some hours later, and made my way up to my own bed, feeling a little unwell, undressed, slid between the sheets, supperless, and slept soundly.

Next morning, a contrite Janet had made me a substantial breakfast, and sat with me while I asked her how she felt about our session with Peregrine. She was enthusiastic, to my surprise.

"See, I've never done it before with someone watching, especially when you see them getting excited like that. That gave me a real thrill." Her face clouded a little. "You're certain that no one will ever recognise us?"

"Cast iron certain. Peregrine is a genius at changing faces, and his clients are all in London. They couldn't possibly recognise you." No, more likely they'd recognise me: we had included some well-known public figures in our London circle. But I had faith in our photographer.

I told Janet about my own excitement at having sexual control over powerful men; that the very thought aroused me. We giggled like girls, but time was getting on; I needed to prepare for the picnic. I must say the prospect of an afternoon with Tristan did not thrill me, although the girls promised to be fair company. Janet had selected a few bottles of wine, and food suitable for a picnic, all wrapped in brown paper. We went upstairs, and, removing my dressing gown, started to don the many layers of underwear.

"No need for all that!" Janet cried. "It's a picnic on a hot day. Just your camisole and drawers."

"Really? Are you sure?"

"I've been here all my life. I know what they wear to picnics or on the beach. Trust me, and I think this should do for a dress." She'd picked a blue and white striped cotton affair from the depths of my wardrobe. I'd forgotten I even had it, or why I'd bought it in the first place.

"I really don't think—"

"It's perfect. You've seen what they wear on the beach, haven't you?"

True, there were any number of fashion rules flouted and flaunted there. I must remember that this is the British seaside, not London. I decided the general effect was quite acceptable when I looked in the mirror.

Topped with a a simple sun hat, I decided I looked quite racy. I remained a little nervous, though, especially when it passed eleven and still no sign of them. Perhaps they had forgotten.

At eleven forty-five, there was a commotion outside the door and a blaring of a motor horn. I picked up my wicker basket and went outside. An enormous motor car was waiting. I approached it with caution. I had never been in one before. In London there had been no need to own such a thing. I had got used to seeing them drive up and down the promenade, but to be this close…

Izzy had opened the door in the back for me. I saw that Tristan was at the wheel and wearing some sort of outlandish Indian robe. Beside him was a rather slight and thin-faced man in a blazer that was far too loud and hearty for his features. Izzy gave me a squeal and a hug and pushed me into the large leather bench seat in the back beside Lavinia, who kissed me on both cheeks and lips. Izzy stowed away my basket, and with completely unnecessary blares of the horn, we waved goodbye to Janet, who waved from the steps. After a few genuine squeals from me, unfamiliar with this mode of transport, we were headed out of Brighton, eastwards.

Izzy was dressed in the strangest of garments — a long white cotton affair with a plunging neckline tightly lashed with red cord. It was rather obvious that there was nothing underneath. Lavinia wore baggy Turkish trousers in a striped material, and a chiffon chemise which again blatantly revealed her lack of underwear. I felt very overdressed.

We climbed out of Brighton, heading towards Piddinghoe and the River Ouse. The noise of the motor made conversation impossible but they shouted and hooted at anybody we passed. After a bit of initial embarrassment, I joined in.

The picnic spot was by the river in a secluded clearing surrounded by woodland. The motor car stopped noisily and we carried the baskets and rugs to the riverside. I gathered that they had come here many times. Free of the noise of the motor car, we began talking excitedly. The aesthetic young man in the loud blazer was introduced to me as Charles Morgan, a painter, they said. He was actually quite charming, complimenting me on my dress and taking my basket off me. I noticed that Tristan did not carry anything but busied himself with directing operations.

We sat on the rugs and laid out the picnic. There was a substantial amount of food and an even more adequate supply of wine. We talked as we ate, Tristan waxing loquacious and waving his chicken drumstick like the conductor of a large orchestra. They were explaining their creed to me, their new potential recruit.

"It is up to us, the artists and visionaries, to seize this time and push forward the bounds of expression," Tristan was saying. "This is a time of progress and new liberties. The hammers of industry have beaten down the people and it's time to free them! It is the artists' task to point the way."

"You may be wondering why we dress and behave as we do," Lavinia said, stretched out and eating grapes, "We want to show people that there are alternatives, that there's no God-given reason why people can't be free to choose what they wear. Who says we all have to go round covered up from head to foot with our behinds sticking out?"

This did make sense to me. Indeed, it fitted very well with my own ideas. I did wonder, though, why I had been invited: one of the upper classes who, to all outward appearances, was the epitome of polite conservative society. Now was not the right time to ask, though.

I leant a little more about them. Tristan had trained in music at the Paris *Conservatoire,* and was building up a good reputation as a concert pianist. He was also writing his own compositions. I began to warm to him as I saw the idealism behind his strutting. All of them, it seemed, were prepared to sacrifice reputation in order to demonstrate their convictions. Izzy was a writer, chiefly of essays and articles for the political press, propounding the views of the group and other, similar conclaves. Lavinia was, predictably, a poet, while Charles was a rather controversial *avant-garde* painter.

I wasn't surprised that many people, Margaret and Peregrine among them, were wary of these people. Both in their ways, depended on the social structure of the day, one feeling that a rigid class structure was the glue that held society together and made it work, the other dependent on a veneer of respectability to hide the more adventurous aspects of his trade. Here were these people, clawing away at the very fabric of society. No wonder they felt threatened!

After lunch and quite a lot of wine, Tristan invited us all to get closer to nature. Izzy took me by the arm some distance away into the woods and explained that this would involve some baring of flesh and if I felt shocked by that, I should perhaps wander into the woods and sit there awhile. I could read one of her tracts, if I wished. I replied that I would be perfectly happy to do as they did. I was aware of a German movement that advocated the removal of clothing to free oneself from the constrictions of society and return to the natural state, and was somewhat intrigued by it.

Izzy removed her gown and stood naked by me. Her short figure was stocky, but not unappealing with her dumpling breasts. She stood with me while I undressed and returned to the others. They looked up appreciatively. We lay naked in the sun, feeling the warmth and listening to the small sounds of nature. After a while, I opened my eyes to observe Charles' hand had strayed to Tristan's penis which was stiffening under his teasing. He in turn, did the same. I closed my eyes again, thinking I should not be witnessing this, but opened them again, fascinated.

Beside them, also watching, Lavinia's long white body lay stretched out and her hand was pulling gently at her pubic hair. As the men stroked each other's genitals, I felt Izzy's body roll up against mine, her breasts pressed against my side. I stretched my arm over hers and started stroking her back. Her hand reached for my breasts and started to fondle them. All so gentle; all so natural. Charles shifted his position so that he was kneeling between Tristan's legs, taking his member in his mouth and sliding his lips up and down the length of the shaft. Lavinia grasped Charles' stiff cock and was milking it in time with the movements of her other hand which was now working her prominent slit.

Emboldened my response, Izzy straddled me, rubbing herself against my thigh while she bent to start sucking at my breasts, then lifting herself a little so that I could suck hers. I reached out to run my hand over Lavinia's lean body and small breasts. We remained like that for some time, lazily caressing each other in the sun with the birdsong in our ears. My own quim was tingling and moist. Then Lavinia let go of Charles who stood up to let her straddle Tristan and guide him inside her. Charles came over, and Izzy moved aside for him. His prick was twitching as I rolled over and presented myself on all fours to him. His hands prised my buttocks apart and he entered me. Such a sweet sensation! Izzy lay on the ground, legs apart with my head between her thighs as I lapped up her juices.

One by one, we reached our climaxes with a roar, a whimper, a silent spasm or shuddering moan. I pulled Charles out of me as I sensed him climaxing, and felt his seed spurt between my buttocks. We released each other and lay back in the sun in the same positions as before, sipping the last of the wine as if nothing had happened.

At last, as the sun started to dip into the west, we gathered up our belongings, and left.

Chapter 4

After these tumultuous few days, I had plenty of time to think. I was in a dilemma. Do I follow Margaret's path and reject the excesses I was enjoying, settle down and become a respectable, and probably married, woman? Reason said I should. My own sense of propriety, or what little I had of it, said I should. Then I should be back where I had started: bored with polite society, frustrated with a dull marriage and angry at a world where women were the dutiful chattels of men.

Or do I follow my natural instincts and become marked down as an outcast from respectable society? Talking with *Les Mouettes* as Tristan's set were pleased to call themselves, I was happy that there was nothing subversive or dangerous about them. They were artists and free-thinking intellectuals who refused to be tied to the rigid conventions of the time and were not afraid to be different. And how easily I had taken to their group sexual activities! One thing troubled me, though: why should they want someone like me with them? Did they suppose I had a lot of money, and want me to fund their lifestyle?

I decided to ask them directly, so a few days later, I sent a note to Izzy who seemed to me the thinker in the group, and had given me her address. I received her reply within the hour: I was to go round immediately, as she was keen to talk to me. Her house was a little way off, so I took a cab and was soon knocking on the door of her apartments. It was a modest affair for I suppose a writer earns little for her labours. She seemed genuinely delighted to see me, and gave me a warm hug as soon as I crossed the threshold. She led me into her study, apologising for the mess, but what a nice mess it was. Books and papers everywhere, pictures all over the walls and all surfaces covered with curiosities. She cleared some books off a chair and bade me sit while she made us some tea.

"I've been so anxious to talk to you," she confided as we sipped our tea. "I've been wanting to know what you thought of our little crowd, but thought I should wait and see if you got in touch. I was so afraid that we might have shocked you away. It was perhaps too abrupt an introduction to our values."

"I admit it was a shock, but a pleasant one," I replied, "and an experience I would happily repeat. I would like us very much to become very good friends, Izzy, and be a part of your group, but there are some things that worry me."

"Tell me, and be honest."

"Well, firstly, I came down to Brighton to start a new life after my husband died, and wanted to become part of a new society. Now it seems I have to choose whether to be part of that society or part of yours."

"Why?"

"Lady Margaret tried to warn me off you. Not you, but the group as a whole. She seemed to think you were, well, hypocrites."

"I know! She's a scream at times. I'm a great friend of Margaret's and she agrees with so much of my thinking. She loves Charles and Lavinia, too. She finds Tris a bit of a bighead at times, but so do we all, but that's how he is, and he's the bit of grit in the oyster that forms a pearl around it. No, she's rather fearful of us all, *en masse,* frightened that we'll upset the order of things. She thinks we're hypocritical because we don't go round blowing up things and because we enjoy ourselves, and I keep trying to explain to her that we're not trying to destroy anything but push the world in a better, more enlightened, direction. I've obviously not convinced her."

"You've convinced me. I should very much like to stay friends with her and a few other worthies while sharing your company. Something else concerns me though. May I smoke?"

"Of course! I will too. Try one of mine." It was a loosely packed affair. It smelt different.

"Herbal?"

"You could call it that. It's marijuana. It helps me think."

I took it and we smoked together. it was rather pleasant.

"You were saying?"

"I'm curious as to why you should like to include me in the group. What have I to offer? I'm no painter, poet, or anything really. I began to think you wanted me for my supposed wealth."

She laughed. "You are a doubting Thomas! No, Cordy, we don't want your money, we want you. Lavinia and I took an instant shine to you at the party. You have an aura of independence and being nobody's fool. And you could talk about ideas. Tell me, what did you think of Tris's recital?"

"I thought he was being a bit of a show-off, to be honest."

She laughed again, and I laughed with her. The cigarette was making me feel so relaxed.

"So we wanted to get to know you for no better reason than we liked you."

"Is there just the four of you?"

"Oh no, I suppose there must be about thirty of us. We're not a secret society or anything like that, just a circle of like-minded friends. We all need encouragement and criticism from the right people. Think what it's like for me, in here day upon day, trying to keep my thoughts disciplined and clear. I tell you, writing's the loneliest job in the world, and I need to know my friends are out there, and they will support me and call on me sometimes."

We drank more tea, for I was feeling thirsty.

"I'd like to be able to call on you often," I said, meaning it.

"Oh, I would so love it if you did." She came over to me and knelt with her head in my lap. I stroked her hair. "Can I lie with you?" she murmured. "Just lie quiet for a while?"

I kissed her head, and she led me to her bedroom. We took our clothes off, and lay against each other in her narrow bed. We lay motionless for a while, just enjoying the press of the other's body. I began to stroke her hair again, and her ear. Her breaths began to deepen as she moved her hand over the bottom of my back. She lifted her face to mine and we kissed gently. And that was it, we just lay there, kissing and running our hands slowly over the other's body, my first lesson in tenderness.

After perhaps an hour, who knows, we dressed and went back to her study. We smoked another of her cigarettes, she handed me some printed manuscripts that she'd written, hoping I might find the time to read them. I kissed her again and said I'd call again very soon.

Janet had cooked an excellent dinner that evening, and I did it justice, for I was ravenously hungry. I felt jubilant, for, after this afternoon, I was sure my future path lay with the *Mouettes,* and Izzy in particular. I had told Janet about the picnic, omitting the afternoon's gambols, and now told her about my meeting with Izzy that afternoon, leaving out my personal involvement, but just seeking her views on that set. She was quite interested.

"I don't know about all their artistic ideas, but I hear they make free love sometimes. I like the sound of that."

"I'm sure that's just a rumour," I lied. "But we might have them round here one evening."

"Well, if it's more than a rumour, just ring for your maid, who will assist in whatever way she may." We laughed, and we drank more wine.

I asked about her mother's health, and she turned serious.

"She's no better, thank you, and I'm fretting about her, I don't mind admitting."

"What's the matter with her?"

"Pains in her belly, bad pains. Making her sick, too."

"She should take some laudanum."

"She takes gallons of the stuff. Doesn't make any difference. And she can't work with it, so I'm having to pass all my pay to her."

"Have you called in the doctor? What does he say?"

"Doctor? We can't afford a doctor!"

"For heaven's sake, I'll pay for a doctor! Anyway, have you tried Doctor Martindale?"

"Who's he?"

"Not he, she. She's a lady doctor, set up in Lewes Road a couple of years ago, specialises in women."

"Could you do it? Get her seen?"

I realised how little the lower classes knew about the medical aid available to them. They could never have considered it before, but thanks to the new wave of enlightenment and the likes of the *Mouettes,* their plight was being catered for.

"Of course I will. Will you take me to your mother tomorrow? I should like to meet her before I call the doctor."

"I'd be so ashamed. It's not the finest of places at the best of times."

"Rubbish, we'll go tomorrow. Now, I don't suppose there's been any word from Peregrine, has there?"

"No, there's been no message."

"No, well, he said he'd be away for a while. He's got some hot stuff to sell, hasn't he?"

"Two irresistible beauties who can't even resist each other? Who wouldn't pay a lot of money to see them, eh?" She got up and stood behind me, kneading my breasts. "Let's take a bottle to bed and have a look at these two beauties, eh?"

I followed her obediently upstairs, she with a newly opened bottle of Bordeaux and our glasses, me with a packet of cigarettes.

We were in bed. Neither of us ever wore nightdresses now. We threw the bedclothes off, for it was getting unbearably close, and lay naked, drinking the wine and smoking one cigarette after another, chatting. It was too hot to make love; we were content to run a lazy hand over one another's bellies and pudenda. I was reminded of the curiously chaste embraces with Izzy earlier. Suddenly, in the darkness of the bedroom, we saw a prolonged flicker of lightning, and seconds later, a distant peal of thunder. Successive peals of thunderclaps grew louder and louder. Janet cowered under the bedclothes, I rose and flung open the shutters and opened the window and stood on the balcony, watching the lightning play over the ocean. It was like the heavens were telling me something. Then, while the thunder grew louder, the rain came. I called for Janet to join me. Fearful, she joined me as we watched the flashes light up the sky while torrential rain soaked our hair and ran in rivulets down our bodies. I licked up the rain from her hardened nipples as a great thunderclap shook the balcony.

Our pent-up sexuality, galvanised by the lightening, washed over us both as we ran our hands over each other's slippery bodies, exultant. Janet pulled me inside, closed the shutters, and fetched two towels.

We dried each other off roughly, then tumbled back into the bed and gave each other hard, intense and noisy orgasms as we listened to the thunder dying away while the rain thrashed at the window.

Janet slept, snoring gently after all the wine. I kissed her between the shoulder blades, then rolled over, thinking of Izzy; of the rich confusion of her study, and the beautiful simplicity of her little bed.

I read Izzy's writings with growing wonder. She was such a lucid thinker, and her arguments were impeccable. Here were essays on the Suffragettes, the rights of women, the inequalities of wealth and the stifling class system. The extent of her learning was remarkable, and I wanted to tell her so and to discuss her ideas with her. There was nothing I disagreed with. I thought of my own attitudes: being raised among the upper classes, it never occurred to me that it was at the expense of others. I had never really considered that servants had a life of their own. Not, that is, until I met Janet and became her lover.

This had been brought home to me even more when we visited Lisa, her mother. The house was a poor affair, and although Janet had tried to clean it, nearly all her time had to be spent with me, attending to my wants. Her mother was a bedraggled wasted mess. She could only have been about forty, but looked twice that. She had taken to her bed, taking the edge off her pain with laudanum. A look at her swollen belly and withered limbs told me that something was seriously amiss. The cut flowers I had sent her were dead and withered in a makeshift vase, and the room had that peculiar odour of death. We sat with her awhile and tried to get her to take a little broth. Janet was blind to the obvious, she insisted that her mother would be up and about soon. "She'll be all right in a day or so, won't you, Mum?" she kept saying, over and over. I wondered about offering taking her into my house, so that she could be properly looked after, but the thought revolted me. No, I would get her examined by a doctor.

The next day, in answer to my urgent request to the Lewes Road Dispensary, Dr Martindale herself came to visit Lisa at home. Janet and I stood in the background while she examined the poor woman, talking gently to her while she poked and prodded. Lisa began to moan under the examination. The doctor took us outside and explained that her swollen belly was caused by a build-up of fluid — ascites, she called it — which very probably signified an advance cancerous growth in the abdomen or pelvis. She would make arrangements for her to be admitted into the hospital right away, that they might at least make her more comfortable, although she feared it was too late to save her. She bade us goodbye, and we went back inside to tell Lisa what was happening. Janet struggled to hold back her tears as she tried to reassure her half-conscious mother that, "Everything's going to be all right." We organised some transport, and accompanied her to the hospital to see her tucked in bed in a long, cheerless ward. They sent us home while they did what they could.

Looking back, that day marked a change in our relationship. Before, we had been each other's playthings, but now another dimension had been added, and I don't think we found it easy to cope with. Janet slept in her bed, and I in mine.

Lisa died a few days later. They had drained nearly a gallon of fluid from her abdomen after which she had rallied a little, but Dr Matindale found the fluid was teeming with cancerous cells, and so they merely kept her asleep with opium until she stopped breathing. Janet was with her at the end. She came back and sobbed for hours while I plied her with tea and wine and held her hand. I let her talk: of her childhood and her remorse at not having visited her mother earlier. Eventually, she slept, and I went out to dine.

Over the next week, I helped her to organise the funeral and clear out her home, as well as doing what I could in the kitchen. I found all the activity oddly satisfying, doing something useful was a novelty to me and I'm sure would have been met with raised eyebrows by my peers locally. But I'd decided I'd had enough of that sort of thing, hadn't I?

I did find time to visit Izzy again to return her literature. In fact, I spent most of the day with her. She gave me such a hug, and we ensconced ourselves in her study to talk about our convictions. I mentioned Lisa's death and Dr Martindale, and it turned out that Izzy was very well acquainted with her. She rummaged around and produced another manuscript: a large bundle of typed pages entitled *Under the Surface*. It was written by Dr Martindale herself and exposed the shocking plight of working-class women, advocating that women should be able to work and earn equal pay to men, that they shouldn't have to resort to prostitution, or if they did, then their health should be a primary concern. I flicked through some pages. It was quite outspoken.

Izzy chuckled. "It's going into print in a few weeks. It's going to cause a bit of a stir, I think. Take it back with you, have a read. Now, let's have some tea and one of my cigarettes."

As we smoked, I told her that helping Janet out had made me realise I needed to do something useful with my life. I had so much stifled energy, which usually rose to the surface as sexual urges, that I wanted to channel into something fulfilling.

"Let's not channel too much away from your urges," she smiled, looking into my eyes. "But yes, if you want to get your teeth into something besides me, I'd like you to help me spread the word."

"I'd love that!" I cried. "As well as getting my teeth into you."

"Good, on both counts. These smokes always make me feel aroused. Do you want to come to bed with me?"

So without any more ado, we helped each other out of our clothes and into her bed. We kissed passionately and held each other close, rubbing our bodies together so that we could feel the other's breasts and pudenda. I reached my hand down to her mound of love while my mouth worked on her nipples. She started to moan, it was almost a growl as her hips responded. My hand worked further down through the wiry hairs of her bush to toy with her clitoris, that little sentry at the gates of pleasure. Her hands played with my breasts as I worked her, sliding three fingers in and out of her. To get a better view, I knelt between her spread legs. She had such nice plump inner lips. She brought her knees up to her chest, still making that low growl of pleasure as she pulled those lips wide apart. My fingers were glistening with her profuse juices. I stirred them round the fleshy walls of her passage, watching as a small rivulet trickled out of her over her tight little anus. As she bucked and writhed in her orgasm, I withdrew my hand and, lowering my face to her, licked up that lovely liquid.

She put her face against my quim and pushed her tongue inside me, one arm around my thigh and the other hand teasing my clitoris, rolling it between her finger and thumb. Then she swapped, licking my little button while pushing her fingers inside me. Her other hand strayed to my breast and rolled my engorged nipple around until I felt the sweet spasms take over my body. We lay in a close embrace.

"I've never come like that before," she murmured. "That was unforgettable."

"I want to make love to you over and over and over," I whispered back.

"Mmmm" she said, as we dozed for a while. *La petite mort.*

It was rather late for lunch by the time we were dressed and downstairs again, so Izzy scraped together a makeshift meal, which we ate while discussing what I could do to help. She spoke rapidly, earnestly.

"We really need someone to help whip up some local support. Louisa Martindale's book is coming out next month. We want it launched with a bit of a splash."

"We?"

"Louisa and I, and you if you're keen. I'd like to find a worthy as well, if I can find one, and get a talk from a working-class girl with a tongue in her head and who can speak for her peers. We want to show those people we're on their side."

I considered this for a minute. "I'm confused. Who do you want in the audience?"

"How do you mean? Anybody."

"No point in having working class women there, they already know how disadvantaged they are, and there's no point in whipping them up into a frenzy because they can't change anything. So who are we trying to win over? The people who have the power, but they also have the money and don't want to share it.

They don't want the status quo changed. We need the politicians and the people with influence."

"You're making sense. Go on."

"I can't, I don't know about these things. But it can either be yet another boring diatribe from a soapbox in a dingy hall, or it can be a memorable evening which will make everyone think and get articles in the papers."

"You're exciting me," Izzy leant forward, then said with a wink, "Again."

"Look, leave me to work something out. I still have some contacts in highish places. Let's try and create a stir."

"I like it. Although Louisa's not exactly a showman."

"Which is why we need some that are."

We talked on. It was quite late when I got back. Janet had a good meal waiting. We sat eating, a rather quiet affair to start. Janet was still struggling with guilt and a brooding anger that hadn't found a target, yet. I tried to cheer her up with wine. I also had an idea.

"Janet, I've been talking to Izzy today—"

"Not just talking, by the smell of you."

"Janet!"

"Sorry. I shouldn't have said. I don't care a toss anyway."

"Look, I know you're hurting and I feel for you, but just listen to me, please. I've been talking to Izzy, and Dr Martindale's written a book all about the hardships and injustices working class women face. They want me to organise an evening to make sure people know about it."

"Bit late now, isn't it?"

"Stop that, Janet. Yes, it's too late for your mother, God rest her, but the problem doesn't end with her. Wouldn't it be good to be able to help people like her?"

"Yes, 'course it would. I'm sorry, I don't know why I'm being such a cow."

"Well, I do, lovely. It's perfectly understandable. I want to help. Seeing your mother like that, in her house in that state, it's not right, and people like me, or the person I was, just turn away and blame it on the moral degeneracy of the working classes."

"So what are you going to do?"

"I'm going to organise a big evening to make sure the world knows about it, and I want you to give a sort talk about it."

"Me? No. Absolutely not. I couldn't."

"All right, as you wish."

We finished our beef stew in silence. I poured us another glass of wine. At last, "What could I say? I'd be a laughing stock."

"I don't think you would. You know what life's like for the underclass. You're angry about it just now. This would be a good chance for you to put your anger to good use."

It took a good few more glasses of wine to persuade her, but she agreed. We went to our separate beds, but in the night, I was aware of her quietly slipping into my bed and snuggling up to me. When I woke next morning, she was gone.

As I expected, she regretted her decision the next morning, but I persuaded her round again. When we breakfasted, she seemed much more her old self. It was also the morning I was to meet Margaret at another art gallery, one that specialised in more contemporary work. We met for coffee and cake at a nearby café, chatting about this and that. I had written to her, telling her an expurgated version of my contact with Tristan's group and my meeting with Izzy. Now I spoke of my second meeting, and my involvement with Louisa Martindale's book launch. She was surprisingly enthusiastic.

"My dear, I'm delighted! I may not be too happy with some of Tristan's posturing's, but Izzy's a brick, and Louisa and I are great chums. I've read the manuscript of her book and I think it's marvellous! And here you are, signed up to doing 'Good Works' already."

I took advantage of her words to enlist her help. I explained my ideas and that I wanted the evening to persuade people with influence to come along. She stole my thunder by telling me that Louisa had already asked her about this — they were both magistrates on the

Brighton bench. I might have known. I told her about Janet's mother, and she grew quite serious.

"I know people laugh up their sleeves at what we try to do on our various committees, and I admit committees are not the best answer to getting things done, but we do try. The council try and sweep the poverty under the carpet as it doesn't help the town's image, and God knows I've nagged them enough. I even got myself elected onto the council for a while, and what a waste of time that was. I'm happy to say a few words at your evening, but the best thing I can do is to drag the right friends along, I think. Things will change."

We toured the gallery. It was like a repeat of my encounter with her at the city gallery. Only this time it was me she was talking to in a loud voice as we walked arm in arm. These paintings were more contemporary, and there was much to admire. Then I spotted a painting, one of those that transfixes you the instant you see it and you know will haunt you for a long time. It was in the modernist style, but carefully executed, depicting a small boat floating away from a shore — or was it floating towards it — with a woman with a parasol seated in it, but it exuded such an air of loneliness and despair, despite the warm pastel colours it was painted in. I stood, transfixed, as I drank it in. It was speaking to me, mirroring something visceral inside me.

"Go and look at the signature," Margaret said, suddenly lowering her voice, and there, with difficulty,

I made out the small letters: C. Morgan. Christ! I'd had him inside me, had his ejaculate spattered over my backside.

"You've met him, I think," Margaret said, resuming her loud authoritarian tones. I think she did this to annoy the gallery attendants. "Nice chap, but I worry about him. Such despair! Very unhealthy. There are a few more of his further on."

There were. One showed a woman and I could see it was Lavinia. On her lap, a letter, and in her hand a posy of wilting flowers, and a face that said nothing but made me want to cry. Another showed a number of couples on Brighton beach; at first glance a happy scene, but the second closer look made you notice the physically small but emotionally huge distance between them. Again, it was painted in colourful dabs of paint that belied the awful loneliness of everything. I admit to being quite dumbfounded and more than a little affected by them. I must talk to him, and see more of his work.

We parted outside the gallery, and I went home to see how Janet was faring. Tomorrow was her mother's funeral, and she was obviously anxious. We sat and talked awhile, and dined together. I tried to keep our conversation light, but Janet was sunk in her thoughts and eventually I gave up, and retired to bed.

The funeral was a muted affair. Besides Janet and I, there were twenty or so there, the rest, judging by their clothes, were from the same shabby part of town that

Lisa had lived in. The minister in the little chapel at the borough cemetery intoned the service with no emotion. Why should he? He didn't know her, he probably thought little about these people. They came and went, their lives meaningless. I thought of Charles' paintings; he'd seen the hollowness of it all.

It took a few days for Janet to throw off her truculence, but she slowly returned to her former self, or as close as she was ever going to get to it. We even got back to making love, although it was more restrained, more comforting than ecstatic.

It was almost an irrelevance when I received a message from Peregrine, so much had changed since I last saw him. He was back from London, the note said, and he was looking forward to seeing me again, perhaps tomorrow afternoon?

He was in a cheerful and expansive mood when he ushered me into his dark domain. His trip had been successful, more so than he could have dreamt of, which was the reason he'd been absent for three weeks rather than two. His photographs had been snatched up by the appropriate people and his client numbers and prices had risen most satisfactorily. I began to feel that old excitement between my legs at the thought of all those men gloating over my body. I had such power over them! Over wine, Peregrine handed me an envelope with a cheque inside it. It was for ten pounds. That was an enormous amount of money, especially for just a few hours of enjoyable work. He chuckled, and pressed his hand against my breast.

"You have such valuable assets here," he said. "May I refresh my memory?"

"You may." I unbuttoned my blouse and undid my camisole, revealing my heavy breasts to him. He reached to touch them, but I moved his hand away.

"I thought you said you were only going to screw me that once."

"But you may touch me." He took my breast in his hand, running his finger round my areola and watching as my nipples grew prominent. He leant over to lick them, but I drew away as he did, and I began to grow excited, I wanted to bait him.

"No. First take off your clothes." He did so, understanding the game. While he stripped, I took off my blouse and drew my dress up to my hips, revealing my drawers. I played with my breasts to tempt him further. Naked, he approached me, his prick half erect.

"No. Stand in front of me! I want to see you play with yourself. Show me how much you want me." He stroked his penis until it was erect. "Good, now, kneel." I parted my legs and he knelt down between them. "Suck my breasts. Now stand up and put your cock in my mouth." He obeyed each instruction, then, at my order, lay on his back on the studio bed, and watched while I slowly and deliberately teased him as I took off my skirt, petticoat and finally my drawers. I knelt by him on the bed. He reached out to hold me, but I pushed his hand away. "No touching. Don't move." I grasped his manhood and began stroking it, then leant forward so that my breasts swayed and brushed his face, then his body and his cock. I could see he was struggling to keep still, but still I teased him this way, until neither of us could hold back.

I straddled him and lowered myself onto him, inch by inch, partly to tease him but partly to be able to accommodate the sheer size of him. I gasped with the delight of having a large cock driving deep into me. I put my hands on his shoulders as I rose up and down on him, slowly at first, feeling the walls of my vagina opening up to take in this welcome visitor. Then faster as the pleasure welled up, so that my breasts swayed back and forward at first, then in mad circles as I bucked and slid up and down him. I started to quiver and reached the point of no return first, then quickly pulled myself off him — I wasn't going to risk a pregnancy — and knelt over him again, taking him into my mouth and milking him with my lips. After a few moments he shouted and I felt his warm, salty semen in my mouth. There was such a lot of it, I had some difficulty swallowing it all, but I coaxed the last drops from him, and stroked his twitching penis until it started to droop.

We dressed and resumed our wine. He politely complimented me on my lovemaking, and I politely complimented him on his restraint and the size of his member. He asked if I would care to do some more poses with Janet. I certainly would, and I would broach it with Janet. I intended to split the money half and half with her. Given that inducement, I was sure she would agree.

I left it until we were sitting in the gaslit twilight, eating dinner. I told her that I had been to see Peregrine, who was back from London. She was curious to know how he'd got on.

"Oh, so-so." I shrugged. She looked a little deflated. It wasn't right to tease her any more. I passed her the envelope and she took the cheque out. Her eyes widened and she gasped unbelievingly.

"Half for you and half for me." I smiled. Considering I paid her thirty pounds a year, it was a fortune to her. To my embarrassment, she started to cry.

"It's not that bad," I joked, and she shook her head, smiling.

"Happy tears," she managed to say. When she'd recovered, I told her that Peregrine had asked if we wanted to do more sessions. She didn't take much persuading. I also asked her what she would do with the money: a few more sessions and she couldn't really keep it all under her mattress. She also needed to decide if she was going to continue to pay the rent on her mother's house. At three shillings and sixpence a week it was probably an unnecessary expense. She lived here all the time, and I had the idea that I might assign a proportion of the house (which was far too large for me, anyway) to her private use, and she could pay a portion of the rental. That would help us both. She would continue to perform her duties, but we might then afford some help for her.

Janet was a bit baffled by my suggestion; the weekly budget was the limit of her financial acumen. I promised I'd come up with a proposal, but she was to give notice to her mother's landlord straight away.

We had drunk more wine than was proper by this time, and our talk turned back to our future photographic sessions. I thought we had reached the limit of what could be shown, but no doubt Peregrine had other ideas. We joked about what else we could do and the talk had us both going. We both had one hand under the table, I noticed. I got up, a little unsteadily and stood behind her. I unbuttoned her chemise and slid my hands over her breasts. She leant back and looked up at me.

"Shall we go upstairs and have a little practice?" she said.

Chapter 5

I needed to organise Dr Martindale's book launch. Margaret knew the right people to invite locally, but I wrote to some influential people I knew in London, including some members of parliament. The liberal government, led by Asquith, was making some sweeping changes. Lloyd George and Churchill had just brought in the 'People's Budget', taxing the rich to fund sweeping reforms to help the poor. The timing couldn't be better: the Labour party largely supported this movement. All the parliamentarians I knew were Tory, for those were the circles I'd moved in, but I decided that was a good thing. It was the deniers we wanted to influence, not the converted. I wanted that hall packed with doubters, and to field a strong team to sway them. I made a list:

1. Dr M
2. Izzy F
3. Local councillor?
4. Janet?

I sought out Janet in the kitchen, and asked her if she would speak on behalf of her class. She adamantly refused, even after I invoked the plight of her mother. I sent notes to Margaret and Izzy, asking when it was convenient to discuss this with them. Margaret replied by return messenger: she would be in that afternoon, I could call anytime before five. Izzy's reply came a little later and promised a meeting with her and Dr Martindale in the next day or so.

I took a cab to Margaret's house. She ordered tea for us both, which we took on her balcony overlooking the sea, for it was a warm day. I explained my thoughts to her. She listened, nodding thoughtfully.

"I agree with you that the doubters should be there, but we need a sprinkling of converts as well. You should make sure there's plenty of time for a bit of a public debate. Your maid and mine will both know some unfortunates to invite as well. As for sympathetic councillors, now you have me. I told you I gave up on them. I can't think of one who isn't a self-serving smug parasite. But I'm happy to stand up and say that, if you'd like me speak as an overprivileged old fossil. I'm going to ask the councillors along, though. They need shaming! Ah, do you think I might have one of your cigarettes? Philip disapproves, and I do so like them."

We smoked, drank tea and chatted. We discussed where the meeting might be held. She offered her house, but I thought it better somewhere neutral. She mentioned a few church halls, then blew out a cloud of smoke and beamed.

"No, what am I thinking of? Of course, the pavilion! Where better to shame them? Ha! Listen to me. Not them, us. I must admit I bridled somewhat when the People's Budget came in, but you know, my dear Cordelia, it may not be a bad thing. I shall be dead in a few years, and I suspect one way or another, so will our way of life; there are the rumblings of an earthquake. Can I have another of your cigarettes?"

We discussed a buffet. Perhaps we should serve potato stew to show what the working classes had to survive on, but decided that might be a step too far, but we would paste photographs of what the workers could afford to eat around the serving table. We knew a photographer who might do this…

Feeling very buoyant, I kissed her goodbye and left her a handful of cigarettes.

Izzy arranged a meeting with herself and Dr Martindale and in two days' time, I went to her house at three as arranged. The doctor was already there, and Izzy had at least cleared chairs enough for us to sit on. Such is the mark of that woman than she remembered me instantly and the sorry circumstances in which we'd met. I shook her hand. Her smile wasn't particularly warm, but it was genuine. She asked me to call her Louisa, and looked at me. I felt as though I was a book she was reading. I'd read her treatise, and was moved by it, and I told her so. I told them both of my ideas and they both very much agreed with them, and complimented me on my efforts so far. Louisa felt sure she could find a suitable person to speak on behalf of the oppressed, and left after an hour of discussion for her work kept her very busy. How she found time to write was a wonder, said Izzy, but I'd seen the fire in Louisa's eyes and could understand. The great majority of us paddle along in the stream of life, but the truly great are propelled along by unimaginable forces, with convictions stronger than all the rest of us put together. It is something special to know them and be warmed by their fire.

After she left, we smoked Izzy's special cigarettes. I was getting to want these, and asked her where I could obtain them. She promised to get me a supply for they were not easily obtained. We decided a few more details about the launch — posters, articles, entertainments, that sort of thing. I asked her if the *Mouettes* were meeting again, as I wanted badly to talk to Charles. I told her what an effect his paintings had had on me, and she talked about him. He was not easy to talk to, she said; he spoke through his paintings and what he was saying wasn't easy, but, yes, it was time for another meeting. Perhaps…?

Of course I'd be delighted to host an evening. We fixed up a date for the following week, and Izzy said she would contact them all and arrange it. Then she asked if I would like 'a little lie down'. Oh yes, Izzy! Yes, I would.

Because I'm falling in love with you.

I had trouble sleeping that night. So much was happening. I tossed and turned, thinking of the launch, the *Mouettes* evening, how to divide up the house to accommodate Janet, the next posing session, and should I ask Izzy to move in with me, except…

"You all right?" Janet murmured. "Oh yes," I replied, stroking the back of her neck as she snuggled onto my breast. "Go back to sleep."

I spent the next few days addressing these issues. I told Peregrine that Janet was agreeable to further sessions, and we arranged a day in the following week. I asked him what he had in mind, but he simply smiled and told me to wait and see. I pencilled in the date in my diary. I worked out what changes we could make to the house to accommodate Janet, and that turned out to be surprisingly simple. My financial position was such that I had been able to buy the house, although it had cost me nearly five thousand pounds, and I had precious little to squander after that. With rent from Janet and my earnings from our photographic ventures, we could live comfortably. I would have to reduce her salary, of course, and between us, we could employ another maid. The sums added up.

Izzy called round to tell me that the *Mouettes* evening had been fixed for next Tuesday. Janet had ushered her into my day room, where I was writing letters, with a rather bad grace, I thought. I wondered how much she had deduced. Izzy appeared not to have noticed, thankfully. She kissed me on one cheek, then, when Janet had left, tenderly, on my lips.

I opened the door to call down to Janet to fetch us some tea. She was outside, pretending to dust. She stomped off. Izzy and I sat down to talk about her writings, the group's meeting and the book launch, but she seemed abstracted somehow. I felt emboldened to tell her this. She was about to answer, when Janet appeared with the tea tray and a plate of cakes. She put it down between us without a word, fixed me with a look, and left. Izzy produced a bulky package from her handbag. It was a large quantity of her marijuana cigarettes. We smoked while we took tea and ate the cake. The herb relaxed us, and I repeated my observation that there was something on her mind.

"Astute as ever, dear Cordie. Look, I don't know how to say this, but you've woken something up in me, certainly some slumbering beast, but it's more than that…"

I put my finger on her lips, and went to open the door. Janet was not in sight, but I heard the angry clatter of pans in the kitchen. I went back and sat beside Izzy, and held her hands in mine.

"Sorry, I have to be careful," I said. "Go on, tell me." She just sucked nervously on her cigarette for a few minutes, looking at the ceiling. I waited.

Eventually, she continued. "Sod it, Cordie, I'm in love with you. There, I've said it. Isn't that a ridiculous thing to say?"

I looked her in the eye. "About as ridiculous as me saying I love you too, Izzy. I think about you all the time. I want you."

I'd never meant anything more sincerely in my life. I leant towards her and kissed her, tenderly at first, then with a passion as she pushed her tongue into my mouth, and we held each other close. We smoked another cigarette, then she left, after I'd promised to see her tomorrow. Janet saw her out, and gathered up the teacups. She didn't say a word. I put my head in my hands and sighed. I was getting into such a mess. Janet was no longer just a maid, she was my companion, my lover, and partner in our photographic adventures. She was from the class that I was trying to help. But there was Izzy: I'd felt an attraction to her from the first meeting and my liking and respect had grown into love. True, her body couldn't compare with Janet's, neither could her sexual acrobatics, but she offered something much deeper. But I was here, living with Janet, and inextricably entangled with her, and needing her for our sessions with Peregrine. I'd steered myself onto some dangerous rocks, and no mistake.

I called on Izzy as promised next day. She had cleared a worn sofa of its piles of books and pamphlets, and we sat side by side. She was wearing a strange, long embroidered gown with obviously nothing underneath. It was from Arabia, she said, and called a kaftan. We embraced warmly and discussed our feelings for each other. She'd obviously given the matter some thought. "We should live as we are for the moment," she ventured, and I agreed.

"The thorny question arises, though, about our sex lives. I should warn you that free sex among the group happens quite frequently. No-one is hurt by it, and it is simply for our hedonistic enjoyment with no emotional entanglement. I don't know how you feel about it, but if you're agreeable, I think we should continue the practice. It has no emotional depth to it, and is a very different beast from our lovemaking which, for me, means so much more. What do you think?"

"I'm very happy with that," I replied. "I think we should continue to be regarded as good friends with a common cause. This is a small community, and homosexual love is only tolerated if kept discreet. Anyway, I found the activities at the picnic very enjoyable."

"I'm so glad! Then outwardly, as you say, we are just the best of friends, but knowing inside that we are so much more than that."

She drew me to her and kissed me passionately. I ran my fingers over her face and through her hair, and was about to take matters further, but she pulled away gently. She picked up her cigarette, took a thoughtful puff on it, and said, "Then there's your maid, Janet. I assume you're in a physical relationship with her."

That took me by surprise. "Why do you say that?"

"Because of the way she behaved, the way she looked at you, and she's rather irresistible."

"You are clever and observant, Izzy. Yes, I'm sorry, we are — were — intimate."

"I'm not surprised, I'd have a go at her like a shot if I could. But I sensed perhaps more of an emotional attachment?"

"I don't love her, if that's what you mean. I was completely on my own when I came here. She became my companion and friend in addition to her household duties. I've never felt entirely comfortable with the relationship; she has too much of a hold over me."

"I would hate to think I was competing with a scullery maid for your favours, that's all. No, that sounds so snobbish, and I hate such class distinctions, but you know what I mean. When it comes to real, meaningful love, I want to be wholly yours and you to be wholly mine."

"Then I shall keep her at arm's length in future, I swear to you. I know it's been sudden, but I know I love you very deeply."

I didn't mention our involvement with Peregrine. That had never to be mentioned. Izzy smiled and sat back on the sofa; a silent invitation. I kissed her again, and this time our hands wandered over the other's body, rubbing and squeezing. This wasn't the frantic, cold-blooded lust of my encounters with Janet, but with Izzy it was where minds met though the medium of the body. We took it slowly, relishing each touch, going into the bedroom to disrobe: she in a second, simply pulling the kaftan over her head while I wrestled with the various hooks and buttons and layers of my clothing. Finally, I stood in front of her, naked. We looked at each other's bodies. She had a well-fleshed body, certainly not fat, but rounded. Her breasts were a good size, with large puffy nipples and only just beginning to sag. Her stomach had a roundness to it, and below it a generous triangle of dark pubic hair. While I stood there, she closed her eyes and ran her hands over the con- tours of my body: face, neck, shoulders, breasts, stomach and thighs, then my back and bottom, as though committing them to memory. We pressed our bodies together and kissed. Our tongues explored while our hands caressed each other. We lay on her bed and played with each other's breasts, sucking and licking them. Izzy had such sensitive nipples, and started to make that curious growling sound as I worked on them. She reached down between my legs and teased my clitoris. I heard myself repeating her name over and over as she massaged it before sinking her fingers into me. First one, then two and finally most of her hand; I was so ready to take her into me. I thrust my pelvis against her hand as she moved it in and out of me. I was doing the same to her, pushing against the walls of her vagina with my fingers. She was awash with her juices, and my fingers made the most arousing squelching noises as she and I bucked and worked each other to a noisy and simultaneous climax. As she came, her juice spurted out of her, making a large wet patch on the sheet. I licked her clean, although I was still twitching and shuddering. We lay, still stroking each other's wet slits, and soon became aroused again. We pleased each other with our tongues, and after the second orgasm, lay happily back in each other's arms. We were glistening with perspiration.

Janet must have sensed what was going on. She became monosyllabic, just performing her duties with polite indifference. We needed to talk, but there didn't seem a right time to broach the subject, and the longer I left it, the harder it became. Eventually, it was Janet who proved the stronger. She had served me my lunch, and I noticed her hand was shaking as she placed the plate in front of me. She stood over me, one hand on her hip.

"All right, what's going on?" she demanded.

"What do you mean?"

"You know damn well what I mean."

I looked down at my plate. "I'm sorry, Janet. I should have talked to you before. The fact is that I've rather fallen in love with Izzy, the lady that called the other day. Trouble is, I think the world of you, too."

"I thought that was it. Well, here's a to-do." She was nodding her head rather intensely, her lips set thin. "What a to-do… a right to-do." Her eyes suddenly flashed angrily. "Well, screw you, and you can stuff your precious meeting!"

She stormed out, slamming the door. I got up, catching the plate of stew and sending it over my dress and the carpet as I hitched up my skirt and ran after her into the kitchen. She was hunched over the sink, her hands gripping the wooden counter, her shoulders heaving. I put my hands on her shoulders to calm her, but she shrugged them off and moved away.

"Janet! Calm down, for heaven's sake!" I pinned her against the wall. She tried to free herself, but couldn't. She was weeping, her tears running down her cheeks. "Listen to me, Janet. Listen!" She calmed down enough for me to be able to speak.

"My feelings for you haven't changed at all. You are the best friend I ever had. That's why I've wanted to help you and raise you up all this time, and I hope you think of me as a good friend, too. Nothing will ever, ever compare with the sex we have together, but it's not real love, and you know it."

She was now just staring at me with a child's eyes. I let go of her and took her by the hand to sit at the table, and drew up a chair to sit close to her, holding her hands.

"It's my fault, I shouldn't have broken the boundaries, but I was desperately attracted to you from the start and we led each other on along a path we shouldn't have travelled. We both knew it was wrong. Then I meet Izzy, and it seems so right."

"Oh, does it really? You hardly know her."

"One just senses these things."

"Oh, does one? I should give my notice, I suppose. I can't stay here, watching you with that woman."

"I hope you don't, for I value your friendship too much."

"How could I go back to just being your maid? It would be too strange to bear for both of us. Best I go. I knew it would all go wrong one day. Suppose that's the end of our posing sessions, too."

I thought about that. "It needn't be. I'm not going to tell Izzy about those, am I? If you want to continue them, then we can. It'll be our secret."

She seemed mollified by this. "I want to. The money's good, and I love our little you-know-whats. But I don't think I could bear being your maid if she were here."

"She's certainly not moving in here, and I shall be visiting her at her home in future. Let's give it a try. Please, Janet?

"All right. I will, but if it feels bad, I shall have to look for another position."

It did feel a little awkward at first, trying to maintain the proper relationship of maid and mistress, and we would both at times look at one another, remembering our times spent rolling together in my bed.

All the more strange, when we arrived, separately, for our next session with Peregrine. He had decided, he said, to do a last set of poses today, but would we be amenable to performing in front of a moving image camera? He had obtained such a device and was convinced it was the way forward in artistic entertainment and he wanted to be a pioneer. A rival in the town, Esmé Collings, was already using it, but who wanted to see pictures of children playing on the beach?

Janet and I looked at one another enquiringly, both uncertain what the other would think. I had heard of moving pictures, and peered into the mutoscope machines on the pier, but not seen one before.

"I suppose it would be all right," I said, "I don't really know anything about them."

"Same here," Janet added.

"Then let me enlighten you, ladies!" Peregrine exclaimed, and moved to the door which led to his darkroom. We followed, intrigued. In fact, the door led to a corridor with a number of doors off, but he led us out into a small courtyard containing a number of outbuildings. I was amazed: his premises were vast. He led us into one of the outbuildings. It was even darker inside than his studio, but as our eyes became accustomed to the darkness, I could make out a taut white screen on one wall and a number of chairs facing it. Behind them was a mechanical apparatus of some description. He sat us down on the chairs and busied himself with his machine. After a few minutes the screen lit up with some random squiggles, then the figure of a woman appeared. Janet and I gasped, it was like a photograph, but the image was moving! The woman was in her undergarments, sitting languidly on a chair. A man appeared with two glasses of champagne. With jerky movements, they drank them at a gulp, then threw them down. The man bent over her, his hand finding its way into her camisole. She pulled it down, revealing her bosom. Janet's hand grasped mine as we watched, mesmerised, while the woman pulled down the man's trousers and took out his prick. She sucked it while she rubbed at her crotch. She stood up, took off her drawers, and sat back on the chair, her legs over the arms and resumed sucking his swollen penis. Janet's hand had now pulled mine towards her crotch, and I began to massage it, while her hand did the same for me. The woman in the picture knelt on the chair and the man entered her from behind, as he jerked back and forth, he winked at the camera, and the picture went dark. Janet and I hastily withdrew our hands as Peregrine's voice came from behind us.

"Well? It is impressive, is it not? Not my work, you understand, but I have acquired the most up-to-date equipment to make such things. This is but the beginning of a revolution and we should be there to all profit from it. Are you interested?"

"Oh, yes!" we both said.

Peregrine led us back into the studio, and we went through another session of poses. This time, I think he was rehearsing us for a moving picture, for he talked us through a scenario. As in real life, I would be the mistress, and Janet my maid. She would drop a vase and look horrified while I looked angry. I pulled up her skirt and tore down her drawers, then put her over my knee and spanked her. She went to bend down to pick up the pieces of the vase, and I lifted her dress again and caressed her buttocks before ordering her to strip. Things just progressed from there.

Peregrine had his pictures and was happy with them. I felt the idea was a bit weak, and determined to work out something stronger with Janet. Peregrine asked if we could make the film in my bedroom, and I couldn't think of a reason why we shouldn't. He said he would have the equipment delivered in unmarked packages by carrier next week — it would arouse too much curiosity if he were to bring it himself.

Janet and I ate together that night, just to discuss possible scenarios for a film. One thing bothered me: Peregrine would be unable to alter all the many images on a moving picture — he had explained how the apparatus worked. The faces of the actors in the film we had seen were clearly visible. Janet had no reservations about this, she would be completely unknown in London and, she joked, who knew what handsome millionaire might see her and ask for her... I however daren't be identifiable, although it struck me, if a gentleman of my acquaintance did happen to see me, he wouldn't dare to speak of it and admit he had seen such a forbidden film.

Janet came up with the idea that she could be the maid folding up her mistresses clothes and sniffing her drawers, then hitching up her skirt and lying on the bed to masturbate. I would then come in behind her in my nightdress, unnoticed, and looked shocked but then start playing with myself before kneeling over her with my slit over her mouth. She would startle, then start licking me while I bent over and started tonguing her. We thought of more elaborations and became more excited as we drank more and more wine, before I pulled her to me and kissed her. She responded, pulling my hips towards her and grinding her pelvis hard against mine.

Oh dear, I thought, here we go again.

I felt too guilty to see Izzy the next day as I'd planned. Instead, I salved my conscience by making preparations for the book launch, now only a week away. Margaret had booked a room in a large church hall, and I had arranged caterers, placed advertisements in the papers, and received many replies to my invitations. Now to distribute the posters. I had thirty printed off, so went around the town pinning or pasting them up with a satchel of pins, paste, string and scissors. People read them with curiosity as I put them up on trees or the side of buildings. I'd made sure that 'Free Buffet' was printed clearly, which should draw quite a few in, I thought. I went onto the pier and posted some around the amusement arcade.

"Sounds fascinating," said a voice behind me. I turned round to see the loathsome Nicholas smiling nastily at me. "Hello, Mrs Cordelia Edwards. Remember me?"

"How could I forget, much as though I'd like to. Now excuse me, please." I tried to step past him, but he blocked my way.

"I liked what you did to me. I liked it very much, and I want you to do it again, my sweet." I was beginning to panic, but hid it.

"Thank you for the invitation, but I must decline."

"I don't think you will. You see, I've been watching you, and I think you're straying from the true path of the light."

"What are you talking about, for heaven's sake?"

"I'm talking, my lovely, about your visits to the photographers. I ask myself, 'Now what's she doing in there so often?' and I tries and tries to think what it could be, then you go in with another lady, but you go in separate, so I think, 'What could they be wanting to hide?' and there's only one thing I can think of. Such a shame if it got out."

"Ah, but you can't prove anything. I have been having some portraits taken, that's all."

"And some very pretty portraits they are too." He produced one of the photographs of Janet and myself. I tried to grab it, but he whisked it away and replaced it in the inside pocket of his blazer. Panic set in. If he did go to the police, that was the end of my place in Brighton society, and the end of Peregrine's business and career.

"How did you get that?"

"That's my little secret. Let's just say locked doors and drawers don't present a difficulty for me. Neither does developing a negative."

"If I come back with you, will you give me the photograph?"

"Of course."

I was thinking quickly, very quickly. If I complied now, he'd be back, again and again. I had my long scissors in my satchel, I could kill him here and take a chance on not being noticed, but suppose he had more photographs in his room… There was only one answer I could see.

"Then I have no choice, have I?"

"None. But don't pretend you didn't enjoy it. I could tell."

He was right, I had. I walked with him to the house and up the stairs that stank of cabbage and into his room which still smelt even worse. That, and the task ahead, was making me feel quite sick.

"Help me to the divine light," he said, "You know what I want. I must be purged through the swamp of sin and humiliation and pain to reach the true path to the light of forgiveness." I played my part. "For one so wicked and sinful, the swamp is deep and deadly and only harsh punishment shall cleanse your wickedness and place you on the shining path."

"Then punish me, mistress."

"Undress, and kneel before me!"

I might as well make it worth his while. As he turned away to remove his clothes, I did the same, and faced him, naked except for my stockings and black leather gloves. He knelt prostrate before me, his eyes on the floor.

"Look at me! Look at me and confess your wickedness. Do you not lust after my body?"

"Yes," he croaked.

"Look at my woman's breasts. Have they not tempted you?"

He nodded.

"Say it! Confess!"

"Yes! I confess I am weak and have been tempted!"

"Look at my cunny, worm. Closer! Smell it! That's right, smell the foul vapours that rise from my swamp of temptation." To tell the truth, I was enjoying this. He gave a cry and, still kneeling, threw his scrawny body backwards and thrust his arms out, his little penis erect.

"Cleanse me! Wash away my sin with fire and pain! Help me to the shining light!"

He got up, fetched the black leather whip, then threw himself onto the bed, on his back.

"Time to be cleansed and purged of your sin."

I started to whip him as hard as I could, raising great red wheals on his pale body. He cried out in a mix of pain and rapture. He was a madman. I beat him until his whole front was covered in livid stripes, then turned him over, and did the same to his back. Between lashes, I picked up the poker from the fireplace. I rolled him back over, and whipped his erect member. Eventually, I think the pain became too great, and he ejaculated.

"I am purged! I am purged!" he cried.

"Not quite," I replied. "One last punishment, I think."

I brought the poker down as hard as I could on his head, and again, and again. He lay still. He deserved to die and was probably happier dead. I replaced the poker, dressed, then took the incriminating photograph from his blazer pocket. I began to search his room in case there might be others.

As I did, I heard a sound from the bed. Unbelievably, he was still alive. I seized the poker again and beat his head until his face was an unrecognisable mess.

I put the poker back and resumed my search. I found them under his pillow, and took them. Even so, I made a thorough search, but there were no others. I did find a kitchen knife and used that to cut off his genitals and stuff them roughly into the space where his mouth had been. I had to escape without being noticed. It was five o'clock and I would be sure to be seen.

I went down the stairs, and knocked on the door of one of the downstairs flats. An elderly lady answered.

"Excuse me," I said, "I'm most awfully sorry to disturb you, but does a Mrs Anderson live here?"

"No, dear, no-one of that name here. There's a Mrs Atkins…"

"No, the name's definitely Anderson, Rebecca Anderson. 17, Grove Hill."

"Oh no, dearie, you've got it wrong, this is Grove Road; Grove Hill is back down there, turn right, and it's on your left."

"Oh, I am such a fool! I'm so sorry to have troubled you. My name's Sarah Bannerman, by the way."

"And I'm Elsie Binks. Hope you find your friend all right."

So I walked away in that direction, and back home. I'd reckoned that, if the police did ask questions and if anyone had seen me, my engineered enquiry and false name would throw them off the scent. Once home, I told Janet I needed a bath. She prepared one, soaped me and rinsed me down. I relaxed as she rubbed the sponge over my skin, then towelled me off and draped me in my dressing gown. She placed the velvet choker around my neck, and put hers on. Dinner was all ready, and another masterpiece it was. Oysters, I remember, some late asparagus in butter, then a suet and beef pudding followed by a trifle. I had a fair idea why I was being treated to such feasts. The more we talked and drank, the more urgent my need for her became. I needed her to blot out the images of the afternoon. I stood up and let my dressing gown fall open.

"Bring the wine up to bed, will you?" I asked her. "And some of my new cigarettes."

I called round to see Izzy the next day, to confirm all the arrangements were in place for the launch. I let myself in and called to her. She called back. She was at her desk, and dressed in that fetching kaftan. We hugged, and kissed and stared into each other's eyes. I asked where she had obtained the kaftan, for I rather wanted one of my own. She chuckled.

"You'll have to go to Arabia if you want one."

"You've been?"

"Oh, yes. Five years ago. Now that was something. I'll tell you all about it sometime, naughty bits and all." We discussed who should say what, although she reminded me that the evening was to launch the book, and underline its message with some contemporary examples, and not to try and make it a political rant. I'd been working on it so hard that I had, I suppose, rather lost sight of the purpose of the evening and was seeing it a chance to shame my own class. Bless the woman, she had such a sharp mind!

"Just trust Louisa to do the talking," she said. "It's her night, and we just have to make sure the right people hear her message. You've informed the newspapers, of course."

Damn! I'd completely forgotten that, but I told her I had. I'd do it that very afternoon. "I've written a pamphlet which we can distribute on the night, but it could do with being circulated to the papers beforehand. Time's a bit short, but I wonder…"

"Of course. Leave it to me. A hundred?"

"Make it two — we can always distribute some afterwards. I've been in touch with the publishers and I think they'll stand the printing costs. Go to Edwards' in North Road and mention my name, they'll do it quickly — I'm always late for deadlines!"

"Right, and don't worry about the money, I'm happy to pay. After all, Margaret's paying for the room with a few of her friends. Louisa is obviously well regarded in these parts. I've agreed to share half the cost of the buffet with her, as well."

She gave me a hug. "Oh, Cordie, you are lovely! I do love you so much. One day, it can be just you and I, free to be together. Won't that be wonderful?"

I kissed her and reached for her breast, but she pulled away.

"I want you, dear Cordie, believe me, but I've an article to write that has to be in by tomorrow. We'll have to defer the pleasure, I'm so sorry. Tomorrow, if you call round, I promise you."

She handed me the pamphlet for the printers, kissed me again, and showed me out. I felt slightly disconcerted for no reason at all, but walked round to the printers, not far away, and explained our needs. The man, a rather large and red-nosed man with an inky apron, laughed knowingly and said he couldn't recall a time when Miss Fallon hadn't wanted them in a tearing hurry. Two days, he said. I asked him where the local newspaper offices might be found. He directed me to the Brighton Herald and the Brighton Gazette. I walked home for luncheon first, and found Janet had prepared a real feast of lobster soup, game pie, and a lovely strawberry flan to finish. Janet had placed a large red rose by my table, too. After a rest to digest that, I ventured out to the newspaper offices to tell them of the meeting and request that a reporter attend.

When I returned, I found the hall full of the packages that Peregrine had sent round, and Janet keen to see what was inside them. There was an envelope attached to the biggest of the boxes and a note inside which simply said, 'Thursday, 2.00pm'. Two days' time! We carried the boxes with an effort up to my bedroom, and opened them. There was a large tripod, a machine which we supposed must be the camera itself, a tape measure, another tripod, a lamp of sorts, a box of lenses of different dimensions and some disc-like metal canisters which we supposed must contain the film. It was so exciting, but we dared not fiddle with any of it, so put it to one corner, and covered it with a cloth.Over dinner, I made a rough sketch of a kaftan and showed it to Janet. I'd rather taken a fancy to such a garment, only for day wear inside, of course. I asked her if she would be able to make such a garment. She looked at it curiously, and said she could, although looked a little askance when I told her where I'd seen it, but yes, she could purchase a length of heavy coloured cotton and would see what she could do. She might even make one for herself at the same time, she added with a wink.

I persuaded Izzy to put down her pen and come for a stroll into town with me the next day. We would take coffee together, then go and try on some dresses, then have some lunch at one of the many eating places near North Street. Worth trying, she said: shopping was a bit of a novelty for her. We walked to the Lanes and drank coffee, talking and laughing, pointing out various characters in the street around us. Arm in arm, we walked to North Street, where the most alluring dress shops were to be found. We called at Ernest's, Harrington's and Joseph Smith's. I dived into racks of dresses, holding them up for Izzy's opinion. Initially entering into the spirit of a ladies' day at the shops, I sensed her enthusiasm was waning quite early on, and by the time we entered the fourth shop, she was positively truculent. I tried to whet her appetite by offering to buy her a fetching lace blouse, and a delightful silk dress in the most gorgeous deep cerise. Not even that raised her interest. Rather deflated, I suggested we find a restaurant for lunch. As we headed back into the Lanes, we passed a bookshop, and Izzy asked if we might go in to browse the books. We were in there for what seemed like hours. Izzy perked up and burrowed around the shelves. It was her turn to ask whether I had read this, or what did I think of that writer. She left, happily clutching three books. It was my turn to feel discomfited; I hadn't heard of any of the writers that she'd mentioned. I resolved to try a little harder and widen my reading.

Our lunch was a little restrained: I was making an effort to discuss the books she was reading, she to talk about dresses. She offered to go back with me to the last dress shop to get the outfit I'd admired so much for her. I asked her if we might go to the bookshop so that she might pick out a suitable primer that I might educate myself on social injustice. She laid her hand on mine. "Let's go back, then, we have much to learn from each other. Isn't that enriching?"

So we went back, and she recommended a book to me, and I bought it, and a small volumes of poems by W B Yeats that she'd selected. I also purchased the blouse and skirt for her — she hadn't the means herself. We walked back to her apartments, clutching our purchases. Once back, I persuaded her to try on the skirt and blouse. She took off her drab, grey dress, and put on the new garments. She looked into a mirror, and saw me approaching from behind. She arched her back as she saw my arms encircle her waist and move her hands to her breasts. She watched as my fingers undid the buttons which she had just fastened, watched as I removed her new blouse, and her camisole, and cupped her breasts in my hands, rolling her nipples between my fingers. She watched as I then lifted up her bright new skirt, and placed my hand on her mons. She stood, transfixed, as she saw me pull her drawers down and unfasten her dress. She stepped out of her clothes, and stood aside to watch me in the mirror stripping off my clothes behind her. She shuddered as she watched and felt my hand reach between her legs and my finger stroking her slit, my other hand toying with her breast. She moved her legs apart so that my fingers could push deeper inside her, all the time looking in the mirror and bending forward so that her breasts swung in time with my fingers. Her generous juices ran over my hand and down her leg as she orgasmed. She led me onto her bed and licked at me until I too reached my climax. We shared a cigarette, lying there on her bed before I dressed and, kissing her fondly, left.

Janet and I waited in a state of excitement for Peregrine's arrival the next day. I spent the morning reading the book I'd bought yesterday. It was very hard going, I thought. I put it aside and tried to read the book of poems she'd recommended. This too was perhaps a bit opaque for me, and I decided my mind was more fixed on the afternoon's adventure than anything more spiritual. Janet and I ate a leisurely lunch together, and she'd excelled herself again. We decided we might benefit from a glass of wine to aid proceedings, which turned out to be a lot more than a glassful. She also showed me the material she'd bought for the kaftans: a pleasing mid-blue and a burgundy, with some white piping to go around the edges. I rather liked the idea of the two of us, sharing a dinner, identically dressed.

At exactly two o' clock, Peregrine rang the bell. Janet let him in, while I tried to look like a lady in my day room pretending to write a letter. He made approving noises about the house, and the three of us made small talk for a while. We escorted him up to my bedroom, and he busied himself assembling his equipment, placing the camera onto the tripod, measuring the distance to the bed, opening all the blinds and shutters so that the maximum amount of light would fill the room. He loaded one of the canisters of film into the camera.

We discussed our ideas for various scenarios with him. He liked most of them, and rejected the rest for technical reasons. Besides, he knew his market well. He knew what titivated his customers the most. We were to start with his original idea: Janet was to drop a vase — he'd brought one — and I was to spank her, then take it from there. He drew the blinds so that we could rehearse in a reassuring darkness. We went through the motions. Janet pretended to drop the vase, for it had to be saved for the real shot. I walked in and looked horrified, while she looked contrite and bent over to pick up the pieces, and while she was doing so, I lifted her skirt and smacked her bottom. I dragged her over my knee while I was sitting on the bed, and continued to smack her exposed rear until the strokes became caresses and she would arch her buttocks up so that I could kiss them, then stand up and take off my nightdress and force her to lick me off. And that was about it. We'd already decided we thought it a bit weak, but didn't dare say so.

It was very odd, having to go through the motions in such a cold-blooded way. But, after a few tries, Peregrine was satisfied. He opened the blinds, then we did it all over again, with the camera turning. There is such a strong part of me that responds to an audience, even if unseen, and I think Janet shares this need, that the thought of an audience for our capers aroused me. We followed the plan for a while, but then Janet and I got immersed in the scene, and drifted off the script. Peregrine didn't stop us, until he announced that the reel had run out. He had stopped us just when it was almost impossible to, but we were supposed to be actors. He liked what we'd done so far, but could we carry on after he'd changed the reel? We relaxed while he fussed over the camera and changed the reel. He said the second reel would contain some closer shots, so we should be prepared to stop whenever he said.

We resumed where we had left off, then Peregrine would shout "Stop!" and we would freeze in mid-thrust. He would then move his camera close to us, and with a tape measure determine the distance from his lens to our privates, and adjust his camera accordingly. Then we had to continue where we had left off. It was so contrived and trying to keep everything spontaneous was hard, but I told myself, we were actors and the film wasn't about our feelings, but just exposing ourselves for the punters. While we messed around on the bed, Peregrine would cry, "Keep going! Another three minutes left! Start your orgasms now! More! Now collapse and kiss. Now wink at the camera."

Peregrine was very happy with our efforts, and we relaxed while Janet put on a *peignoir* and padded down to the kitchen to make a pot of tea. She reappeared with a tray laden with tea and fancy cakes. I provided my herbal cigarettes. We sat around, chatting. I realised I was becoming a professional at this. It was all such a cold-blooded pretence, but if it paid, then why not?

Then, suddenly, I was gripped by a worrying thought.

"You can't disguise my face! I should have worn a mask or something! What if someone recognises me?"

"You need not fear on that score, my dear. I fear that the technical quality of these films is not precise enough yet. Your face will not be distinct enough to be recognised, and, even if it were, what man is going to admit that he's been watching an art film?"

I wasn't that convinced, but then thought that I really didn't care that much about any of my London acquaintances. Let them gawp and gaze! I really didn't care, they weren't in a position to tell anyone, were they?

We decided to film another two-reeler. (You see how quickly one picks up the right phrases!) We decided on a variant of Janet's and my idea — me undressing, Janet sniffing my drawers, pulling up her dress to reveal herself and masturbating. I returned, naked except for an open gown and, discovering her, placed my hand on her quim as well. We improvised expertly after that.

It must have taken us two hours to do that one simple sequence. I think Peregrine must have been learning as he went, for this time, there was far more stopping and starting, moving camera distances and angles. By the time we'd finished, it was getting late, and we were all tired. I invited Peregrine to share dinner with us, but he declined — there was much to do in the darkroom. He left with his spools of film, and Janet and I lay down on my bed and slept. By the time we woke, it was too late for Janet to cook dinner, so I suggested

we went out to the nearest restaurant to eat. By this time,
I didn't care who saw me on the film, or who saw me
out with my maid, or anything really.

Chapter 6

It was the day of the book launch, and I spent the day getting everything ready with Izzy. We'd decided that Izzy should introduce Louisa, who would talk about her work, and her book, then Janet would give her few words affirming the difficulties facing the working classes based on her first-hand knowledge. One of Margaret's Tory councillors would then say what measures the council were taking to improve matters, then finally invite questions before the buffet. We had plenty of copies of *Under the Surface* available to purchase, and the leaflets to hand out.

It was late in the afternoon by the time we'd laid out a hundred chairs, arranged cloths over the tables and placed the books and leaflets in a prominent position. Peregrine had done us proud with a number of photographs of the squalid side of our society. They were extraordinarily powerful — the man was a genius. We'd also been able to indulge in a few passionate embraces during the afternoon. We returned to our respective homes to get ready and take tea, returning at seven to greet visitors. Louisa Martindale was already there, looking approvingly at our efforts. One or two people had already arrived and sat waiting. More and more people started to arrive, and I breathed a sigh of relief: it looked like we were going to get a full house. There were the upper classes, Margaret and a considerable circle of her friends, MPs from London and locally, councillors and charitable committee ladies. Tristan, Charles, Lavinia, and a few others with them that I hadn't met were also there. I managed to have a quick word with them, especially Charles. I told him I was most impressed by his paintings and wondered if I could see some more of his work. He'd be delighted, he told me. If we could talk after the meeting, he'd tell me where his studio was and arrange a time for a visit. I gave the others a quick kiss on the cheek and exchanged a few words before having to welcome other guests. Then there were a lot from the working classes. Bless her, Janet had been whipping up support among her peers. I chatted to some old acquaintances, but it was time to start.

Izzy rose from her seat at the speakers' table.

"Good evening, ladies and gentlemen, and thank you for turning out in such large numbers tonight to celebrate the launch of Dr Martindale's new and I think highly significant book: *Under the Surface*. I am Isobel Fallon, a writer and political philosopher as I'm sure most of you know. I have long championed the rights and true worth of the labouring classes, and now we have a book that gives factual evidence of the problems facing them, and indeed our whole society. I'm sure you are all familiar with Dr Martindale. Ever since she arrived here, she has worked tirelessly at the Lewes Road dispensary, and has been the driving force in converting it into the Lady Chichester Hospital, which should open next year. Her special interest lies in the treatment of women's ailments, a subject too long neglected. I would ask you give a warm welcome to Dr Martindale."

Louisa stood up to polite applause.

"Thank you so much, Miss Fallon, for you kind remarks. I will blow my own trumpet and confirm that I do indeed work tirelessly at my job, not because I have any natural inclination to hard work, but because there is so much work to be done. In my previous practice in Hull, and in my three years here, I have been struck, and indeed sometimes horrified, by the neglect of the health needs of women by a profession that only admitted women into their ranks thirty years ago, and still show little interest in it.

"Now, I'm a rather hands-on sort of doctor, and like to visit my patients at home when I can in order to understand them better. I visit duchesses and I visit paupers. Now the duchesses can afford medical attention and demand it in a timely fashion, but for every duchess, there are thousands of working-class people who can ill afford medical intervention. They also can't afford proper sanitation or nutritious food, and when your family is starving, you have to turn to petty crime to survive. Then, when you're caught and put into prison, what does you wife have to do to feed herself and her children? She can take in laundry, or she can sew, but those occupations are not paid well enough that she can survive on that, and so she turns to prostitution —" One of Tristan's weak- chinned friends gave a childish guffaw at the word. Every female in the room turned and glared at him. "Not because she wants to, but because that's the only way to survive."

There were a few cries of, "Hear, hear!" from some women at the back. Otherwise, you could have heard a pin drop.

"It is my privilege to visit these people, and to learn from them just what life is like for the majority of the population: the unseen, the unnoticed, the ignored. They only matter when they have to steal from the rich, that's when they're noticed, and they pay for it dearly. I sometimes feel such a sense of hopelessness when I stand in the path of this tidal wave of poverty and sickness, which I think is totally unacceptable in the civilised society we claim to be, but I have to stand and try to fight it. It was seeing these terrible things day in and day out that drove me to write this book. It is not a sensationalist book for I am not given to overstating facts. It does not point any fingers, it merely serves to reveal the uncomfortable truths that are kept hidden from us, or that we'd prefer not to see."

She went on to read some passages from the book. They were the more lurid passages about prostitution and venereal disease, but that was deliberate. I'd suggested that they might tempt people into buying the book.

"Now, I'm glad to say I have allies in this battle. There are some very good people who recognise that there is a problem and do an immense amount of work to help the worst off. People like my friend Lady Padgett over there, who has devoted much of her life to raising funds and donating a great deal of her own money to help. Fundraising will help individuals, but it won't change society. For that, we need government, local and national, to stop me from seeing these appalling sights every day."

She spoke for a while longer, in fact longer than we'd allowed, but there were no signs of restlessness in the audience. She was rivetingly sincere. She wasn't trying to be a great orator, she was just talking to each and every one of us. She finished her talk and sat down.

Izzy introduced Janet, which made us all feel slightly awkward, I think, and poor Janet looked terrified, but stood up hesitantly, looked round the room, paler than ever, but I'd told her to do this for her mother. She spoke with a confidence that surprised me.

"I've been asked to say a few words, because I'm working class and was born into a poor family and I know just what poverty looks and smells like. I'm one of the lucky ones, and found a position as a maid to a kind employer who pays a fair wage, thank you, Mrs Edwards. But I've known hunger, and despair, too. I'm just here to tell you that everything in Dr Martindale's book is not only true, but repeated a hundred times over in every street where I came from. I've had to go out begging when my sailor father was drowned at sea, I've had to see the last of our money spent on cider because what else is there to keep you going when there's no hope. I've seen my own mother forced into prostitution to keep us alive, and I've seen so many neighbours die because they couldn't afford a doctor. I've seen husbands beating wives until they're unconscious. And it's all put down to weak moral fibre. Well, it isn't. It's desperation. I think people are the same underneath it all. The upper classes are no better or worse than the working classes when it comes to it. It's the circumstances and the measures the poor have to adopt to survive that make our so-called superiors look down their noses. We can't afford moral fibre, but I see so much strength and kindness and spirit among my sort and they do what they can to help in hard times, but there are times when it gets too much, and you do bad things."

She described the conditions they lived in, the uncaring attitude of landlords, and painted the most vivid of pictures of life in that side of town. I was astonished: she was wonderful. She sat down to great applause. Izzy then called on Councillor Burnham to say a few words. Margaret had done her job well; he was the epitome of arrogant self-satisfaction.

"I am very grateful for the invitation to be able to talk to you tonight," he said. "I have the honour to represent the Brighton Town Council, who are, I think, rightly proud of their progressive, yes, progressive, attitude towards the social problems that face, not just this town, but this country. It is a problem that has always been with us down the long march of history, and, I fear, always will. But your town council has agonised, yes, agonised, over what we may do within our means to minimise the plight of working families. Perhaps they might be persuaded to do a little more to help themselves? Alas, our resources are limited by the meagre allotments from Whitehall, but let me tell you, we have plans for modernising the sewage system…"

He carried on in this vein for a while. Sewage, subsidised health care, food vouchers, all sorts of things. I could sense unrest at the back of the hall.

"Excuse me," came a woman's voice. "I've lived here all my life, and we've been promised all these things for as long as I can remember. But nothing ever happens, does it, eh?"

"These things take time to implement —"

"Rubbish!" shouted another. "You couldn't care less."

"Put 'em on a list so you can trot them out, feel good then forget about them!"

"When have any of you talked to us about what we need?"

There were shouts of agreement. Councillor Burnham tried to talk over them but the pent up anger had been unleashed. Then there was uproar. The shouts became louder, and the councillor got in the way of a slice of pie from the buffet table. Izzy stood up and banged on the table, to no avail. Then a large man with an imposing presence stood up.

"How dare you!" he shouted. "How dare you!" The protestors quietened down and he stepped up to the speakers' table. "This evening is to hear about Dr Martindale's new book which seeks only to point out your plight. I am Sebastian Fairweather, as you know, your member of parliament for Brighton, and I hear with great interest what Dr Martindale has to say and intend to bring it to the attention of the house. Drowning out this meeting with your grudges is no way to behave when people are trying to help." He had to shout the last sentence, and with the pleas of the rest of us, the room quietened down. Mr Fairweather continued. "I have to say that I fully share your exasperation with the town council, who have done nothing to help your plight, despite my earnest endeavours—"

"Now, just a minute!" Councillor Burnham turned to face him. "Our town council are hamstrung, yes, hamstrung, by your lack of any effort to help us achieve our heartfelt, yes, heartfelt, desire to help these poor people." A few other councillors stood up to support him, and so did two other MPs to support Mr Fairweather.

The evening ended disastrously. Parliamentarians and councillors hurled abuse at each other to the great amusement of the whole audience, and most of the people at the back soon came down to the front and joined one side or the other. The prodding and pushing came next, then the punches. The buffet at the back became ammunition. Izzy was screaming at them to stop and Janet was grinning. The rest of the *Mouettes* were laughing, and Tristan was lobbing egg rolls at the councillors. The two reporters were scribbling frantically. Margaret sat with her head in her hands. Eventually the police, hearing the commotion inside the hall, stepped in and restored some sort of order. Tristan and the others were ushered out with the rest. They were still laughing, much to Izzy's disgust.

Everything stopped, and Izzy, in tears, stood and said, "Go home, all of you. I feel ashamed at what's gone on tonight. All we wanted to do was to celebrate Dr Martindale's book that seeks to draw attention to the plight of the working class, and especially the women. It's a sad reflection on our human species that we blame any problems on someone else and then wash our hands of it. You disgust me! Just go! Go home and reflect on your stupidity!"

It was Janet who had the wit to shout, "But don't forget to buy a copy of this important book! Two shillings each."

She jumped off the platform and grabbed an armful of books, and as the policemen ushered people out, many of them lingered to buy a copy. I stood beside her armed with the leaflets and pushed them into people's hands as they were leaving.

When they were gone, Izzy tearfully announced that she was going home: the whole evening had been a disaster, thanks to my bright ideas. Dr Martindale thanked me, rather stiffly, for my efforts and left with her. Only Margaret remained.

"Public houses are still open," Janet said. "Come on, both of you."

We found seats in a nearby public house and sat with our drinks. Margaret wasn't happy, obviously, and I wasn't feeling very bright myself. Only Janet seemed in a cheerful mood. We congratulated her on such a good speech.

"It was from the heart," she said, "Anyway, it was a great success, wasn't it?"

"Don't be so silly," said Margaret, "It was an unmitigated disaster."

"It might seem like it now," Janet said, "but think. If we'd had a straightforward meeting, then there'd be five lines in the papers, a few books sold, and they'd all forget about it tomorrow. Now it'll be splashed all over the papers, people will be talking about it, the council will be stung into action because they don't want to look like the old humbugs they are, and I reckon the MPs won't want to be outdone and it just might get somewhere. I reckon we had the best outcome we could have hoped for."

Margaret threw back her double brandy and clasped Janet's hands.

"My dear, you are worth your weight in gold! How right you are! Let's have another drink. My turn."

We had another. And another. Under the table, I placed my hand on Janet's thigh and slowly worked it upwards. I loved her. She was one jump ahead of all of us. Notoriety is the best publicity of all, I thought.

At last, we left, feeling pleased with ourselves. Margaret's cab dropped us off at my house and we kissed her goodbye. As soon as we got inside the hall, we kissed and fumbled. Janet dug out a very good claret and the glasses, and we went upstairs. While we lay naked on my bed, I told her I thought she was wonderful. Her speech was wonderful, her mind was wonderful, her body was wonderful…

"Shush," she said, "and give us another of your cigarettes, please."

We tried to make love, but the excitement of the evening and the wine rendered us incapable of anything more than the clumsiest of gropings.

The morning, however, was a different story. It was late when we woke up, around half past nine. The sun, absent for the past week, penetrated the blinds making wonderful patterns of light on the walls. I rolled over to Janet, and put my arm around her, and she put hers around me. We lay like that, slowly wakening, then she rose and went down naked into the kitchen. It was half an hour before she returned with a large tray, announcing that we were to be very decadent, because we'd earned it, and would have breakfast in bed. We ate our way through macaroni with bacon, Swiss eggs, crumpets and bread steaks, all with a large pot of coffee.

It was one of those perfect mornings. I opened the blinds and the shutters so that the light and the air flooded the room as we ate, and our thighs rubbing together. When we had done, Janet put the tray aside and put her arms around me. My own hands traced a path from her shoulders, down the length of her spine and into the cleft of her buttocks. She twined her legs around mine and pulled my pelvis towards hers. She rubbed her pubis against mine, then shifted her position so that the lips of my vulva were kissing hers. She started to circle her hips, so that out cunnys rubbed together, slowly and deliciously at first, then faster and faster as we became absorbed in the delicious sensations that were overcoming all else, until all we could feel was the pressure of crotch against crotch, her clitoris against mine, juices flowing, sweat, grunts, breasts flailing, until we both cried out in one ecstatic moment and lay together, content.

We slept a little longer: there was nothing to get up for, until I remembered I should go round to Izzy and put things right with her. Janet provided a light luncheon, after which I declared I would take the air that afternoon. I could see that Janet knew what I intended, but she just smiled.

Izzy was in her study with Louisa when I called. They were both looking a little grim-faced, and had been discussing the events at the meeting. I felt like the prisoner in the dock, but I wasn't having any of it.

"No, sorry, I organised the meeting, I arranged the mix of audience we wanted, and it's worked out rather well, don't you think?"

"You call that a good result?" cried Izzy, "It was the biggest humiliation I've ever suffered!"

I then explained Janet's theory — what happened would gain far more attention and interest than a staid public meeting which would soon fade.

"I don't think it's the right sort of publicity we need. I have a reputation to maintain, even if you have not." Louisa's words stung me. I started to get angry inside, but kept it hidden.

"Your reputation is unblemished. The humiliation is entirely heaped on the heads of our councillors and MPs. The papers will love it, the word will spread and I wouldn't be surprised if it was debated in parliament. What more do you want?"

"Dignity," Louisa said firmly. "My professional reputation depends on dignity, and it is not at all good that I'm now viewed as the instigator of a public riot."

My anger was beginning to come to the surface.

"So, despite the fact that some of us have worked very hard on your behalf, and the whole issue you write about has now been dragged into the light and is the subject of controversy and even hopefully change, all you care about is your bloody dignity?"

I shouldn't have said that. I knew I was wrong, and apologised to her. She smiled that cold smile of hers.

"It's not my dignity, but that of my profession. I am an ambassador for women doctors, who are still viewed with great scepticism by my male colleagues, and if I become a laughing stock, then all the women going into medicine will be discredited."

"I realise that, but there was no possible slur on you. You conducted yourself with the utmost dignity. It was the men who made fools of themselves, and that is what the newspapers will report."

Izzy chipped in. "I certainly hope you're right, Cordie. But what happened, happened. We shall put it behind us and move on. Louisa and I are devising a list of practical and affordable measures that the council can take to improve the lives of working people. We intend to present it to them in a few weeks."

"Then I'm sorry to have disturbed you. I'll leave you to your work."

"I'll see you out," Izzy said. I took my leave of Louisa, and went to the door with Izzy.

"Don't be cross with me, darling. I've been having to soothe her ruffled feathers. Come to me tomorrow and we can talk properly, eh?" She stroked my cheek and kissed me on the lips.

"It's all right, I understand, my love," I said, "You'll just have to make it up to me somehow, won't you?" I drew my finger over her bust, and she smiled.

I walked home, I passed Peregrine's studio, but decided not to go in. He wouldn't have had time to develop the film yet. I must be patient.

The next few days were leisurely ones. My visit to Izzy was highly satisfactory, both in terms of affirming our great affection for each other, and a gentle and prolonged session of lovemaking. With her, sex was slow and sensuous. She liked me to put my fingers inside her and work them in and out slowly as she became increasingly moist and the love juice started to flow out of her. I could never tire of feeling the slippery fluid on my fingers, or the taste of it. How different from Janet's wild, savage fornication. Both equally pleasant in their own way. Izzy got her pleasure from vaginal penetration, Janet from, well, anything, but especially her clitoris. Izzy would lick me only with some persuasion, Janet revelled in cunnilingus. Janet's breasts jutted out aggressively, Izzy's were comfortable little plump cushions. Luckily, all three of us had an insatiable appetite for sapphic love.

I learnt something of Izzy's background. Her family were from Derbyshire, and quite well-to-do. When she told me, I could identify her accent, which was not from these parts. They owned a cotton mill, and treated their workers harshly. Izzy had grown to detest the way her family had grown rich by depriving others of all but the basic essentials to keep them alive to work the mills. She had been a very bright child and her parents were all too keen to comply with her requests for a university education. She was accepted into Somerville college in Oxford to study moral philosophy, which made her even more aware of the social injustices her parents were perpetuating. On returning home, her outspoken views caused major arguments with them, and five years ago, she had left them on bad terms, and indeed had had no communication with them since. She had secured a job as a columnist for the Essex County Standard newspaper. She had started up a socialist newspaper at the same time, which had not succeeded, but had kept herself by writing articles for magazines, as well as publishing some short stories. She had met Louisa Martindale a few years ago, fell in love with her and moved to Brighton to be with her. Alas, soon after, Louisa met another woman, Ismay Fitzgerald, who became her lover, and Izzy had gone through a period of depression. But she and Louisa had remained friends, united by their political ideals. She was committed to a simple, plain life, and a determination to stay true to her political ideals. That at least explained her reluctance to trail around the dress shops.

I told her a little about my history, albeit rather modified. We talked of what the group were doing these days, for we had not met for a while, and I was beginning to wonder if they had quietly excluded me. I asked her if I might visit Charles, for I was still haunted by his paintings. She gave me his address, but warned me not to call on him unannounced: his moods could vary. She also gave me a large parcel of the herbal cigarettes, which I paid her for, and we parted fondly.

The carriers never came for the film equipment, and I wondered whether Peregrine was leaving it with us for another session. Still I refrained from contacting him to see if it was ready. He would let us know in good time. In the meantime, I sent a message to Charles, asking to see his work and to name a time when it might be convenient to call. Ironic, I thought, writing a polite and formal request to a man, a stranger really, who had screwed me from behind and shot his semen all over my back entrance. I dispatched it, wondering if he'd reply. He did, very quickly. He'd be happy to meet me at his studio tomorrow; he'd be working there all day and would be glad to show me his paintings whenever I cared to drop in.

Over breakfast the next day, Janet raised the subject of altering the house so that she might have more living accommodation, in return for a decrease in her salary, she hoped we could both continue to earn from our acting. I hadn't given it much thought, and as we were both tired from a night of wine and marijuana and repeated bouts of sexual activity, I deferred any decision until later that day. I took a cab to Charles' studio, for it was some way out of the town, but found it easily enough.

It was a large but ramshackle wooden construction which had probably been a barn, but large windows had been inserted under the eaves. I knocked at the door, and Charles ushered me in. It was a remarkable space inside: the wooden walls had been painted white, which, with the windows, gave the space a marvellously light and airy atmosphere with canvasses stacked around the walls, and a gramophone was playing something by Brahms. A long bench was covered in tins of paint and varnish while against the opposite wall, in a corner, was a bed, a table and chair, and a small stove. I fell in love with the place immediately. Charles shook hands, rather formally I thought, and bade me sit on the chair while he made some coffee and took the needle off the recording. He wore a plain white shirt which was covered with smears of paint. We talked about the group and the disaster at the book launch. I told him I'd seen some of his paintings at the gallery, and admitted that they had a powerful effect on me. He was a good-looking man: his dark hair fell over his forehead and his youthful face was delicately featured, apart from his eyes which were dark and so intense I couldn't take my gaze away from them. They drew you into them, like whirlpools. His voice was cultured, and pleasing to listen to. I remembered his sun-browned, lean body and recalled the feeling of his cock inside me. I tried to push that from my mind as we talked about the various activities of the group and what they were up to at the moment. He asked what I took away from the paintings I'd seen so far.

"They're very eye-catching at first glance, the colours are so attractive that you have to take a closer look. Then it strikes you: behind the prettiness there's such melancholy, and the more you look, the sadness takes you deeper and you see despair and hopelessness. At least that's what I've seen in them."

"Then you have a good eye, and I have done a good job!"

"And is that how you see the world? As a place of despair?"

"I do. It's the way I am, and I wish it were otherwise. Artists are trained to see the spaces between objects. I paint the gulf between people."

"Are there not times when minds meet?"

"I don't think so. We are all tiny little islands in a vast sea. Even at our most intimate moments, our thoughts are our own. We can never know other people, or their thoughts. We are ultimately totally alone, each one of us. You cannot ever know what I think or feel, and I cannot ever know you."

"That is a poor way of thinking, surely?"

"But it's my way of thinking!" He paused and shook his head. "I am sorry, Cordelia. I am a gloomy companion. Forgive me."

"Not at all, I think there's a lot of truth in what you say, but very few dared speak of it, and it takes a rare artist to paint it. Now, treat me to some more of your pictures."

He showed me what he had in his studio, about twenty canvasses, and they all had that same unsettling effect on me. There was one, of a couple on a bed, the woman lying, her modesty just covered by a sheet, and the man sitting on the other side of the bed, that seemed to convey it all. It was ambiguous: you couldn't tell whether they had just made love or had an argument, or even were just obeying their usual routine of going to bed or getting up, you couldn't tell, but the sense of unspoken, desperate isolation was so acute it again made me want to cry. Most of his paintings did, and I told him so. I asked him how much he wanted for the painting of the couple and he named a price which was a lot less than it was worth, I thought. I told him I'd like to buy it, and he smiled for the first time.

"If you want it, have it with my compliments, if you will look at it often and understand it."

"Nonsense! I shall look at it every day and see more than I'm seeing now, but I insist on paying you what it's worth."

"No!" He was quite adamant. "I shan't be needing any money. I'll have it sent round. It would make me happy to know you had it."

Further protestations were fruitless. I thanked him and implied I could pay him in kind, if he wanted. He appeared not to understand. I told him I was planning a *soirée* for the group shortly. He said he'd look forward to that. I gave him my address, kissed him politely on the cheek, and turned to go. As I was leaving, he cried "Cordelia!" and I turned back. His whirlpool eyes looked into mine.

"Thank you. I wish—"

"What, Charles?"

"I wish there could be a bridge over the chasm, and that you and I could walk from each side and meet — well, you know what I'm trying to say."

I gave him a hug, and left to catch the omnibus home.

As I sat on the crowded bus, I tried to make sense of it all. I felt such an affinity with Charles. I understood him, or so I thought, and felt such pity that a man could be so attractive yet feel so isolated. Then I thought of Janet, then of Izzy. I loved them, too, but in such different ways. Was that it? Did we all need different people to satisfy all our needs for love? Not one bridge but several? The carnal, the comforting, the intellectual, the artistic, and the other myriad shards of the splintered mirrors of our personalities? Do you strive to find 'the One' who satisfies all these, or do you find a lover, for each shard of your complex soul? I decided after today I was not a little in love with Charles for his good looks and ability to look into the blackest depths of the human condition. I was also in love with Izzy and her crystal-clear intellect, and Janet for her easy companionship and uncanny ability to cater to my physical needs. If only you could take them all, knead them into a single clay, and mould a perfect Pygmalion from them. It struck me that I fell in love too easily, or what I called 'love'. Was it just sexual attraction? Was I that shallow? Love is a slippery concept, and people fall in love for so many reasons. Lust was just as valid as any.

These daydreams caused me to overshoot my omnibus stop. It was a considerable walk back to my house, but the afternoon was sunny, and the walk enjoyable. I walked along the promenade, past the small groups of people, and I thought of Charles' painting of the beach. Yes, I thought, he has captured it perfectly.

Janet had a cold collation ready for lunch when I got home, and I suggested we might take it onto the beach and enjoy the sun while we may. She packed it into a hamper and, dressing as lightly as we dare, we headed to the beach and found a space to spread ourselves out. I remembered it was Wednesday, and the newspaper would be out. I sent Janet off to buy a copy.

We scanned the paper eagerly. There was a considerable amount of space devoted to the meeting, and I was pleased that the paper was very scathing about the local council. I got the impression that there were other issues to settle with them. They gave Louisa's book a glowing and sympathetic review. Altogether an excellent outcome, I thought. I also read through the rest of the paper in case Nicholas' body had been found. There was nothing.

As we ate our lunch, Janet gleefully handed me a note that had been delivered that morning. It was from Peregrine, and simply stated: 'Wonderful! 10.30. Studio, Friday'. We giggled and exchanged glances.

"I can hardly wait," Janet whispered. "To be able to see yourself making love. Now that's a novelty."

Eventually, Friday morning came, and we slipped into Peregrine's studio. We were both excited, and not a little nervous. Peregrine, I could see, was nearly as excited as we were, but still insisted we should take coffee first, while we talked about anything but the purpose of our visit. Refreshment taken, he led us through the yard to the viewing room, Janet and I holding hands like two nervous schoolgirls. We sat down, and watched, mesmerised, as the screen flickered into life.

It was astounding. The moving pictures we had seen before were remarkable enough, but when you become your own *voyeur* the sexual thrill is overwhelming. Janet gave a cry of amazement and delight and had to bite her handkerchief to quiet herself. While we watched the film, she pulled up her skirt and toyed with her slit. I copied her while we both watched ourselves kissing, licking and fingering on my bed. When the first film had finished, Peregrine spoke from the darkness behind us.

"I see you enjoyed the entertainment. What you have seen represents a milestone in moving pictures. It is the best there is! You, my dears, were quite, quite, magnificent! Now I will load the second film. Just watch."

While he changed the reel of film, I did have a qualm. The film he had showed us two weeks ago was quite blurred, making faces difficult to make out. His film, by contrast, was much clearer, and it was all too easy to recognise our faces. I would discuss it with him afterwards.

The second film was even better than the first, with more varied camera angles and close-ups. I could imagine what it might do to an audience, the spellbinding hold we would have on the gentlemen who watched it. While we watched ourselves writhe and buck, the excitement took over again and by the time the film finished, I was very damp. Janet and I, rather incongruously, clapped.

Afterwards, we sat in his studio discussing what we'd just seen. I did mention my anxiety about being recognised, but he waved his hand dismissively.

"Don't worry about that. These films will be shown only in private smoking clubs, and there is a strict code of secrecy about what goes on there. Besides, if by a rare chance someone were to recognise you, they wouldn't dare speak of it if they wanted to maintain their position in society. You are very safe on that score. So do you agree to these films being shown, but only to the most discreet and discerning of gentlemen?"

We did. Peregrine assured us that he would draw up proper contracts for our signature specifying the restricted nature of any showings, and the terms of payment for our work. Janet asked if we might know what those terms might be.

"I shall give you a flat fee of twenty-five pounds for each film and ten percent of the net takings after that. Would that be acceptable?"

It would. It most certainly would. I thought Janet might have another orgasm there and then. Peregrine went into his darkroom and returned with a roll of banknotes. He handed us fifty pounds each for both films.

"It won't have escaped your notice," he said, "that I haven't taken the equipment back. This is because I wish to make some more of these art films. Would you be agreeable?"

We both nodded. "Good! Now I would like to introduce some variety into them: I would like to film you with a gentleman. One film with all three making love, and one with just one of you. What would you say to that?"

Neither Janet nor I wanted to answer first. I was equally at home with men, and I knew she'd have a number of men in her life, although they hadn't been particularly happy experiences. I broke the silence.

"I wouldn't have any objections. Would we know him?"

"No, he would be a complete stranger. I can guarantee he will be free of disease, and will perform well."

"And what about, er?"

"He will only spill onto your breasts or back, and he will wear a protective during penetrative scenes, if that's what you mean."

"I did, yes. Then I think on those terms I would have no objections. It might be quite fun."

Janet, too was quite amenable. For the amount she was getting paid, I think she'd be amenable to a monkey. I was beginning to wonder, if we were getting paid the sort of money, just how many Peregrine's London clientele numbered. I said nothing, though. Janet and I arranged a time with him for the next filming session to take place. It was not to be for another fortnight, as he would be going up to London with his films.

We took our leave, and walked back to the house. It was lunchtime, but we had a greater appetite than for food. Without saying a word, we climbed up to my bedroom and undressed each other hurriedly. As my breasts tumbled out, Janet cupped them from behind rolling my hardened nipples with her fingers as I reached round and clasped her buttocks, pulling the cheeks apart and drawing her close so that I could feel the scratch of her dark bush against me. She licked and nibbled my ear, knowing how quickly that aroused me. My fingers worked their way into her cleft and stroked her tight little anus. We stayed like that for a while before she broke away and threw herself onto the bed, her thighs parted in a lewd invitation.

The curious thing was, there was something different about our lovemaking. Instead of being wrapped up in our own and the other's pleasure, it was as though we were performing to someone watching. That's how I felt, and I'm sure Janet was experiencing the same strange transformation. It added another dimension; spurred us on to greater excesses still. One orgasm followed another, until we were exhausted and covered in perspiration. The doorbell rang at one point, but we were in no state to answer it.

That evening, I found a note pushed through the front door. It was from Izzy: 'You are elusive! I called this afternoon to see if you wished to play hostess to a meeting of the group, but you must have been out — or otherwise engaged. I shall be at home tomorrow if you care to call. Your affectionate friend, Izzy'.

I felt a small pang of guilt that I had been 'otherwise engaged' when she called. I would see her tomorrow, of course. It would be rather fun to have *Les Mouettes* around for an evening. I would ask what the form was, and how many to expect. I would wait until after my visit to inform Janet, but already felt some unease at her reaction to Izzy coming to the house, even with a crowd. Oh, to hell with it! I loved them both, but differently, so they'd just have to get used to it. Izzy was an advocate of free love, after all, although I had seen the jealous side to her.

We ate a hastily prepared but substantial dinner that night. I have to admire Janet: she had to cater for my unpredictable coming and goings and our erratic mealtimes. Not only that, but tonight as we drank wine and smoked after the rabbit pie and trifle, she ran downstairs and returned with two parcels, and handed one to me. I looked enquiringly at her, and she blew me a kiss. A bundle of cloth was folded inside. I opened it out — it was my kaftan! I held it up: it was the most wonderful creation — royal blue shiny cotton with the most intricate embroidery around the neck and down the front seam. I went and hugged her, rather tearfully.

"And a present for me. I wonder what it could be?" Mock curious, she opened her parcel, and held up a similar one, although hers was in the burgundy, and plainer. We stripped off and put them on, then I embraced her. The feel of her body through the slippery material was delicious. The material clung to our bodies,

"Did you do the embroidery?" I asked.

"Ah, no. I've a friend who works miracles with that sort of thing. I drew out the design, though, so it's especially for you."

I looked a little closer. There were my initials, woven into vine leaves and ribbons, with small love birds flying amongst them. It was astonishing, and the colours superb. "You? You designed this?"

"Do you like it?"

"It's utterly beautiful. I can't believe you did this."

"What, the numbskull scullery maid?" She grinned. "Well, perhaps there's a few things you've yet to discover about me. I'll show you my efforts sometime."

We clinked our glasses together, happy, and opened another bottle.

Chapter 7

Izzy ushered me into her house the next morning, with a warm hug. Her study was even more chaotic than before, with many of the piles of books and papers pushed aside to accommodate a Remington typewriter. She was wearing her coarse cotton kaftan, and I could sense her disapproval if I wore mine in front of her. In any case, that would be a betrayal of Janet's dedication.

She pushed one of her straggly locks away from her face and remarked on the heat.

"You look as though you are working hard," I said. "Have I come at an inconvenient time?"

"Not at all, my darling! I welcome the interruption, and would greatly value your opinion. But some tea first, I fancy."

She went to make some tea. Bless her, she was always a little too unworldly to make a decent pot, but it sufficed, and she'd bought some cake. She explained that she was wanting to get out another book which would add weight and economic arguments to come hot on the heels of Louisa's book, which was selling in remarkable numbers, its sordid content no doubt adding to its saleability. It had already been listed for a commons debate.

"So perhaps the evening was not such a failure?" I asked.

"Oh, darling, you were right and we were wrong. The papers went to town on the council in particular and the country at large. It's not how Louisa had envisaged it, but she admits it turned out well in the end."

"Very gracious of her."

"Don't be like that, Cordie dear. I know she comes over as a little frosty, but you've seen her deep compassion underneath. She's just highly driven, and means the best."

"I know, and I'm sorry I took offence, my darling. So, what's your book about?"

"What else? The unequal distribution of wealth. I'm trying to say it's not ordained by God, as they'd have us believe, but ordained by man's selfishness and greed. They think that because you can afford an education that makes you intrinsically better. Well, that's rot, and I think people are beginning to realise. I just want to catch that mood and spread it further."

"I do admire you, Izzy, my love. I wish I were half as committed as you."

"I think you are, which is why I'd like you take the manuscript I've written so far and tell me what you think. I trust your judgement."

That was indeed a real compliment. I felt pleased to be part of this new wave of liberated thought that was slowly but surely taking root, and I told her so. She grasped my hand.

"Oh, Cordie, you and I can make such a difference. Every writer needs a muse, and you are mine. Every word I write, I see you in front of me, and it's to you I write."

She kissed me on the lips and I started to respond, caressing her breasts, but she drew back.

"Oh, I want to do it with you, but I must discipline myself while I am writing. Give me a day or two, my love."

I was actually slightly relieved. My recent exertions had quite drained me, and I was quite sore after yesterday.

"I so understand, sweetheart," I said. "Let us merge minds rather than bodies for the moment."

We changed the subject to the meeting of *les Mouettes*. How many could I accommodate? How soon could I be ready? Did I have a piano? (I did, of course.) The evening would commence with drinks and a buffet, then all present would tell the group what they'd been doing and demonstrate their work. After that, well…

Between us, it was decided that I could accommodate fifteen. Izzy would see that word got round. I was happy to pay for the evening's refreshments, although Izzy said they were in the habit of contributing with a bottle, which, in polite society would be seen as an insult. I just would provide a simple buffet.

"No," she said, "each contributes what he can. We set the example, and perhaps the world will follow."

I asked if I should invite Margaret, as she seemed to know us all. Izzy laughed out loud and said not to be so silly: Margaret would be horrified by our behaviour. The meetings of the group were kept strictly for the group and no one else.

In her hallway, she handed me her half-written manuscript. We embraced, and I lifted her kaftan a little.

"Please, not now," she whispered, so I gave her behind a gentle squeeze, and left.

As I expected, Janet was happy to cater for the party, but not happy about Izzy's presence there.

"Are you still seeing her?" she asked, a bit too directly for my liking.

"Yes, I am."

"And frigging her?"

"Not much," I replied truthfully. "More just talking about politics."

"Do you love her?"

"Oh, Janet, Janet, I don't know! I really don't know what love is, and that's a fact. She says she loves me, so I suppose I love her in return. I think she must be a very lonely person. But you're my best friend, and the best of all lovers. I couldn't let you go."

She looked me in the eyes, then smiled and kissed me.

"Then let's get this party organised, and make it the best one yet, eh?"

I explained about their beliefs, and about their belief in free love. She grinned.

"Lucky old you. Oh well, I'll just have to be the serving maid, and make sure all the glasses are topped up. It should be amusing to watch."

Later, after dinner, she produced a large folder, it must have been three feet across and two feet deep. It contained the designs that she had promised to show me. I was astonished. These were beautifully executed designs for dresses, and for the embroidery that would embellish them. They were done in watercolour and showed real artistry. Mere designs or not, they were special in themselves. There seemed no end to her talents. And then there were all the members of *Les Mouettes,* all with such diverse and brilliant talents, that I suddenly felt a sense of desolation. What had I to offer, to show for all the years of a ladylike existence? Nothing. What talents had I? None. I felt useless: a large slug surrounded by people with drive and talent. I don't know why, for I'm not given to emotion, but I started to cry uncontrollably. The little child deep inside me was wandering, lost and crying out. Between sobs, I poured all this out to Janet, who I noticed quickly removed her paintings from me before my tears could smudge them.

She knelt by my side stroking my arm, trying to comfort me.

"Hey, hey, come on now. Don't cry. You can't reproach yourself. You don't have to prove yourself, either. Shall I tell you what I think?"

I nodded, wiping my tears and laying a hand over hers.

"I think you've never had the need to paint or write or play music. You, well, not just you, but all of the gentility, have no need. The world suits you fine. No need to feel angry or fired up. It's people like me who are desperate to find a voice. I started all this because it was so bad at home, so I'd escape it all by drawing the elegant ladies I'd seen and daydreaming I was one of them. They were terrible to begin with, my pictures, but they got better, and I started thinking one day I could make these dresses, and sell them. It was a way out, a dream. I'm willing to bet that your other talented friends weren't just born with their gifts. They took them up because they needed to say something that can't be said, and just kept saying it over and over again until their talent grew. You've never needed to cry out about anything, and you should be happy about that."

I thought about Charles and how he could only express his black inner world through his painting, and how much practice it must have taken him. She was right. But then I thought of my own circumstances. I had a past that I could scream about, and never talk of it, but

I had sought a more direct way out. Perhaps that was my talent. The thought brought me no comfort, though, and I started to cry again. Janet stood and leant over me, offering me her breasts, and I sucked on her nipples while she cradled my head to her, like a baby.

By the morning, I had regained my composure and was wondering what could have brought that silliness about, although a nagging unease stayed with me all that day, and the next. It was one of those indefinable anxieties; as though your subconscious sensed something but wasn't going to tell your rational mind what it was. I distracted myself with Izzy's manuscript, which turned out to be disappointingly hard work. Oh, the case for radical change in the social system was soundly argued, thoroughly researched, scholarly and very worthy, but so soporifically dull that I had to keep pinching myself to concentrate on it. What was I going to tell Izzy? I could just tell her that it was a closely reasoned treatise and leave it at that, but that wouldn't be honest, and, I told myself, where there's love there has to be honesty.

I visited her a few days later with the manuscript, still wondering what I should tell her. What a change from when I saw her last. This time she was affectionate, chatty and in such a good humour. We drank tea and smoked as usual, and she told me who would be coming to the party. She reeled off names too fast for me to remember, but I gathered there would be poets, other musicians, a couple of novelists, and a number of others who, like me, were just 'free thinkers', whatever that might mean. While she was telling me the who's who, her hand explored my thigh, and soon she stopped talking and began to kiss my neck and my ear, then my lips.

"Let's go to bed, right now!" she whispered. I had wanted to broach my thoughts on her manuscript, but was by that time quite worked up and wished to have her as much as she wanted me. We undressed in her bedroom.

"Excuse me, my love, I need to go to the bathroom," I told her, when we were both naked.

"Me too!" she said, and led me to her bathroom. Much to my surprise, she sat on the closet before me, then made me sit on her open thighs, facing her.

"Now piss between my legs, darling." It was almost an order. I let my jet of piss loose. It sprayed onto her quim as she let go of the contents of her bladder. At the same time, she sucked at my nipples. She moved her hand and placed it in my stream. It was a new and lovely sensation, and even when our flows had ceased, we sat like that for some minutes, relishing it. Her hand began to stroke the open lips of my cunny, and her fingers pushed inside me. I managed to squirt out a little more of my water over her hand. She withdrew it, and rubbed it over her breasts. We went back into her bedroom and finished each other off, slowly, luxuriously, lapping up our juices as they flowed.

After we had done, we sat, naked, in her study, smoking her cigarettes. I would now smoke no other type; these relaxed and stimulated all at the same time, satisfying like ordinary cigarettes could not.

"Did you read my book?" she asked.

"Oh yes," I replied. "It's good…"

She must have sensed my slight hesitation. "But?"

"No, I mean, it's well researched and argued. You have such a brilliant mind, Izzy."

"But?"

"I mean, your readers can have no choice but to agree with you…"

"But?" There was a slightly aggressive tinge to her voice.

"All right, I'll be honest, and I'm being honest because I love you, mind. It was just telling me what everybody knows. The system is unjust, of course it is, but it's only the privileged and the powerful that can change it, and they have absolutely no incentive for doing so, even though they cannot argue against what you say. It's a worthy book, Izzy, love, but it's, well, dull because there are no new arguments in it, just well marshalled reiterations of the same old arguments."

I'd not meant to be so wounding, and I hate to hurt other women. She stared at me in silence.

"Izzy, I'm saying this because I love you, and love means being honest."

She turned away. I felt terrible. Eventually she spoke. "Fucking hell."

"I'm so sorry, darling. Look it's only my personal opinion, and I'm sure there are—"

"Fucking hell, you're right! Why didn't I see that?"

"Sorry…"

"No! Don't be! Cordie, you're something special. Writers have to do their work in a vacuum, and sometimes we get too bogged down in getting the bloody stuff written that we lose track of what we were trying to say. I've sent copies to others in the group and they all say how good it is and well done, but I doubt whether any of them have read more than the first few pages. It's good to have you as my special person. You have such a cutting mind."

I thought back to my tearful outburst a few nights ago. Perhaps I did have a talent after all, just not in one of the creative arts. I allowed myself a little inward smile.

"So, all right, what should I do?" Izzy asked.

"God, I don't know! That's up to you intellectuals. All I'm saying is that there's little purpose to a book that just points out the wrongs that only fools would deny; you need to provide some solutions. Solutions that can tempt the rich as well as the poor."

"How can I do that? Nobody's ever done that before."

"Exactly! That's what can make you an original thinker. Izzy, I know you have it in you! Such passionate beliefs coupled with such an intellect… If anyone can do it, you can."

She kissed me with happy abandon, we bit each other's lips and tongues and pressed our bodies together. She loved to fill my mouth with her saliva — she had such a predilection for sharing bodily fluids.

I suggested we should go out and have lunch at one of the nearby restaurants, and to my surprise, she agreed. We dressed, and I took her to The Flying Fish, which was well recommended. It was a cheerful place, painted in some sort of marine blue and festooned with fishing nets and sea shells.

It was thronged with families and children and echoed with their noisy chatter. She had the hake, and I the bream, while we shared a halfway decent bottle of white Alsace wine. We talked of what the solutions to society's problems might be. The wine emboldened me a little.

"Here we are, me from the so-called upper class and you, God knows, somewhere in the middle, I suppose, talking about what the working class needs. Do we know, though?" I said.

"I need to speak to them, you're right. I need to establish what they see as their greatest needs before we start providing irrelevant answers. I've got a lot of work ahead of me, I think, and no idea where to start."

I had, and had been wondering how to broach it. There was no way but head on. "Why don't you start with Janet?"

"You don't expect me to take that seriously, I hope."

"Why not? She's articulate, and comes from the class you want to talk to."

"You're seriously suggesting I talk to your lover?"

"Well, yes, I am. Look, Izzy, it makes sense for two reasons. She can give you the information you need, but more importantly, you're both dear to me in separate ways, and I don't like to feel torn between the two. I'd like all three of us to be friends and lovers."

"Is that what she wants?"

"I've no idea, but I'll talk to her."

"I need to think it all over. It's a bit of an ask, you know."

"Please think about it, Izzy darling. It would mean such a lot to me."

"I will."

She took her leave. I sat, finishing the wine, and watched her retreating figure walk out into the street.

Janet was amenable to the idea. After the initial display of jealousy, she'd had time to think and realised that, as long as she knew that we'd stay the same, there were benefits in sharing. She was also more than happy to tell Izzy about the real everyday problems of her class.

The doorbell rang the next morning. I was in the living room reading the newspaper, which made rather a meal of the discovery of the maimed body of a man in Grove Road. The man had been dead for a considerable time and had been identified as a Mr Nicholas Fairburn. He was apparently known to the police as a thief and a dealer in stolen goods, as well as a number of sexual crimes. It was presumed that this was a revenge killing by his criminal associates. My mind worked quickly. I needed to think this through. As a bit of human flotsam, and a solitary one, I doubted the police would go to any great lengths to pursue the matter. I'd left no clues, and if I had been seen, I'd left an alibi. And who would believe that a woman could have the strength to inflict those injuries?

There was a murmur of voices in the hall, then Janet showed Izzy into the room. She was about to leave, when Izzy said, "No, please stay, Janet. This concerns you." She turned to me. "If that's all right with you, Cordie."

I was taken aback; I hadn't expected her to call round, I was happy she had, but wondered if there might be a scene and started to speak, but Izzy pre-empted me.

"Janet, Cordie suggested I might speak to you about getting material for a book I'm going to re-write. Now, I don't know whether she mentioned it to you, but obviously we both have a physical and emotional bond with her, and I think we've both resented the other. She suggested to me that it was in all our interests to become friends and share our mutual affection, and after some thought I think it would be very good for us all. So I've come to ask you, Janet, whether you'd be willing to be my friend, and help me with my book. Sorry, it's all a bit sudden, but that's the way I am."

Janet looked like a startled rabbit for a second, then walked over to her and held out her arms. Izzy embraced her, and they were both smiling.

"I'd like that very much," said Janet. We took tea together, ate cake and smoked. I suggested that I should leave them to get acquainted and for Izzy to tell Janet about the book and the material she was seeking. Better still, I suggested they might go to my bedroom while I stayed down to read. Izzy left, and Janet, with a wink to me, followed her upstairs. I smiled; things were going well.

After a while, I heard the springs of the bedstead creaking. Excellent, but should I leave them to it, or join in? Time for that, I thought. Let them enjoy themselves together first. They were up there for a long time. Eventually, when the muffled noises stopped, I uncorked a bottle and took it upstairs with three glasses. They were both naked in my bed and not abashed by my entrance. Izzy's notebooks were open, but she'd taken no notes. We toasted our friendship.

"She's quite something, your Janet," Izzy said, putting her arm around Janet's neck while Janet stroked Izzy's breast with the back of her fingers. I again felt the urge to undress and join them, but no, let them form their own side of the triangle. I suggested we should all go out to lunch at a restaurant in the Lanes. They were both hungry, and agreed like a shot. I had a momentary panic as I realised Peregrine's film equipment lay in a great pile under a cloth on one side of the room and wondered how to explain it away if Izzy should remark on it, but she didn't.

It was the day of the party. Janet and I laid out the 'Old Country Rose' plates, and the Edinburgh crystal glasses, enough for fifteen, and damask tablecloths on the dining table. Janet worked like a navvy in the kitchen preparing the food, while I tidied the living room and unpacked the three cases of half decent wine I'd ordered. I laid out plates of dates and grapes, and made sure there were enough cushions for any eventualities. Izzy called round in the afternoon to help, but we were mostly done. Janet shooed us out of the kitchen, knowing we'd be far more of a hindrance than a help, so we retired to bed for a brief session of fingering and a rest before getting ready for the guests. Izzy had brought another exotic garment to wear — a *kimono,* she called it — as she said the dress code was as casual as could be. I showed her the kaftan Janet had made. She gasped when she saw it — the first time I'd seen her take any interest in a garment. I put it on.

"Ideal!" she said. "It's absolutely magnificent — a work of art. Where on earth did you find it?" I told her it was all Janet's work and design. She pulled me downstairs and into the kitchen. "Did you do all this?" she asked Janet.

"Oh no, I just made it, and designed the embroidery, but a friend did the sewing. She's really good."

I told Izzy that Janet had some wonderful designs. Izzy demanded to see them, so Janet, with a, "What? Now?" wiped her hands on her apron and went off to fetch them. Izzy looked through them in amazement.

"These are quite astonishing. Right, we're going to lay them around in the room for the rest to see! These needs seeing."

"I'd rather you didn't." Janet said in alarm.

"But we must! These show that real talent can reside in the working classes as well as the upper classes."

Janet squared up to her and brandished a whisk in front of her face. "Don't you start on about how wonderful the working classes are. I'll tell you as much as you want about the so-called working class, but don't be so surprised that we can actually produce arty stuff. We can't afford education, or pianos, and we don't have the right contacts, but never assume that we're thick!"

"That's not what I meant at all. Oh, Janet, I'm sorry if I sounded patronising. That's not what I meant to say."

"I know," she replied. "I'm sorry. And yes, why not? Put them on show, if you want." They kissed and laughed. "Now bugger off, both of you," she said, "I'm busy."

I was rather glad that Tristan and Charles were the first to arrive with two others, heralded by some loud bangs and squeals from Tristan's motor car. He bounded in, wearing a loose calico shirt, like something out of Byron's wardrobe, indeed his whole appearance seemed to have been modelled on some vision of the Romantics — the mane of black hair, his large stature and his air of command. Charles, by contrast, wore his usual and now rather grubby blazer over a white shirt and bright blue necktie and bore the picture I'd bought from him. I greeted them both with a hug, and was introduced to their companions: another poet, Edward, who was dressed more like a bank clerk than the way you'd imagine a poet would dress, and Samantha, a small, wiry girl, an actress with the local repertory company, who seemed constantly restless and ill at ease. I chatted with them before Lavinia arrived with a fresh-faced young man called James, a journalist and columnist on the Gazette, and Henry 'just a friend'. A little while later, a strikingly well-built blonde lady, Ellen, strode effusively into the room, calling loudly to one and all. With her was her very antithesis, a small, shy girl who smiled uncertainly around her. She was carrying a violin case. Catherine, I think her name was.

There was none of the usual polite conversation when acquaintances meet at *soirées*. These were all good, uninhibited friends. Rather ironic that the only stranger to most of them should be the hostess, but they were friendliness itself and lavish with their compliments. They drank and ate and mingled, the conversation getting louder. Janet moved among them, filling their glasses and chatting to Izzy. She was attracting some admiring glances from some of the men and not a few of the women. The air grew thicker with marijuana. At last, Tristan seated himself at the piano, playing quietly (for him) at first. The room quietened down; it seemed as though we had moved onto the next part of the proceedings. He launched into a Chopin nocturne with all the finesse of a steamship rolling down the slipway. We applauded politely.

Then Edward stood up, and recited his latest poem; something about church bells ringing and were they ringing in joy or in lamentation? That sounds dismissive, but it wasn't meant to be. It was really very good, and he was heartily clapped for it. He thanked me in front of everyone and presented me with a book of his poems, which made me blush.

Ellen, the large blonde lady who, in the few brief conversations we'd had that evening, had struck me as someone I could get to like greatly, sang Dvořák's *Song to the Moon*. Tristan accompanied her. It is a divine piece, and she sang it superbly, to begin with, anyway. But Tristan was not one to be the sympathetic accompanist, and began to play louder, forcing her to raise her voice to be heard. I was rather tipsy by this time and as the volume increased to deafening levels, I started to giggle, one of those laughs you can't suppress. Other started to see the joke, and soon we were all laughing. Ellen broke off as her voice was rising to a screech, and looked, first annoyed, then she too started laughing. Only Tristan couldn't understand the levity. I went over to her to apologise, but she waved her hand, still laughing.

"I should know better than to let Tris accompany anything! It's always happening. Next time I shall strap his foot to the *piano* pedal! Now, I must get a drink and console poor dear Kate; I think she had planned to accompany me on that one. But what an excellent party you throw, Cordelia! We shall come here often, I hope, if you'll have us!"

She spoke like that, in exclamation marks. She swept off to find her friend. Charles stood up next, with the wrapped painting he'd brought along. I knew what it was. He spoke some nice words about me, then asked me to come forward and unwrap it. Sure enough, it was the painting of the sad couple I'd bought, but the others hadn't seen it yet, and there was quite a lull in the noise as the sheer power of the painting struck home.

Eventually, Tristan said, with a refreshing quietness and sincerity, "Charles, you continue to amaze us. That is breathtaking. I think you are well on the way to greatness. Thank you."

I thought of the mental anguish that lay behind his Charles' work, and had to agree. I went up to him and kissed him on the lips. "Thank you, Charles. It will be my most treasured possession."

"No, thank *you,* Cordelia, you've bought it, after all."

"At considerably less than its value, I fancy."

He smiled and shrugged. "Who can say? But tell me, these fashion paintings around the room. Where did you get them?"

"From someone in this very room." I answered. "You?"

"Ah, no, if only." I called over to Janet, who was still topping up glasses.

She came over. "More wine, sir?"

"No need for the role-play, Janet. Charles, this is Janet, my maid. These are her pictures."

"Well, I'm damned. They're really something." With that, he grabbed some of them and stood by the piano and raising his voice, said, "Attention everybody, thank you for your kind words about my painting, but you may have noticed some rather remarkable paintings around the room. I don't know anything about fashion, as is obvious, but I know a good painting when I see one.

Look at these, and then look at the lovely lady that's been quietly serving our food and drink this evening."

All eyes turned on Janet, who blushed deeply. Everyone, including me, clapped her enthusiastically. Charles laid her paintings on top of the piano and then went over to speak to her. The entertainment continued with Samantha, the actress, giving a speech from *Everyman* that she had recently been touring. I'd seen the original at the Charterhouse in London some years ago, and had been disappointed. I did not enjoy the overly melodramatic posturing of the Victorian theatre, but her performance was stripped down, simple, and spoken with a beautifully modulated voice that sent shivers up my spine. I began to realise that I was in the company of some truly impressive artists, and that I was part of them. I felt my eyes pricking with tears at the thought.

The mousy girl, the violinist, then played an Irish air beautifully, before Lavinia gave us one her poems. I'd not had much to do with Lavinia yet; she always seemed to be in the background and with her tall, willowy figure and gothic pallor, I assumed that her poems would be inferior pastiches of the Romantics. Instead, this one was savage and rang with jagged rhythms, denouncing the blindness and deafness of those in power. Finally, Tristan and the violinist played a duet. Just before they started, Ellen strode to the piano, knelt down and planted Tristan's shoe firmly down on the soft pedal of the piano. There was general laughter, and Tristan himself stood up, smiling, bowed, and said, "Ladies and gentlemen, the hint is taken." Sure enough, he played softly behind the violin, a lively Beethoven sonata, and this time the music drifted over us like a delightful cloud to great applause at the end.

There was a little more, light conversation and drinking, then it all changed. Tristan was seated on the sofa between Ellen and Catherine, chatting, until he turned to Ellen and kissed her. She responded with passion, and he was groping at her breasts. Catherine, on the other side began to massage his cock through his trousers. That was the signal. James and Henry were removing their clothes and kissing. Lavinia, standing next to me pulled up my *kaftan* and began stroking my bare thighs. Soon, we were all naked. Janet was on her knees in front of Charles, sucking his cock. Tristan had his hand between Ellen's legs while Catherine stoked his erect member with one hand while rubbing herself with the other. Edward was behind Izzy, kneading her breasts and rubbing himself against her buttocks. Samantha went over to Catherine and knelt down to lick at her slit. After that, it was impossible to tell who was doing what to whom. people were moving from one partner to another in rapid succession. At one stage I remember Janet and I found ourselves face to face on the floor with our bottoms in the air. Tristan was taking her from behind; I'd no idea whose prick was sliding in and out me. We winked and kissed.

"This is fun," she said, before Tristan pulled out of her and allowed Izzy to suck him while Catherine came over to push her fingers in her cunny. It was only James and Henry who remained together. They must have been strictly homosexual. I was scissoring with Ellen while Charles was fondling and sucking my breasts while I worked his nice large prick. One by one, people climaxed, some with grunts and moans, some with shrieks or profanities, until we all lay panting on the floor, stroking one another gently. It was so enjoyable: no possessiveness, no emotional baggage, just a surrender to the pure pleasure of intercourse.

They wiped themselves with their handkerchiefs, then dressed. One last drink, although most of them were getting a bit unsteady by now. They left in the same groups they'd arrived in, then Janet and I shut the door on them and breathed a sigh of relief. We left everything until tomorrow, then went up to bed with one last bottle and the cigarettes.

"Well, what did you think?" I asked, as we lay in the bed. "Amazing people! So much talent and, well…"

"Well?"

"Nice to have a stiff cock up you sometimes. Makes a nice change. No offence, of course. There was even one up my arse for a bit."

"You are a shameless hussy."

"You didn't look too unhappy about having one up yours, I noticed."

"Oh, you saw."

We attempted sex, but we were both so tired, we just fell asleep in each other's arms, the wine only half finished.

It took me most of the next day to recover, and Janet wasn't much better. Despite her protestations, I helped her clear up the glasses and the food and the encrusted handkerchiefs that were still lying about.

The rest of the week was spent very quietly. There were some lovely letters from the group, thanking us for a splendid evening. I would certainly be happy to host such an evening again, and Janet agreed. I was glad for Janet, that her paintings had been praised by Charles, although, once again, I felt the lack of any recognisable talent of my own rather keenly.

I went to see Charles at the end of the week to buy another of his pictures; one, like the one I'd seen in the gallery, with people sitting on the beach, only this time they were seen from the front, and there were storm clouds approaching from behind. I admitted my feelings of inadequacy to him. He snorted, then said, "*Les Mouettes* are quite a remarkable group. Most of the real talent in this town are part of it, and how many are we? Thirty at most. Given that half of them are hangers-on, that leaves fifteen out of a population of what? Twenty thousand? That means there are nineteen thousand, nine hundred and eighty-five with either nothing to say or no talent to say it with. I was talking to Janet last night about it. She has both the talent and something to say, by the way. You should treasure her."

"Oh, believe me, I do. But what has she to say?"

"Hers is a statement of dreams. Here is a working-class girl with no chance in life who wants fine clothes and dreams of better things. So she works and works to try and say what those better things are. Some artists express their politics, others their rage, or their fantasies. I express the darkness inside me. Janet wants to find the beauty that was — is — lacking in her life."

He fell silent, took a few breaths, then looked at me.

"Look, would you mind awfully if I took her under my wing for a while? I know she's your maid and all that—"

"She's a lot more than that to me, Charles, and yes, of course I'd be delighted to let her come to you for some instruction. Of course, I'm happy to fund the cost of some lessons."

"Hoi! Stop talking about money. I'd have her here as a friend and apprentice, not for lessons. I'd like her to set up her easel in this studio — there's plenty of room. It would be company for me, and she's a very inspiring girl."

I couldn't help a pang of jealousy. I had passionate hankerings after him myself. He read my silence right.

"Cordelia, I'm not talking about anything more than giving her studio space and some guidance. If I had a desire for a woman, it would be you."

"Do you mean that?"

"I never say anything I don't mean."

"But you prefer the solace of men?"

"I am indifferent. Creative people are often bad partners; we are too selfish. I relish the casual embrace, be it male or female. That's why we so enjoy our sessions of detached sex, especially the one we had at your house. Please host another one again!"

"Would you make love to me?"

"I already have. Twice, in case you haven't noticed. But I would like to again. Very much."

"Now?"

He cocked his head on one side and looked at me directly in the eye. A minute must have passed.

"Take your clothes off."

I did so, expecting him to do the same. He didn't, so I stood in front of him and started to undress him.

"No, I want to paint you first, then I will shag you."

He fetched a chair, then went off searching, while I stood around feeling exposed and vulnerable. He reappeared with a rich tapestry rug and an egg. He arranged the rug over the chair and had me sit in it. I had to hold the egg in my left hand, thumb upward, and look at it. My right hand he manoeuvred into position around my left breast. He got annoyed when I didn't understand what he was after.

"The egg will be a serpent in the picture, but due to a woeful lack of serpents, I've substituted an egg just to get the position of your hand. I want it to be completely ambiguous whether you're offering your tit to the snake or protecting it!"

"Well, why didn't you say so?" Then it was easy.

"Perfect!" he cried. "Now think of some sexual wrong that's been done to you. Has there?"

"Huh. Yes."

"Then look at the snake like that."

I did. This was all very reminiscent of my times in Peregrine's studio. "Right, don't move, and remember that exact pose."

He was sketching away on a large canvas. It must have been four foot long and three wide. I looked at his eyes darting from the easel to me. What a lot of fire there was in them! "Look at the damned egg, would you?" he cried.

It must have been an hour before he let me relax. I felt incredibly stiff and wanted to pee badly. He apologised, but said the first sitting was important. I looked at what he'd done so far. Just a charcoal sketch, but I could see what he was getting at.

"That's enough for today," he said. "Can you come back later? Or tomorrow? And bring Janet with you, if you can."

"Perhaps an hour later this afternoon, with Janet," I said.

"Good. Now put on some clothes and let's have a coffee."

"Haven't you forgotten something?"

"Oh no. But you have been my model; an arrangement of body and limbs. Now I want to start thinking of you as a woman again."

I put on my undergarments and we sat talking and drinking coffee a while. The he came over to me, and bent over to kiss me roughly and passionately on the lips. His hand slid under my camisole and onto my breast pinching my nipple painfully. I stood up, and we embraced. I undid his shirt and threw off my camisole. We ran our hands roughly over each other's torsos. Then he suddenly broke loose, took off the rest of his clothes, and came to my arms. This time, his touch was different. It was gentle, reverential. He kissed my lips, my ear, my lips. To tell the truth, I just wanted his cock inside me, but no, he was relishing this in a way I'd never really known a man do before. I fell into his pace, smelling his skin, nibbling his nipples, and kissing his chest before his hands slid down over my buttock cheeks. Gently, so gently! I grasped his erect penis in my hand and led him to the floor in front of my posing chair. I took off the rug and laid it on the floor. I sat, and laid his head on my lap, leaning over him so that my breasts were in front of his lips. As he sucked, I reached down and started to stroke his erect cock as gently as I could. I could have stayed like that for hours, and not even with Izzy had I known such a languid, drawn out foreplay. My initial impatience had gone, and I began to see that this was my initiation into a world of heightened sensuality. This was the same meal I'd eaten countless times, but he was making me relish every mouthful.

He shuffled down and placed his head between my longing thighs, but he stroked and licked the pale, soft skin of my inner thighs for ages, teasing me as my pelvis rose up, silently begging him to reach his goal. I could feel the wetness well up from my quim and trickle over the tight little ring of my anus. His finger started to stroke my vulva, up and down between the black triangle of my pudenda, over my cunt lips and between my buttocks then back again, over and over. I was gently tugging the top half of his shaft all the while, and stroking his balls. I was getting desperate. I was so on fire that tears were running down my cheeks and this assault on my senses took over my whole body. He parted my pussy lips and started to lick the pink flesh within. I could stand it no longer. I guided his prick, now wet with his own juices, towards my cunt, and gave a cry of relief as he slid easily and gently inside me. He pushed himself a long way up me, but not quite to the point of pain. Slowly he advanced and retreated, making me appreciate every inch of him, but, after a few strokes I couldn't hold back a massive orgasm. The walls of my vagina gripped him as the butterflies started, and soon my whole body was convulsing in strong, uncontrollable spasms as one wave of ecstasy after another took me. My vaginal walls were twitching as he stayed inside me, still unspent. He slowly began to move inside me as my wet passage waited for him. As his thrusts became more urgent, I found myself approaching another climax. This time, there was no teasing, just a need to reach an ending. I started to shudder again, as he pulled out of me just in time, and I watched as his copious semen shot in warm spurts over my belly while I bucked and thrashed in another orgasm. As he slumped over to lie beside me, I ran two fingertips over my belly to gather up his spend, and licked it off.

We lay on our backs for a while, in silence. I felt the need for a cigarette. Eventually he said, "I've never felt like that before."

"I don't think I have, either," I told him. "Thank you." I meant it.

Eventually, we dressed and I took a cab home. I looked out at the passing vista of the scenery, but my eyes were blinded with tears.

"Now what's wrong?" Janet asked as I got home. My eyes must have been red and the tears had probably run rivulets though my make-up.

"I don't fucking know!" I said. I waved her aside, and the lunch that she'd prepared, and went to my bedroom. I couldn't tell you how I felt. Muddled, that's what. I had been sustained all my life by a hatred of men, and now here was one who had crept under my defences. Talented, intelligent, and the most sensitive lover I'd ever known — could it be I was falling in love with the enemy? I pulled a pillow over my head to blot out the world, but it didn't work. Nothing but the old sense of confusion and foreboding.

I emerged an hour later, still in a turmoil. I apologised to Janet, and ate some soup (and some fish, then a pork pie, suet pudding and some Turkish delight to finish) in silence while she watched me, her arms folded across her chest. I just wasn't hungry.

I pulled myself together enough to tell her about Charles' offer and our invitation to return that afternoon. Janet was beside herself with joy.

"Really? That man's a genius and he wants to teach me?" She put her arms around my neck, but I pushed her away.

"Yes. Just bring what art materials you have and we'd better get going."

"Right!" She hesitated. "I wish I knew what's got into you, I really do."

"Oh Janet, I wish I did, too."

We caught the omnibus to Charles' studio. He let us in and he told Janet what he'd told me that morning; that she had a genuine talent, and that he wanted to nurture it, in exchange for some company and 'artistic stimulation', whatever that was supposed to mean. Janet looked enquiringly at me, and I nodded, happy for her, well, sort of.

Charles asked me to undress and pose. He also asked me quietly not to move the tapestry from the chair. He'd managed to fashion a credible snake out of bits of an old towel and some string. He sat Janet down beside him with her sketch pad and pencils.

"You need to get the proportions better," he told her. "I know fashion drawings elongate the figure because that what sells dresses, but yours are too out of proportion. Far better you learn to get it right by looking at a real body."

I sat there, holding the pose while they sketched and painted, musing that it was strange to be modelling for Peregrine and now Charles and Janet, now I had screwed them all, too. I certainly wasn't complaining; I had found that few things apart from the act of sex itself gave me as much pleasure as having people gazing at my nakedness. This in itself was a curious compound of vulnerability and dominance. I thought about Peregrine: he was due to return any time soon, and Janet and I had another filming session to look forward to.

I continued to sit for them every day, for the next week. The weather was dismal and it rained most of the time, so we were glad of the distraction. Charles was impressed by the swift progress that Janet was making and seemed quite cheerful at times, apart from one morning when he appeared very subdued. I could tell he was struggling with the painting as he kept letting out grunts of exasperation. Eventually he collapsed on one of the chairs, his head in his hands. Janet put down her sketch pad and went over to him.

"Here, whatever's the matter with you today?" she asked. He just raised a tearful face to her and shook his head. I relaxed my pose and went over to them.

"He just gets like this sometimes, poor love. You can see it in his paintings. Think it's there all the time, but some days it gets a bit much, doesn't it, Charles?" He just nodded. I stroked his head and Janet, kneeling by his side, took his hand in hers. He gripped it tightly.

"Shall we go?" Janet asked. "Or would you like us to stay?" He didn't answer, lost as he was in his own hell which dogged him so. Janet made us all a cup of tea, and we sat and drank, the silence only magnified by the sound of rain on the tin roof.

I looked at the half-completed portrait on his easel. He had painted in the details of my face and it shook me. It was a very good likeness, but more than that, it was like looking into a mirror of all the hidden shards of my personality. Look at it, and you saw sensuousness, look again and there was cruelty. Hurt, longing, lust — they were all in there. Charles had been given the gift of being able to see into people's souls. Or was it the curse? No wonder he suffered so; we're better off in the darkness.

We stayed with him for a while. We played a few records on his gramophone, and both of us stroked him like a mother would. You see, I'm not totally devoid of tenderness. He recovered enough to stammer out some thanks eventually. Janet was very good; she knew when to shut up and let silence do its work, and when to chatter like a fishwife. She coaxed him gently out of his shell, until he started to talk. He was very apologetic.

"I just wake up like it sometimes. Well, quite often, and I still can't deal with it. You must think me an awful ninny."

No, we don't," Janet said. "Tell you what, my dad was like that. He was bright as a button sometimes, and would have all these great plans and ideas, then other times he'd just lie in bed all day and couldn't talk. My mother thought he was being daft and got to despise that side of him, because she didn't understand that he was ill. It was her that wanted him to go to sea, to be rid of him for a while. I never found out what happened to him, but I do know it's not being silly. Don't we all wake up some days feeling terrible? Just some people feel it more."

She carried on like this, talking to him, coaxing him. I saw there was a profound side to her that we never shared. Our talk was always superficial, or lustful, or as a mistress would speak to her maid. I knew so little about what she really thought. At last, we were satisfied that he would be all right, and left him. He said he'd got enough detail down that I didn't need to pose any more, but Janet was to carry on with her practice with him. Of course, he said, I was welcome to come anytime.

I'll admit to feeling a slight pang of jealousy when I saw how Janet had understood him, and dealt with his mood. On the way home, she chattered on about how much she was learning from him, how much she wanted to keep improving and how she could use the money from our work with Peregrine to buy the art materials she needed. The more she enthused, the more irritated I felt and I couldn't say why.

That night, we went to bed after Janet had cooked a fine meal. I'd rather forgotten my earlier scratchiness and mellowed with the wine, although I couldn't get the image of my portrait out of my mind. Although only half finished, it held up an unflinching mirror and I wasn't sure I liked what I saw.

We didn't make love that evening, but just lay in bed together. It had been a day of revelations, and my head was full of my own thoughts, and Janet, I'm sure, with hers. We couldn't talk about them.

As if in answer to my thoughts, the next morning I received a message from Peregrine: I'm back! Can you call round this morning?

I could, and did. Janet was off to Charles' studio again, so I walked round to his studio and knocked. The peephole opened and his eye looked out. He opened the door and welcomed me in with a brotherly hug. I asked how he'd fared and his eyes glittered.

"Better that I could ever have hoped for. We are on the crest of a wave. These films have been groundbreaking. I can't tell you how the select audiences I showed them to, appreciated them. I have been able to charge premium prices and they are so willing to pay. We have seen the future, and we can make our fortunes. Are you still ready to make some more?"

"Oh yes. You know I enjoy it. No one recognised me?"

"No! Do not concern yourself with that. That is London, and now you live here. The capital has a short memory; I doubt even your friends would remember you now."

That seemed a little cruel, but probably true. He had brought back a performer from London with him, so would like to film us as soon as possible, to minimise the hotel expenses. We fixed on the next afternoon. Peregrine handed me a cheque for ninety pounds. He must have done well.

When she got back, I told Janet that we were going to perform the next day. She was happy about that and very much happier when I wrote her a cheque for her half of the proceeds from the film. I asked how Charles was.

"Better," was all she would say.

She went for her lesson with Charles the next morning, so I took myself off to the Flying Fish for lunch. I rather relished my time alone with my thoughts as I worked my way through some properly made Brown Windsor soup, grilled hake, a steak pie and a custard trifle to finish. Truth to tell, my thoughts didn't amount to much, apart from wondering what sort of man Peregrine had got for the afternoon's filming. By the time I got back, Peregrine was already there, talking to Janet. With him was our fellow enactor. He was a rather disappointingly slim gentleman with a handlebar moustache called Dougal. He was a Scot, originally from Glasgow, which I could believe from his rather uncouth manner and impenetrable accent. Peregrine set up his apparatus, this time in the kitchen as he wanted to vary the setting. He outlined the meagre plot. Janet would be the maid, and Dougal a decorator who was painting the wall. He would fondle her as she bent over the sink and as he had her skirts up, I would walk in, pretend to be shocked and order him out. He would then start touching me and start making love to me. I would relent and submit, tearing off my clothes as he undressed and revealed his erect penis. Janet would look amazed and join in while we made use of the kitchen table in various ways. It went well, and when he undressed, I saw why Peregrine had hired him. His prick was a monster. I fell on it greedily, sucking it and massaging it. Under his clothes, he had a superb body. Janet, when she had stripped off her clothes, joined in eagerly. She laid on the table offering herself to me. I bent over her, licking her labia, while Dougal took me from behind. What a feeling it was, to have my hole so stretched by such a prick. We adopted all sorts of positions and combinations after that. Peregrine shot it all, but then required us to repeat this bit or that while he shot it from different angles. Dougal's stamina amazed me: he could stop in the middle of some wild penetration and, with a few stokes of that lovely cock, keep himself erect until the next 'take', as he called it. Finally, when we had done, Peregrine ordered us to kneel in front of Dougal while he masturbated himself into spending his load over our breasts. We didn't enjoy that particularly, and, as the whole thing had been a series of starts and stops, both of us had had to feign our enjoyment.

Janet made us all some coffee while we recovered, sitting on the benches around the table, naked, and chatting as though we were sitting in some polite society cafe. I could see that Dougal was a professional at this and wasn't surprised when he told us he was more comfortable in the presence of men.

Peregrine announced that he was ready for the next film, and asked if Janet and Dougal would perform some straight sex in her bedroom. I volunteered my services, but Peregrine said no, he had other plans for me. Dougal stroked his cock into another massive erection, and they went with Peregrine into Janet's room. Feeling a bit put out, I picked Dougal's now dried sperm off my breasts and dressed. I sat in the kitchen, listening to the shouts and grunts from her room, wondering what Peregrine had meant.

In due course, they emerged, Peregrine happy with his work, and Dougal dispatched to his hotel, no doubt to seek the services of some willing man. There had been no time for Janet to cook any dinner, but Peregrine just waved his hands.

"Fine! Let me take you out for dinner. Let's go to the Fitzroy and be damned!"

With the curtains drawn and the gaslight and candles illuminating the murals, the waiters hovering and the opulent atmosphere, the place looked fabulous. So was the meal we enjoyed. Peregrine was in an expansive mood and ordered two bottles of very fine wine to go with the meal. This was the first time Janet had been in somewhere like this, but with one of my dresses, looked every bit the lady. We ate muesli as inspired by Dr Bircher-Benner, poached turbot, asparagus, lamb cutlets, a fruit confit, then a gorgeous layered mousse before some fine French cheeses. We ordered two further bottles of Bordeaux to wash it all down.

Peregrine left it to the final courses to present his plans.

"There are vast profits to be made from our endeavours, as you've seen, and my business is expanding rapidly. I won't bore you with the details. Now I am going to propose something and I want you to listen. You need not say anything now, but think about it and let me know in a day or so."

We both listened as he said, "You are both in high demand. True beauty, and the willingness to display it, is a rare thing. There are many establishments where bored whores strut their wares in front of bored customers. But you are both something on another plane! You have a power over men's minds. The next step would be for you to pose in front of the most discreet of the smoking clubs in the West End of London. I have an interest in a number of such clubs in or around there, and my clients would be prepared to pay a lot of money to see you. As usual, it would all be very discreet and tasteful. I would pay your fares and put you up in respectable hotels for a week at a time in return for your doing live what you have been doing in front of the camera. No, don't say anything now, but consider it and let me know. It would make you both wealthy."

I saw the bill when it arrived. It was for nearly two pounds.

That night, as I lay with Janet and we sipped our way through another bottle of wine and smoked the marijuana, Janet rolled over towards me, stroking my thigh.

"Well, what do you reckon?" she asked.

"About what?"

"How do you mean 'About what?' About going up to London, of course."

I exhaled a cloud of smoke. "I'm up for it. How about you?"

"Me too. Just for a week, mind. I've never been to London. Never been on a train, either." "It can't do any harm, can it?"

"No, now let's go to sleep."

I sent Peregrine a message to let him know that we were agreeable to his proposition, although just for a week, and received the answer that we should prepare to travel in two weeks' time, on the Wednesday. He would come and collect us and would travel with us. In the meantime, the film equipment would be collected and taken away.

Chapter 8

In the meantime, I caught up on my social round. I visited Izzy on a few occasions, and also took tea with Margaret. She seemed quite happy with my association with *les Mouettes*, and I confessed myself impressed by their ideas and talents.

"They're certainly the harbingers of a new order," she said, "and I suppose it's all for the good. It just seems everything's moving too fast. All over Europe there seem to be rumbles of change. But I suppose I'm just being a typical old lady, scared of where the world is heading. The young have always clamoured for change and I include myself in that. I saw the atrocities the British were carrying out in the name of the Empire, even though we weren't supposed to know about them, and we railed against them. So good luck to them, and you, my dear." She leant over to me and smiled wickedly. "And tell me, are the rumours true: that they indulge in rather modern sexual practices?"

"Really? I've not heard about anything like that," I lied.

She just nodded and smiled.

"Of course not, I'm sure they're just rumours and tittle-tattle. Anyway, that's up to them."

She changed the subject, thankfully, and we talked of her various charities. It was a pleasant afternoon.

At Izzy's request, I took Janet along to talk to her about the social conditions of the working classes. We hugged and kissed like the intimate friends we were. Janet sat beside Izzy and soon became talkative. There was a lot she had to say, and they talked for most of the day. I was interested initially, indeed, quite shocked by her tales of injustice and desperation. I became a little bored with the whole thing after a while, and picked out a book to read until they were ready for lunch. We went to the Flying Fish again, but the earnest discussion carried on between them. When we'd finished, I suggested that my presence was superfluous and announced that I would return home to await Janet's return.

I changed out of my dress and lay on the bed in my kaftan. I tried to read, but it was a warm day, and my attention wandered. I closed my eyes and ran my hands over the cool slippery cotton of the garment. The sensation aroused me, and soon my hands were gliding over my breasts, teasing my nipples until I could see them erect under the material. I put a hand down over my pubic hair, feeling its roughness. I began to feel that delicious tingle, then pulled off the kaftan and lay naked on the bed. I played with my nipples, then opened my legs and stroked my inner lips and fingered my clitoris with small circular movements. I pushed two fingers inside my passage, which was now slippery and ready. My cunny made loud sloppy sounds as I worked my fingers in and out while my other hand rubbed my clitoris. Two fingers, then three, then four went in deeply and easily. I was on the point of orgasm, so stopped to let the tremors die down so that I could prolong the pleasure, just stroking my wet slit gently. Then I set to again, thinking of Dougal and his monster inside me. This time, I let myself come as the spasms started and my thighs clamped shut over my hand while I convulsed with pure pleasure.

I must have fallen asleep, for the next thing I was aware of was Janet in bed beside me, kissing my ear. I turned to her and smiled.

"Hello, I must have nodded off. I was just taking a little nap."

Janet took my right hand and licked my fingers. "Tastes like you managed to find a way to get to sleep. You should have waited for me."

"I am waiting for you."

"Well, here I am," she said, and we put on the black chokers.

I took her proffered breast and sucked on the nipple tenderly at first, then roughly as our passion mounted and we climbed the mountain that leads to ecstasy.

Afterwards, we lay on top of the bed, smoking.

"How did you get on?" I asked.

"I think I must have talked for England. I never knew I had so much to say. Poor Izzy had a right struggle to get it all written down. She wants me to go back again and keep talking. There's certainly a load more I can tell her."

"Did you fuck her?"

"Nah. She sort of wanted to, but I could see she was wrapped up in her writing, so I didn't bother. Anyway, I wanted you."

I squeezed her thigh. "Thank you."

"Anytime." She grinned. "I need to be getting back to Charles tomorrow for a day or so. He's right, you just have to work at it all the time. He is a brilliant teacher."

"How's his mood? I worry about him."

"So do I. He's fine again now, and he sort of knows when he's down that he'll be better in a day or two, but it's still a worry."

"How's my picture coming on?"

"Now that's going to be something. You'll be thrilled to bits. It's a bit different from his usual style, more — what's the word he used? Pre something?"

"Pre-Raphaelite?"

"That's the chap. What does it mean?"

"Oh, a bunch of artists who wanted to paint things as they really were, as opposed to the conventions of hundreds of years before. One of them, Jane Morris, used to be an embroideress. I've a book somewhere with some illustrations. I'll dig it out. So why has he done it like that?

"He just said you were more complex than anything else he'd painted, and wanted to put in lots of detail."

"Can I come and see it?"

"Not until it's finished, he says. I think it nearly is."

"You remember we're going to London next Wednesday?"

"I couldn't really forget that, could I?"

Chapter 9

It was a treat to see Janet's face as she stood with Peregrine and I on Brighton station. The noise and the clouds of smoke and steam were something very new to her, and her nervousness as we got into one of the carriages was apparent. She became almost hysterical as the train got up steam and sped out of Brighton, but soon relaxed, and was as wide-eyed as a child, watching the Sussex countryside go past.

On the train, Peregrine enlightened us a little more about the week ahead.

"I have around five establishments in the best parts of London. Gentlemen's clubs, where the finest in society meet to relax and be entertained. You will tour them all, and put on a few showings each day. I will pay you handsomely for your act, which will be much like you have been doing. Anything else is up to you, if you so wish."

"Anything else?" I asked, curious.

"The influence you will have over these gentlemen will encourage them to stimulate themselves. If you wish to aid them in their endeavours, there is a strict code of payment to the artistes themselves. In other rooms, your films will be shown, and you may do the same there. But it's entirely up to you, although my advice is that it is very easy money. At the end of the week, we shall return home, and if that's what you want, we will leave it at that, otherwise…"

He trailed off. Janet and I looked at each other. Just how extensive was Peregrine's little empire? I realised there was more, a lot more, to his business dealings than we had suspected.

We pulled into Victoria station, a great noisy place where guards' whistles blew and porters shouted, while the monstrous engines let off hisses and billows of steam. "I always thought hell would be like this." Janet shouted over the noise. We took a cab to somewhere off the Tottenham Court Road, Janet marvelling at the sights. Peregrine escorted us to our hotel. This was our first disappointment. The place was rather down at heel, and he had booked us into a double room, which was drab to say the least, with well-worn dark wood furniture and the walls in a tobacco brown. The sounds of the street would be a nuisance. I'd become used to the relative quiet of Brighton, where motor cars were not that common. Here, they were ubiquitous, and clanking omnibuses crowded the roads.

I mentioned this to him.

"Come now, it's good enough, and anything better would reflect on the money you'll earn. It is only for a week, after all. Next time the Ritz, perhaps! I will call on you tomorrow morning, and take you round the establishments so you can get an idea of them."

He smiled a dazzling smile and left us to settle in. I'd forgotten how stuffy London could be on a warm day; we were both glistening with perspiration. To Janet, however, this was all such a novelty. She leaned out of the window, watching the street outside and asking a stream of questions. We lay on the bed and slept for a while; it was too hot to do anything else. Later, we dressed and decided to explore the sights. We walked down to Oxford Street with all its impressive shops, and went into a few, Janet exclaiming all the while at the prices. I was used to London, so it was a delight to view it through her eyes, the sheer scale of everything, the goods that were unobtainable elsewhere, the hurried and impersonal way the shop assistants treated their customers. We didn't buy anything, but I could see Janet taking a careful mental note of the fashions. We wandered down Shaftesbury Avenue as the shops shut and bought tickets for a show, then found a decent-looking restaurant for some dinner. Janet was in a high state of excitement, and I reflected that she'd probably seen more in this one day than in the whole of her previous life. An indifferent meal, served at the same breakneck speed that I'd forgotten, came to seven shillings.

The theatre was a treat, though. It was a silly comedy and not to my taste, although ably performed, but the decor, the crowds and the magnificent sets impressed us both. The air was heavy with cigar smoke and strong perfume. People were there to see and be seen. I was glad to have escaped all this, although Janet was vibrant with these new experiences. Afterwards, outside, we saw the parade of prostitutes touting for custom along the avenue, and the entire nightlife of the city come awake.

Arm in arm we walked back to the hotel, Janet gawping and exclaiming at each new sight.

Once we reached the sanctuary of our room, I collapsed on the bed, quite exhausted. Janet was still in an excited frame of mind, savouring this dangerous new world.

In the morning, after little sleep for either of us, we breakfasted, then waited in the hotel lobby for Peregrine to appear. Eventually he did, and even he, so calm and polite usually, seemed hurried and anxious. We got into a motor-cab, another first for Janet, and drove to Dean Street, in Soho. The cab drew up outside an anonymous doorway which led into a short dark corridor, with a cloakroom leading off to the right. Peregrine opened the door at the end, and we entered a large, surprisingly airy room, although it smelt strongly of stale cigar smoke. It was painted in a pleasing shade of light blue, with gold-coloured fittings, comfortable leather armchairs and some white tables which stood on a dark blue carpet.

There was a bar at the far end. The place was deserted apart from two cleaning women, who looked at us knowingly and disconcertingly as we walked on past the bar and into a similarly decorated dining room. From there, a small doorway led off to the right. Peregrine ushered us through. We were confronted by the curious sight of a wall of black doors, about a dozen of them in this unlit room. Peregrine opened one of them, and we stepped into a small cubicle containing a chair, which looked out onto a small stage area backed by two folding screens. This, Peregrine explained, was where we would be performing. It was festooned with drapes and swags of grubby red velvet of rather inferior quality. We stood on the dais and saw that the twelve cubicles were identical, each with a plain wooden chair, a small side-table with an ashtray on it, and a linoleum floor. Each occupant would be hidden from the view of the others. Only we could see them all. To the left of the stage, behind the drapes, was another curtained doorway. This was our changing and retiring room, and a bleak, functional room it was. A similar doorway on the right contained the props we would need: a bed, a couch, table and chairs, potted palms and so forth.

In our dressing room our costumes were hung on pegs. We were to be two society ladies for one act, and a mistress and maid, predictably, for the other. The clothes were exotic, the society ladies' ones being fashioned from sheer material that revealed the skin underneath, although decorated with enough lace and ribbons as to make it all the more tantalising. Peregrine also proudly showed us a novel undergarment he had imported from Germany, although its name, *brassière,* was French. I'd heard of such things but never seen one, so we tried them on. What a blessed change from the whalebone corsets! We practiced putting them on and, more importantly, taking them off. There was an elaborate *peignoir* for me with slits giving access to my breasts and pudenda, whereas Janet's maid costume was open right up the back of the dress to reveal her buttocks. We were to take these costumes to the other venues, and repeat our act in the same roles.

Peregrine disappeared to have a word with the manager while we changed back into our normal clothes. Then on to the four other venues, all rather similar, although not as opulent as the first.

"Do you own these places?" I asked Peregrine.

"I have a large share in them, yes. I leave the running to others of course, but don't let that concern you. I merely provide the high-quality entertainment. There are other rooms where we show the films. You are proving extremely popular, I am pleased to say. Your appearances in the flesh, so to speak, will create a small sensation."

A cab would bring us back for eight fifteen, ready to perform at nine, after the members had dined. We would perform our first routine, allow some time for a changeover, then perform the second. Peregrine then apologised for having to take his leave of us, as his times in London were rather crowded with various business interests.

I took Janet to a restaurant I used to frequent in Russell Street for lunch, which used to be the haunt of theatrical and artistic types. We chatted about what we should do that evening and decided we should be talking about London society on the couch, as the two ladies talking frankly and intimately about their husband's sexual deficiencies, and wishing for a well-hung rich man to service them, but in the meantime, we'd say, perhaps we can satisfy each other. We'd then start kissing and take it from there. The maid and mistress scene, we decided, would have me instructing Janet to polish the table. She would bend over the table while I looked lustfully at her. I would steal up and part the back of her dress without her knowledge. I would then say that there was something else that needed cleaning, and I would thrust my breasts out of the slits and say "These!" and order her to lick them clean.

I was wanting to go back to the hotel to rest, but Janet wanted to see some of the sights of the city, so I treated her to a cab ride down to the embankment, Westminster, The Mall, Buckingham Palace, Piccadilly and Oxford Circus and then back to the hotel. I smiled and caressed her hair as I revelled in her wide-eyed innocence. It was worth the extortionate cab fare, or nearly.

We rested, although I couldn't sleep. To tell the truth, I was starting to feel some anxiety about exhibiting myself publicly. It had seemed very natural in the private surroundings of the studio or my house and I told myself I would quickly get accustomed to this unfamiliar situation, and wasn't this what I enjoyed above all else? To watch men becoming aroused by the sight of my body? I looked at Janet, lying asleep beside me, seemingly quite untroubled. I wondered what she got out of it. Perhaps it was just the money, or did she share my craving to flaunt my body? We never talked about things like that.

We ate a light dinner before the cab called for us at eight. Peregrine was obviously well organised. My nervousness was increasing, and it must have showed, for Janet asked "Are you all right?"

"Bit nervous." I replied. "You?"

"No, what's there to be nervous about? It's a well-paid job, and we know we're good at it, don't we?"

Peregrine met us at the door, and led us down a side alley to the back of the building, to avoid us having to walk through the club members We entered by a back door — Peregrine's life seemed to be full of strange and hidden alleyways and doors — and into the changing room. He noticed that my hands were shaking.

"Nervous?"

"A little."

"Quite understandable. I'm sure you will enjoy it when you get going. Let me get you a small brandy with a small stimulant in it. Janet?"

"Just the brandy, thank you. I'm stimulated enough already."

"Good girl."

He reappeared with two large brandies, although mine was considerably larger. We drank them down and after a bit my nerves settled as the brandy took effect. We changed into our costumes, put on the chokers and waited. The stage was set with the furniture we had requested, and the electric lights were turned on over the stage. Shortly before we were due to start, I felt a curious surge of energy and my brain started to sparkle. That's the only way I can describe it: it sparkled. I turned to Janet with excitement.

"I'm looking forward to this. We're going to be great!"

She looked a little taken aback. "You've changed your tune. But yes, we'll be special." She kissed me passionately on the lips.

We heard Peregrine's voice introducing us. There was a ripple of applause, and we stepped on to the stage.

I felt exultant, as we launched into our dirty talk, both of us coming up with inventive phrases to turn our audience on. There they were, all twelve cubicles occupied by men in evening dress. Already one or two of them were gripping their crotches. We stood up and talked of having to satisfy each other. We kissed, then started to let our hands stray over the other's body. Janet moved behind me to undo the two buttons that held my dress together at the back, and I slipped it off my shoulders, standing there in the brassiere and some unnaturally skimpy drawers — 'knickers' Peregrine had called them — while Janet cupped my breasts from behind and teased them. I was aroused now, and so, I saw, were the men, some of whom had their cocks out of their trousers and were playing with them. I took off Janet's dress and in our strange underwear we rubbed our bodies together. I took off her brassière from behind to let the men get a good view of her body, then let my hand stroke her bush through her silk undergarments. I slipped it under the material, working her clitoris. We drifted to the bed and took off our few remaining garments displaying our genitalia to the occupants of the cubicles. One, then another and another held up a ten-shilling note, Their trousers were round their knees, revealing their pale skinny thighs. They were working their erections with various degrees of success. Janet left me to cavort on the bed while she stepped off the dais, and one by one, took the proffered notes and sucked their cocks until she jerked back her head to avoid their ejaculations. As more notes were offered, I took over, until we had drained every last one of them between us. I can't describe the elation I felt: to watch these men, normally so proud and dignified, abase themselves so willingly and thoroughly in front of us at the sight of our naked bodies. They were like worshippers at a temple, and we were the goddesses. One by one, they wiped themselves, tucked their little shrunken soldiers back into their trousers, and shuffled awkwardly out.

My only disappointment was that our show had been so brief. We could happily have done a lot more, but, typical men, it was quick up, a few clumsy strokes and that was it: a sticky little discharge before the shame set in, then down again. They could have no idea of the slow intensity of a woman's arousal and the drawn-out delirium of her orgasm. But, if they were willing to pay that much for what little they got, well...

We posed for them until the last one had gone. A young lad came in with a mop and swabbed the floor, trying not to look at us while we retired to the dressing room to rest. Peregrine came in, obviously much happier than when we'd seen him that morning, and congratulated us.

"Bravo, my dears! A wonderful performance. It has been the first of its kind, and it appears that each show will not be as long as I had anticipated, but I have a large queue of gentlemen eager to watch you. The entire club, in fact. If you are agreeable, can we start again in ten minutes, then squeeze in two more performances? You will double your earnings, of course."

We didn't mind one bit. The performance had taken so little effort on our part, so we changed into our other costumes while the lad wheeled off the *chaise longue* and replaced it with the small table and chair. The next batch of men shuffled in and took their seats in the cubicles. They carried their glasses of brandy or whisky and smoked their cigars while Peregrine announced us again. This time, he urged them "to take time to appreciate the timeless beauty of the female form, to savour the delicacy of feeling between passionate women, to share their sensuality" and other such nonsense. His plan, of course, was that we might get the chance to do more than just suck them off.

We launched into the second scenario. I ordered Janet to polish the table. She bent over it with her bottom facing the men. I looked lustfully at her while she wiggled her backside at the men and winked at them, knowing what was coming. I came up to her and parted her dress, revealing her naked cheeks, which she rather deftly twitched. There had been a deal of chatter and coughing when we started, but now you could hear a pin drop. I parted her cheeks to reveal her neat little anus while she pretended not to notice and carried on polishing. I walked over to stand by the bed and ordered her over to instruct her to clean my breasts. Janet was excellent; she was teasing the audience by teasing me. She took a feather duster as I exposed my breasts through the slits in the costume and dusted them off with it. It was strange; shooting the film had required us to do everything in mime, and here there was a natural instinct to do so as well. It seemed more fitting. I shouted to her to stop, as we had planned.

"Not like that, you silly girl! Wash them!"

"But I haven't got a cloth, ma'am."

"Then you'll have to lick them clean…"

As she started to fondle and suck my breasts, we kept up a stream of lewd talk with me instructing her what to do. This time we kept the teasing up, prolonging the chat and the jokes while we removed each other's clothes more slowly and deliberately. Still, they were unable to keep their cocks in their trousers for long. While Janet was licking and fingering my vulva, with her bottom in the air, I was propped up so that I could look the men in the eye, giving them a look that said "Would you like to do this to me?" We lay side by side on our backs, stroking each other, and half feigning passionate arousal before we both went out in front of the cubicles, fingering ourselves. Again, the ten-shilling notes were proffered, and Janet shouted "Double that and we'll double your pleasure!" One man did, so Janet and I worked on his cock, letting him penetrate me while Janet stroked his balls and let him suck her breasts. I masturbated him until his spunk splashed over my breasts. Eventually, we worked round them all until both of us were dripping with strangers' semen. That was a whole pound from all twelve of them.

Peregrine popped in while we were still naked in the dressing room, sponging off the sperm. He asked us if he could buy us a drink before the next showing. Janet had another brandy, and I asked if I could have the same with the tonic in it that I'd had before. He obliged, and I drank the cocktail gratefully, for I was beginning to think I wanted to be tucked up in bed with Janet, rather than to have to repeat the performance. But obligation was obligation, and money was money. Janet seemed quite indefatigable, and after the brandy took hold, I felt more than ready to start again.

The evening finished as successfully as it had started. I felt exultant after two more of my brandy mixtures and could have gone on all night. Janet reminded me we had to be ready to perform at the next venue tomorrow evening, so we purchased a bottle of wine and took it back to the hotel. We lay in bed, drinking and smoking the marihuana, but I was too excited to sleep. I remember telling Janet about my loathing of men, and my desire to goad them with my sexuality. I probably said a few other things I shouldn't, but we were both tired, perhaps a little muddled, and fell asleep.

The rest of the week followed much the same pattern. It soon became chore, and I think we were both ready to go home. Disappointingly, Peregrine came to the hotel to tell us that we couldn't keep all our extra earnings. He had, regrettably, he said, to take half of our earnings to cover his considerable expenses. When we protested, he pointed out the terms of our contract. Neither Janet or I had bothered to go through it thoroughly, and there it was. Never mind, we were still earning silly amounts of money for what was a very pleasant experience, and, he pointed out, there were still our earnings from the film showings. Peregrine was generous with my brandy mixtures, which I was becoming very fond of. It made each performance a new excitement. The only slight anxiety I had was the bond between Janet and I. We faked passion four times a night for what turned out to be the full seven nights, so much in demand had we become. During that entire week, I don't think we had real sex once. The boundaries between real and feigned passion were becoming blurred in these highly unusual settings. We tried, believe me, but I think both of us started to suspect the other of feigning real passion and our attempts at lovemaking didn't work. We needed to return home.

Chapter 10

When we did, things didn't improve much. I rather withdrew for some days, my mind full of the old men's creaming cocks we had tasted and taken inside us. Somehow, we had spoiled sex. What should have been natural and free we had now made a commodity with a price to be sold and bought, and a profit to be made.

Janet resumed her lessons with Charles. She seemed to have put London behind her very quickly, as though she'd done a job, taken the money, and, well, just got on with her life. Our talk became spasmodic and estranged. I persuaded myself it was only temporary, I was just tired. Janet told me excitedly that my portrait was now finished, and invited me along to Charles' studio to view it and pick it up. I should have been thrilled, but wasn't. I was irritable and aimless. I should have gone to see Izzy, but didn't feel like it. I couldn't face Margaret, as I couldn't face her kindness and wisdom knowing what I had been doing.

Was it shame? I don't think it was, for I felt no inhibitions then, only exultation at the ultimate humiliation I had provoked in rich and powerful men. I had wished to taste life in all its aspects, but now I was left with the feeling that I had tasted something delicious, but poisonous.

As soon as I could, I went round to see Peregrine, who had accompanied us back from London. He welcomed me with his usual bright aplomb, and we went to sit in his studio.

"I do hope you enjoyed yourself in London, my lovely Cordelia. It was a unique experience, I think you'll agree."

"It was certainly unique. So unique that I'm having problems returning to ordinary life. I don't suppose you have any of that tonic, do you? I need a bit of a lift."

"That is something you will only find in those clubs, but I have the same thing in another form. Would you like to try it?"

"I should, very much."

He disappeared for a little time. I heard him open the door into his courtyard. He returned, smiling, with a small twist of paper. Inside was a white powder.

"What is it?" I asked.

"It is an extract of the leaves of the coca plant, much used in the South Americas to increase stamina and as a euphoric. It is quite harmless."

"What do I do with it?"

"Take it home with you, then you can either rub a pinch of it on your gums, or some prefer the anus. Or you can put a little powder into a thin line and sniff it into your nose with a drinking straw. I would try the gums first."

I took the small package and placed it in my handbag. I asked the price, but he waved his hand dismissively.

"A little gift from me, dear Cordelia."

"You are a dear, sweet Peregrine. Thank you."

"Not at all, although if you require any more, I shall have to make a small charge, I'm afraid."

"Of course, I quite understand."

I hurried home. Janet was in the kitchen, preparing dinner. We spoke a few words, then I went upstairs to my bedroom. I opened the package up, licked my finger and dabbed it in the powder, and rubbed it into my gums. It didn't seem like much, so I tried another dab. It didn't take long before I felt more relaxed than I had since I came back from London. I sat on the bed, relishing the moment and feeling my sense of self-worth returning. Why I had become so withdrawn I couldn't understand. I was beautiful, and had driven men mad with desire, and I suddenly wanted to do it again. I was still feeling in an ebullient mood when we sat down to dinner, and started chatting to Janet in the way we hadn't done since before the London interlude. Janet looked a little puzzled, but we had so much to talk about. I drank a lot of wine as I asked about her lessons and all sorts of things, but only toyed with the food. I got a little argumentative when I asked Janet if she would go up to London again with me and she shook her head.

"No, it was fun in its way, I suppose, but I've got my little nest egg saved up, and I said I wasn't going to do any more."

"Oh, come on. We made a heap of money and we had a good time. You and me, eh? Why are you being so stupid? It makes sense!"

"Does it? Really? I don't think I'm being the stupid one. I think that was a dangerous world we entered, and I'm not venturing there again."

I got annoyed at that. She had no right to talk to me in that tone. I got up and roughly seized her by the hair with one hand, forcing her head back to look at me, while my other hand clutched her breast, hard.

"You're hurting me! Let go of me!"

"Listen to me. We're a double act! I want to do more of it, and that means you'll do more of it, too. I'm your mistress, remember, and you'll do as I say!"

She hit me in the stomach with her elbow. I gasped and let go of her. She stood up and faced me.

"Not any more, you're not."

"How dare you!"

"Listen to me, *Mrs Edwards*." She spat my name out, her expression like a mask of iron. "I've had enough. I am giving you a week's notice, as of now. I don't know what's got into you, though I can have a good guess, and you need to stop it at once. You know it's cocaine he's got you on, don't you? I've seen what that stuff does to people. But I'm not staying here, that's for certain."

"Bugger off then! See if I care. And where would you go? Nowhere! You need me, you stupid girl."

"I'll tell you where I'll go. I'm going to look after Charles. He needs someone to look after him. I actually care about him, but you couldn't possibly understand what it means to really care for someone else. You think you're in love with us all, but it's just a one-way thing for you! We all serve your warped ego."

I couldn't believe she was standing there in front of me, saying these things. Even so, she hadn't finished.

"And I'll tell you something else — I've put a deposit down on a shop. That was my dream and now I've saved enough to get a tidy little business going. So you see, *Mrs Edwards,* I don't need you any more." She flung something at my feet. It was her black choker.

I stared at her, not sure if all this was real. I picked up the black band, winding it round my fingers as I felt the tears running down my cheeks.

"Janet, don't say these things! You can't leave me. I mean, we love each other, don't we? Of course we do. I love you and you love me. We're great together, you and me, aren't we? I'd love to help you in your shop. It'll be such fun, we'll run it together…"

"Oh yes? Who'll do the books? Not you: you're useless with money. Who'll do the designs? Not you.

Who'll cut and sew? Who'll kow-tow to the customers? You can't do anything except flaunt yourself naked. Don't make me laugh!"

Seeing me sitting there, sobbing, she softened a little.

"We've had a good time together, and you've been very good to me, and my mum, but it's over and done with, don't you see? It was only lust, and we knew it. And lust never lasts. I'm grateful, but you've changed, and so have I. Time we both moved on, I think."

"Oh, Janet, come to bed. Let's make love like we used to? Bring up a bottle and we'll have a smoke and a cuddle. We'll make it good again, I promise."

"Sorry, but no. Go to bed. I'll help you up, and I'll bring you a fresh bottle and your smokes. There's no point in talking any more."

Dazed, I let her help me into bed. She went downstairs and returned with the wine and cigarettes, dumped them roughly down beside me, and disappeared.

Fuck her, I thought, after swallowing a few mouthfuls of wine. Who needs her? There's plenty more nice-looking servant girls out there. But I knew none of them would match Janet, and I started to cry all over again.

I didn't sleep much, and just worked my way down the bottle and smoked one cigarette after another until I must have dropped off in a stupor when the first light of dawn cast its grey light in the room. It was ten when I woke, hoping that last night had been a dream, but it hadn't been. I felt dreadful, and dressed myself in whatever came to hand. Janet had laid some breakfast out on the sideboard, but I had little appetite for it. I ate what I could, and decided to venture outside to pull myself together, to walk along the promenade and let normality seep back in.

But the sight of normality only heightened my pain. Couples walked up and down, children played, old ladies gossiped; the normal world was a foreign land, and I was not part of it. I began to glimpse the nightmare that Charles must be living through every day. I went back inside, grabbed a bottle of wine, and retired to my bedroom. I rubbed the last of the powder onto my gums, and soon the world shifted back into its proper perspective. I lay on my bed, trying to work out what I was to do. I would have to advertise for another maid, for I knew that Janet had meant what she said, and I knew that she was right, what was past, was past. It was time to move on. I wondered how I could word an advertisement to suggest what I needed. 'Willing young girl to cater for the needs of a single lady…' That would do. I wrote out the advertisement and placed it in an envelope for Janet to take to the newspaper offices. I felt a surge of energy again, and went outside. A group of children were playing on the beach, throwing a ball between them. Their laughs and shrieks of delight were a clarion call back to the normal world. I rushed down to the beach and joined them. They were a bit puzzled, but accepted me into their game and we threw the ball to each other. I admit my aim could have been better, and my catching skills, and once or twice I fell over, until some parents came over and moved them somewhere else, giving me some disapproving looks. I struggled to my feet, and made my way along the beach to the pier, and up to Peregrine's studio. He answered my knock, but said "Not now, I have a family portrait. Wait on the pier until you see them go."

I leant against the railings a little unsteadily, until I saw a man in a top hat, with a pretty little wife and their two smartly dressed young children leave his studio. He let me in, and I asked him if he had more of the tonic powders. I told him that Janet was leaving me, and he tut-tutted with regret, but said there would be more work for me if I wanted it. There was no shortage of people willing to model for good money. I told him I would welcome another week in London. He disappeared again, and returned with a larger package, about the size of a domino. I took it gratefully.

"That will be a pound," he told me.

"How much?"

"A pound," he replied. "I know, it is not cheap, but it has been harvested in Peru, shipped here with no little difficulty, and laboriously converted. This amount should last you some time. And I would ask you to keep these transactions between ourselves. If it became known, there would be grave consequences for me. And you." He added pointedly.

I didn't have that much money on me, of course, but wrote him a cheque. He took it, and bade me good day with a smile.

Janet appeared later that afternoon, emerging from a cab with a large parcel which must have been my portrait. I was in the kitchen, resting my head on the table. She looked at me, and sighed.

"This should have been a happy occasion. This is your portrait and it's magnificent, but look at the state you're in."

"I am not in a state."

"Then why is your dress undone, and gaping open at the back? Everyone can see your backside."

She was angry with me, I could tell, but it was her fault. She should have been there to dress me, and I should have been asked along so that Charles could reveal the portrait to me in person. Instead, she placed it on the table, still wrapped. She stomped off into the dining room to clear up the remains of the breakfast, and lay out some cold meats for my lunch.

"How's Charles?" I asked, trying to be conversational.

"Not very good. He put a lot of himself into your picture, and it's left him in a poor way. I don't think he should have bothered."

I wasn't going to rise to that. "Does he want anything for it?"

"Of course he does! He's no good at asking for payment, but I've no qualms. You've no idea, have you? How much time a brilliant artist has devoted to it. His whole experience and knowledge has been poured into that—"

"Spare me the talk. How much?"

"Twenty pounds."

"What?"

"Twenty pounds, I said. Cheap at the price. It's worth a lot more than that on the open market."

I had no choice. I sat and wrote out a cheque. Janet took it, folded it, and placed it in her cleavage.

"Thank you. Charles would like to see you at the studio. Just come when you've sobered up a bit."

She left, leaving me alone with my portrait. I was sufficiently sober to want to wait until I was in a better frame of mind to look at it, but for the moment, I was tired and just wanted to go to sleep. I laid back on the rough wooden bench I was sitting on, and laid out on it, my legs parted on each side of it. I hitched up my dress and toyed with myself, but found my finger strokes, instead of arousing me, just caused me pain and an intolerable itch. I had to stop, and fell asleep where I was.

I woke up some time later, stiff and uncomfortable and still aware of a stinging between my legs. I forced myself to get up, and dragged the wrapped portrait upstairs to my bedroom. I was feeling terrible. I needed to connect with reality again. I opened the small parcel of coca extract and this time tried rubbing it into my anus. The effect was swift. I tore off the wrappings of the portrait and propped it up against the bedroom wall, then sat back on the bed to look at it.

It made me gasp. It was truly a masterpiece. I was sitting in the chair, a queen, naked but strong and grasping the powerless serpent. I was dominant, my expression blankly scornful as I sat amongst the rich tapestries and drapes. He had caught my inner essence, I thought, as I kept staring at it. The image stared back at me until I fell asleep again.

I stayed in my room for some days, trying to pull myself together. I would look at my portrait for hours on end. It was as though Charles had placed some black spell in it. Sometimes I was the haughty queen, but at other times it seemed the serpent was about to bite me, as I put a protective hand on my breast. Sometimes my expression seemed to betray fear, at others, rage or boredom. There was all of me in there, and all the 'mes' were sitting in judgement. I knew I had to break this cycle of despondency, although, with Janet's going, I had every reason to feel despondent. There had been no answers yet to my advertisement for a replacement, but the papers had only just come out. There was still time.

Janet had warned me about taking cocaine, and I wrestled to stop taking the stuff, but sometimes, the world seemed such a dismal place that I had to give in and take some. The lips of my vulva continued to sting, and when I examined myself with the aid of a hand mirror, I saw the cause: clusters of small blisters had erupted on the delicate skin, although they looked as though they were healing. I placed a tentative finger inside the opening and moved it around. It didn't hurt, so I continued — I needed some sexual relief, and when it came, I felt a lot better. I dressed myself, and ventured downstairs. Janet was out, but had left some lunch for me. I had been eating very little for my appetite had disappeared latterly. There was a small pile of mail which Janet had put on the table: a letter from Izzy expressing concern for my wellbeing, as I had not been in contact with her, a letter from Charles informing me that my picture was ready and he would dearly love to see me, a few circulars, and a letter from Margaret, inviting me to another *soirée* at her house next week. Finally, a letter from the bank, informing me that my funds were running low and inviting me to talk to them about rectifying the situation.

My heart began to race and I broke into a sweat. How could this have come about? I'd had a comfortable amount in there when I moved here. True, I hadn't been very diligent about my finances and had left Janet to sort out the household budget. A statement was enclosed. I looked down it, not wanting to face the truth. I'd never had to bother with things like that in the past. The men took care that sort of thing. The household expenses were considerable. I normally liked to eat well, and drink good wines, and here it was in cold black and white, quietly mounting up. But things like insurances, Janet's wages all mounted up during the months, as did my little extravagances such as my dresses, the pictures, the party.

I relaxed a little. I hadn't paid in nearly one hundred pounds for the London venture, which still lay in cash in my room. That would see me through for a while, but I reflected wouldn't keep me going for ever. But how was I to earn a living? Janet had been brutal, but quite right. I had no real talent or training. In fact, the only thing that had seen me marry into money or earn any was that precious little hole between my legs.

Curiously, my very real money worries spurred me back into life. I was forced to sit down and confront them. I needed to cut back on my expenses for a while. In a sense, it was fortuitous that Janet was going, that would save a wage if I coped for myself. After all, Izzy did, Charles did, in fact all *les Mouettes* did. It would do me good, I decided. I could reduce the food and wine bills. No more new dresses, or at least, fewer. I even contemplated selling the house and moving somewhere considerably cheaper, but that would be a last resort.

All that was on the debit side. Was there a way to earn some regular money? Well, yes there was. The same enjoyable way I'd been earning it over these last months. I needed to see Peregrine again to talk about getting some more work, as well as buying some more tonic.

Later that afternoon, Janet returned from Charles' studio, or wherever it was she'd been. I heard her let herself in, and the kitchen clatter. I stood at the top of the stairs, frightened to go down. I told myself not to be so ridiculous, but still had to go and take a small amount of the tonic to do so. Janet, to my surprise, was quite friendly and chatty about the progress she'd been making. Charles, too, it seemed was much recovered, but was still anxious to see me. For the first time since London, we ate companionably together. She could stay on, she said, until I'd found a replacement maid, and even volunteered to find one, but then I told her of my financial difficulties, and told her I needed to dispense with the services of a maid in future.

"Are you sure?" she asked. "Could you cope in a place this size?"

"Why not? I'm sure I could learn to cook."

"And wash and scrub pots and clean and polish and lay fires and order groceries and meat and drink and keep accounts?"

I hadn't really considered all these. Funny, I thought, I'd assumed they just happened.

"Either you get another maid, or you move somewhere smaller and stop trying to be a lady. This place is beautiful, but in winter it'll be full of soot and smuts. More cleaning and more laundry in the cold dark mornings."

"If I decide to move somewhere smaller, would you stay on here until I move, and teach me?"

"That depends. I've signed the papers for the shop, and I want to be open while the crowds are still here."

"Two weeks?"

"That wouldn't be a problem. No more than that, mind."

I would have asked her into my bed that night, as it had been so nice to be friends again, but I sensed that neither of us relished the idea particularly. We shared some wine and smoked a cigarette, until we kissed and went our ways. I took up another bottle of wine and drank it with another application of tonic and thought. The idea of somewhere new, smaller and manageable grew more appetising the more I thought about it. I wanted to be a 'sleeves rolled up' person like Izzy, and if I sold this place, then there would be a lot of capital released to keep me comfortable.

The next morning, I woke with a feeling of being on top of my destiny. I got rid of the after effects of the wine with a little more tonic, and tackled what needed doing. I banked the cash, I put the house up for sale, and made enquiries about other properties. I wrote letters to

Izzy, apologising for my absence and promising to call in the next day or so, and accepting Margaret's invitation. I told Janet that I would accompany her to see Charles the next morning. Later, when dark doubts set in, I took the last of the cocaine, then felt sure I'd done the right thing.

The pressing thing was to see Peregrine, and I called round that afternoon. He seemed a little distracted, but listened to my tale nevertheless. Dear Peregrine, I felt he was the one who knew me best and who I could trust with my dilemmas. He listened, making small sympathetic noises.

"It seems to me," he said, "you need have no worries. I can find you work in London, although the capital is always hungry for new sensations and new performers, but I think I can guarantee you at least another week's work, perhaps with Dougal or on your own. Also consider this: there is a large local market…"

"Are you suggesting that I flaunt myself in a small town like this? Like a common prostitute?"

"No, no, no! Not at all. I'm simply suggesting that there are local gentlemen in need of female companionship, that's all. Prostitution is such an ugly word, and I would never be a party to such a thing."

"Then what are you suggesting?"

"Consider this. How many men here want a female companion just to be seen with and talk to? So many single gentlemen, and not a few husbands. You are educated, and delightful company, if I may say so. You would just have to eat and drink at their expense and inflate their wilted egos. You would be their partner for formal occasions — beautiful, witty and charming. Anything else would be up to you. I would have to charge an introducing fee, of course, just to cover my time and costs. You are known to be quite young and still single. What more natural than you should be seen in good restaurants with similarly desirable gentlemen suitors?"

The idea was appealing, and sounded more tempting than the crude offerings in the London clubs. It was agreed, the clients would pay one pound, and we would take half each. Any further charges I might make for additional services would be up to me. We shook hands on it. I bought some more tonic from him, and left.

That, at least, had secured an income of sorts. I went back to the house and took a little of the cocaine before looking at my portrait. I was the haughty one again, gripping the serpent and in control once more.

I spent another week in London, and I rather wish I hadn't. The accommodation made the previous hotel look like luxury. It was a seedy room in Soho, and the remainder of the rooms were taken by prostitutes. I could hear the grunts and moans through the thin walls. The schedule was punishing, and, without Janet, I became one of those dull-eyed performers, taking off my clothes and going through the motions of arousal without feeling anything but contempt for myself and the men who were watching. Sometimes I performed with Dougal, who managed to do the job with complete professional detachment, yet still look as though he enjoyed our sexual acrobatics. I had to admire that, for I had completely lost the feeling of control over the punters. My thoughts remained fixed on the money I was earning. Peregrine had established a large network of shady and probably illegal nightclubs, and the clientele was now certainly not confined to the rich and powerful any more. I was now just a grimy little slut performing in grimy little rooms to grimy little men in a vast grimy city. I was so glad when the week was over and I could return to the fresh air of Brighton.

Chapter 11

I lost no time in looking for another house. Property prices were plummeting, and I went to see a few quite suitable properties over the next few days, and put my house up for sale with few regrets. It was an unaffordable luxury, and empty without Janet. Happily, the house sold very quickly, although for less than I'd paid, but I'd settled on one in Edward Street, quite a way back from the promenade, but nicely anonymous, and a lot cosier. The next few weeks were spent in arranging removals and selling off my excess furniture.

In between, I went with Janet to see Charles. She was worried about him, she said, and when we got there, I could see why: he looked terrible. He face was haggard, and it seemed as though he couldn't look either Janet or myself in the eye.

"Dear Charles!" I tried to be cheerful. "I'm so pleased to see you again. I want to thank you for painting such an extraordinary picture. It is a work of genius. It quite unsettles me how uncannily you have caught so many aspects of me." I rattled on in this vein, and eventually caught his gaze.

"Thank you." He spoke slowly, as though his thoughts had come to a halt. "Glad you like it. Sorry… I'm not quite…"

He trailed off. Janet went up to him and put her arm round his waist and her head on his shoulder. They had obviously become good friends.

"Come on, Charles, come and sit down. There. I'll make us some tea, shall I?"

She was speaking to him like a mother trying to comfort her child, but there was an edge of desperation in her voice and she was near to tears. She bustled off into the little kitchen, and I sat down next to him.

"I hate to see you like this, Charles. It's really bad, isn't it? Really dark where you are now?"

He suddenly gave a disconcerting laugh which made me jump. When he spoke, it was as though another being was speaking through his mouth.

"Not… dark… enough… I… see… everything… shine… pain… much."

He was suffering from a tormenting madness, it was plain. I wondered if he might benefit from a little of my cocaine, which I had taken to carrying with me, but decided it might be risky. I felt a little scared. Janet came back with the tea things. We sipped our tea and tried to coax Charles into drinking some, but he wouldn't.

"We have to do something," I told Janet. "We can't leave him like this."

"But what? I don't know what to do!" It was the first time I had ever seen her out of her depth.

"Perhaps we should tell Tristan. Or Izzy. No, Louisa! Dr Martindale. She'll be able to help. We must send for her."

"But she'll have him in the asylum; we can't afford that and it would kill him."

"Well, we can look after him and she probably has some medicine that would help. We can watch him until this bad patch passes."

"All right then," Janet said. "Fetch her, and I'll stand watch here."

I took a cab to the Lewes Road dispensary, and asked if I might see Dr Martindale. She was away at a conference, the receptionist said, but would be back tomorrow morning. In the meantime, there was her apprentice, Dr Simkins.

I took a gamble. I trusted Louisa, and one night shouldn't make a difference. I gave the receptionist Charles' address and asked that she call as a matter of urgency as soon as she could the next morning. I called round to Izzy on the way back. She opened the door and said, "Why, hello, stranger," before I interrupted and told her about Charles.

"The damned fool!" she cried, and changed into outdoor clothes, and together we returned to the studio. I reckoned that Izzy had known Charles in similar states before, and might be able to advise us.

Janet had got Charles into his little bed, and was crooning over him, trying to comfort him, although I think it was more for her benefit. Izzy tried to speak to him, but couldn't connect with him, he was in a trance-like state. The three of us sat looking at him, helpless. Izzy, bless her, was the more decisive one.

"There's no point in us all sitting round gawping," she said. "Someone needs to stay with him until Louisa gets here in the morning. I've seen him withdrawn and a bit disjointed in the past, but nothing like this. Let's see, it's five o' clock, someone should sit with him until ten, then someone else take over the night watch until six tomorrow morning, and the last one come and stay until the doctor gets here."

We agreed that Janet would take the first watch, I the second, and Izzy would come in the morning to await Louisa. Thus agreed, Izzy and I left Janet to it and went to eat at a nearby restaurant. We talked about Charles' sad state. She had known him for some years, and they all knew and understood his lapses into black depressions, but apparently these had been slowly worsening, and this was on quite another scale. She gently upbraided me for not getting in touch sooner, and I lied my way out of it by telling her that I had been catching up with London acquaintances, and been much distracted by a search for new premises. I told her about Janet's leaving and my decision to dispense with a maid and live like her, independent in somewhere small and manageable. She was heartily in agreement, although, she said, *les Mouettes* would miss my fine house. We finished the meal and I had another bottle of wine while we talked of her book and how much Janet had contributed, of some new ideas and movements from the continent, and what the other members of the group had been doing. I paid the bill, although with a mental image of it appearing on my statement of account in impersonal figures, and went back to her rooms.

We sat together in her study, and kissed. I wanted to make love to her, although the image of Charles in that state rather hindered us both, I think, but as we continued to kiss and fondle, the old embers burst into flame again. We went into her bedroom, undressed each other, then sat on the edge of her bed. I kissed her breasts, sucking her nipples into hard bullets while my hand stroked and kneaded the lovely pale flesh of her inner thighs. I sunk to my knees between them and coaxed out her juices with my tongue while she clamped my head firmly against her opening. As she moaned, I lapped up the salty discharge, until she collapsed back on the bed, shouting my name. I lay beside her while she worked on me with her fingers inside me and her tongue licking me until I too cried out in joy and we curled up closely in her cramped bed, contented.

The next thing I knew, she was shaking me awake. It was time for me to go and take over from Janet. I dressed, kissed Izzy passionately, borrowed a bottle of wine from her, and hailed a cab. When I got to the studio, Janet seemed very glad to see me. Charles had just laid inert, staring with unfocussed eyes, for much of the time, but sometimes he would become agitated, leaping from his bed and pacing the studio, thumping his fists against the wall and quite beyond her powers to restrain him. She'd been through his effects, and removed any sharp objects like cutlery. At the moment he was quiet and back on the bed. Janet offered to stay with me, and I was tempted, as the thought of being left alone with him in this condition filled me with some apprehension. But if she could do it…

"No, I'll be fine, don't worry. I've left the cab waiting outside and paid the fare back, so go and get some sleep. I'll see you tomorrow." She turned to go, then came back and kissed me on my lips as she hadn't done for a long time. I stroked her cheek. "Thank you, Janet. Friends?"

She looked at the floor, then into my eyes. "Best friends." Another peck on the lips and she was gone.

I looked at Charles: he was curled up facing the wall, dressed in a loose shirt and his long underwear, and making small cries from time to time. I found a glass and opened the wine, then sat on the chair beside his bed, sipping and thinking. My life was certainly changing, and perhaps quicker than I'd have wished, but hadn't I made drastic efforts to rid myself of my previous stultifying life, and vowed to cast myself on the sea of life and go where the waves took me? Even to sitting beside the bed of a mad genius? I refilled my glass, then dived into my bag and took a little cocaine. By now I had discovered that the best effects were to be obtained by inhaling it through a straw into one nostril. My gums had become rather sore and ulcerated. I divided up some of the powder into two thin lines on one of his plates, and inhaled them. These days, it only took a few minutes to feel the familiar racing of the pulse, and that wonderful rush of confidence and the obliteration of all doubt. I got up and started to wander the studio, looking at the finished and uncompleted canvasses propped up against the walls and in racks. It was a priceless treasure hoard. The man just painted because he had to. He didn't care if they sold or not. Under the influence of the cocaine, I began to understand more about him. His painting was just a way of expressing the nightmare of his all-encompassing vision.

As I was looking at one of his paintings, I felt a hand on my shoulder, screamed and turned round. Charles had risen, removed his clothes and come over to me, naked. His eyes still stared into some nightmare world.

"Charles?" I asked. A bit stupidly, really. He didn't respond, but ran his hands over my neck and shoulders, then my face, like a blind man trying to make contact with reality. He stroked my face again and again, while the panic grew.

"Yes, Charles, it's your Cordelia. You know me, don't you? I'll make it better for you."

I carried on in this vein until I thought he almost recognised me. He abruptly turned around and began to punch the wall with his bare fists. Hard, so hard that the skin on his knuckles tore and his blood was running down the walls. I heard myself wailing while he hit first one side of his head against the wall, then the other until his temples too were raw and bleeding. He sank to the floor and didn't move. I didn't know what to do: I tried to lift him but he was a dead weight and I was sobbing as I failed to move him. I went to get a pillow and a blanket from his bed to cover him, but he was up again, and thankfully returned to his bed with very little guidance from me, and settled down again. I washed some of the blood off his hands and face, then took a large gulp of wine and took another line of cocaine. My hands were shaking as I did.

He seemed to sleep for a while, and after some time, I felt my own eyes getting heavy. I was jolted alert sometime after by his voice, crying out in the most hideous way, like a man going through all the circles of hell. I flatter myself that I am not a soft or sentimental creature, but his cries were unbearable. I took some more tonic and finished the wine, to blot it out. He was hardly conscious, but in some other world. As the cocaine took hold, it dawned on me that the stuff gave me so much relief that it should have the same effect on

Charles. Anything to ease his torment. I took a sizeable dose and, lifting his upper lip, rubbed it into his gum, then some more, and more again.

After a while, he seemed to wake. He swung himself round to sit on the side of the bed, shook his head and looked at me.

"Cordelia?"

"Yes, my love, I'm here."

"Are you real?"

"Oh, yes, Charles. You see, it'll be all right. Forget the dreams, I'm here."

He stood up, almost exultant. He stood before me, then tore my dress off with a startling force. My underclothes likewise he ripped off, until we both stood facing each other, naked. I saw his erection bobbing up and down hungrily. He grabbed me very roughly and threw me on the floor. He turned me until my bottom was in the air and he took me up the back way. The pain made me shout out, but he kept pounding at me until he shouted loudly and I felt the spit of his semen inside me. He pulled out, then grabbed my hair and dragged me to the studio to look at the picture on the easel which had been obscured by a sheet. He tore it off, and forced my head up to look at it. I recognised the two subjects: Janet and I lying naked on the bed side by side, but not touching. It nearly made me sick to look at it. An art study at first glance, but it spoke of the futility of love, and of life itself.

"It's — powerful," I said. "You are a genius, Charles. I understand what you're trying to say."

"No, you don't!" he cried. "Nobody will ever know, but I give you one last painting that you will understand in time."

He still had me grasped painfully by the hair, pulling my head back from behind. I saw to my horror that on the shelf of the easel was a pallet knife — one of those diamond shaped ones to smear the paint onto the canvas. Before I could move, he'd grabbed it, and held it at my throat for a moment before plunging it with great force into his own throat. I whirled round to see him repeatedly plunging the knife into his throat as his blood spurted over me. I sank with him to the floor, trying to tear the knife out of his hands, but it was too late. After some seconds, he was dead. I lay on the floor with his corpse in my lap, wailing at the loss of the one man I had really respected and a friend.

I don't know how long I sat there, crying. These were the only genuine tears I'd ever shed, or would do. The grey light of a new day came, and Izzy with it. She had let herself in, and her voice was a shock.

"Jesus Christ! What's happened?"

I explained as best I could the events of the night (omitting the cocaine) while I cradled him. My whole front was covered in his blood, now drying and cracking off. Izzy was in tears as she stroked his dead body. I kept saying, "It wasn't my fault!" like a child caught with a broken ornament. I dressed, while Izzy stood beside him, frowning. We decided to go back to my house, and tell Janet.

She was up and about, and took the news very badly. I saw just how deep an affinity she had with him, and thought his suicide was going to cast a long shadow over all of us. I washed, and we breakfasted. Then I went to inform the police, Izzy to let Louisa know, and Janet to tell Tristan, who would contact the rest of the group.

He was duly removed to the mortuary. The three of us were questioned by the police, who seemed satisfied with our explanations, although you can never tell with them. I think they still had lingering suspicions that I might have killed him. My fingerprints were on the handle of the knife from when I'd tried to wrest it from him, but the inquest absolved me. Only I secretly wondered if the cocaine had had anything to do with it, and wonder still to this day. I have looked at my portrait often, and it's there, concealed from all but mine and Charles' eyes. Guilt.

Charles' funeral was well attended, by all *Mouettes,* contacts in the art world, by quite a large family presence. I don't know why, but I was a little surprised to find he had a family. How close we can be to someone, knowing them intimately and yet not know anything about them. Tristan gave an excellent eulogy, while Izzy, Janet and I wept throughout, like the three queens on King Arthur's barge. We had all loved the man, and his death was proved to be a turning point. Over the months to come, the group drifted apart; our confident lust for life overshadowed and turned grey.

I moved house shortly afterwards, saying a tearful good-bye to Janet, who had fitted out her shop with great flair and style. She had one of Charles' paintings on the wall behind the counter, and some of her designs framed on the other walls. There was a large stock room, and a sewing room, where three women were employed making up her dresses and embroidering them.

My new house was humbler than I had ever been used to, a small terraced house with a small garden, and for a few days I felt wretched there, and sat among the packing cases, too downhearted to do anything. I ate out at various cafés, and took far more tonic and wine than I should, often stumbling over the boxes and cursing. The painful blisters on my privates reappeared. Izzy announced that she would call round, and that galvanised me into action. I didn't want her to see me in this state of squalor. So, with the help of the powders, I unpacked the boxes, and arranged my belongings as best I could. I hired a man to put up the pictures, bought some flowers, arranged the books and went on a little spree for some ornaments more suited to the place. It looked better, but still rather drab after my previous house.

Still, Izzy wasn't one for decor, and she seemed to approve. We talked at length about Charles and *les Mouettes,* and both agreed that it shouldn't — couldn't

— continue as it had. The town still needed a nucleus for the arts, although, she pointed out, we had been inward looking and indulging ourselves for our own pleasure. We weren't known locally as anything other than a hedonistic group of inflated egos, with just cause. As we talked, we persuaded ourselves that we wanted the town to be a focus for art and new ideas, and that meant looking outwards, not inwards, attracting artists to the town, and giving the working classes the opportunity to shine, like Janet. We started scrawling the ideas down on some paper, and they flooded out: a Charles Morgan art gallery, perhaps an orchestra, a writers' group. I felt revitalised. There was no shortage of rich potential patrons in Brighton, if they could be persuaded that our ideas were sound, and we were determined enough to make these things happen.

I'd done my best to cook us a meal. My lack of any culinary skill and the length of time we talked made the results inedible, so we laughed, and went out to eat to discuss how we should make a start. I wanted to make love to her, but the blisters were at their painful worst. We parted. She would write a manifesto, while I would spread the word around.

That Sunday, Janet called to see me. It was the first opportunity she'd had after opening the shop and a very successful first week. She certainly looked tired, and admitted it had been hard. She had been devastated but Charles' suicide and opening the shop had been exhausting, but sure that she'd gauged the public taste correctly, and her sales had been twice what she'd predicted. I showed her round my little house, while she nodded at each room, but refrained from commenting until I served her some tea.

"Don't take this the wrong way, and you've done a good job, but this old decoration is so depressing. Why don't you have it done up a bit, eh? Make it fresh and yours."

"What do you suggest?"

"Think of a room you've really loved to be in. Go on."

I thought. Then I knew. "Charles' studio."

"That's what I wanted you to say. Let's paint it white and let the light in!"

"White? Are you sure?"

"Come here…"

And we kissed, tentatively at first, then with a hunger we hadn't felt for some time. We went upstairs, undressed and lay beneath the blankets to explore our bodies once again. I ran my hands over her shoulders, breasts, belly and thighs, while she did the same to me. I knelt beside her and rubbed my breasts up and down her body, then dangled them over her mouth for her to suck, while I worked my fingers inside her. She tried to do the same for me, but I had to push her away.

"Sorry, it hurts down there just now."

She dived under the bedclothes and emerged after I could feel her fingers parting my lips. "You've got the cunt-pox! A souvenir from London, I'll bet. Well, I don't want it!" So we just stroked and cuddled. It was too bad: I had been starved of gratification for weeks now, and needed attending to. But there was something missing now, as there had been with Izzy. Perhaps too much repetition? I don't know. Sexual intercourse had become somehow mechanical and predictable. While we lay back afterwards, I thought back on the giddy days of our relationship and felt sad.

She arranged for some decorators to come round and in a few days the transformation was complete. It felt so much better, and I had my pictures rehung, my shelves restocked and the ornaments replaced. The effect was breathtaking, and armed with a purpose, and pleasing surroundings, I felt very much better.

I still needed more supplies of cocaine though, and called upon Peregrine. He supplied me with two more packets, announcing with regret that he had to increase his prices somewhat, as supplies had been harder and more costly to secure. He kept the same tone of regret as he expressed sorrow at Charles' death, and my need to move to inferior premises. He was also sorry, he said, that he'd only been able to secure five appointments so far for my professional services as a gentleman's companion. I was surprised that there were even five such trysts arranged. I'd rather forgotten about that aspect of my life, but welcomed the new experience, and, who knows, I might find a rich patron for our art centre idea?

He handed me a list of the five names with times and dates. I was to meet them outside his studio and they would escort me to whatever function I was required to attend. I would proceed from there. The first client was in two days' time, at six o'clock. A Mr Percy Oliphant. I pressed him for more details? Where were we going? Was he rich? What were his requirements? Peregrine just smiled and shrugged.

"That's for you to find out—"

"All right."

"—and charge accordingly. Don't undersell yourself, that's my advice. My clients are well off. He will pay you the agreed rate for the consort service, and you will pay half to me. I shall be keeping a tally, of course. Anything else, as I've said, is up to you. Now, I have arranged a further week for you in my clubs in London. I have approached Janet, but she, sadly, is adamant that she will not repeat the experience as she is now running her own business, and I congratulate her on that. A pity though, she was a natural performer, and most attractive. This time you will perform with Dougal and another girl called Elsie I have secured."

Suddenly, I wished this would all go away. I wanted to do "Good Works" as Margaret would say and make the town a vibrant arts venue. But I needed the money, and yes, I admit, the excitement. Peregrine pushed another contract under my nose, and I signed it. He'd always played fair; I trusted him.

Chapter 12

My meeting with the first client, this Percy Oliphant, was not as successful as I'd hoped it might be. He was a gangly, slack jawed man of around thirty, and rather shabbily dressed. I noticed the dirt under his fingernails and tried to hide my distaste. He simply wished to be seen in a decent restaurant with an attractive woman. He lived with his mother and worked as a clerk. I suggested we went to a medium-priced restaurant I knew of. I didn't want to be seen with him in any of my usual haunts. I took his arm, trying to be the perfect escort as I could imagine Peregrine didn't undercharge for my services, and I guessed that Mr Oliphant had had to save up for the evening. The dinner was hard work: his life was not something that lent itself to much discussion, nor was he much of a conversationalist. I worked hard to keep up a flow of small talk and gaze adoringly at him, probing him for any hint of something which might excite or interest him. There was nothing. I felt sorry for him, unblessed by any talent or personality. A life with no ambition or hope.

We struggled through the meal. I couldn't tell whether he was enjoying it or not. I wanted to get away and go home, but laid on the flannel as much as I could.

"What a lovely evening, Percy. It's been enchanting, thank you, and what a stir you made in the restaurant."

"No, I didn't," he said. "I'm boring, and I'm sorry. You've been very good to me." He smiled a rueful smile. "I'll never do anything, or be anything, but tonight's been special for me."

I tried a sales pitch. "Then why stop the evening here? We could go back to my place, if you like."

"I'd like that. That's what I really wanted."

So I took him back to my house, and up to my bedroom. Suddenly, he started talking, pouring out all his frustrations and yearnings.

"Why didn't you tell me earlier?" I asked.

"Why should it interest you? Why should anybody care?"

"Come here," I said. "Give me a cuddle. Ten bob extra, mind. I have to earn a living too."

So we hugged a bit, then I took my clothes off, undressed him, and laid him on my bed. His little prick stayed curled up, although I thrust my breasts at him and fingered his small pale slug. It didn't work. I stared at it, while he propped himself up and stared at it too, as I tried to coax it into some sort of life. It was not going to happen, so I settled for trying to please him by stroking it and rubbing myself against him. Eventually he pushed me away, got dressed, and paid me the fees for the night. I gave him back the ten shillings for 'extras', thinking that all the evening had achieved was to humiliate him more than the rest his life had done. He left, leaving me naked on the bed, and thinking what a painful world it was that we live in. How would the poor man feel after this night? Don't think about it, I told myself. It doesn't do to think. I took two lines of the blessed cocaine and tried to blot everything out, but I couldn't. I kept thinking about Charles, and seeing his torn throat and the blood everywhere.

I called on Janet at her shop. It was busy, and Janet herself was rather hurried. I asked how she was doing, and she waved at the ladies in the shop.

"See for yourself. I've done it, lovely, I've made it work! I've had to take on two more staff, and the way we're going I might have to take some larger premises. Now, do excuse me. it's rather busy. Have a look, and if there's anything you fancy, I'll give you a special rate." She winked and went to attend to another customer. I looked around the shop. She had done a wonderful job: the interior was quite unlike any other. The walls were painted cream, with panels of light blue which framed her designs. She had installed electric lights which emphasised the bright colours of the dresses. I noticed a padded velvet board on the counter on which were pinned rows of different coloured velvet chokers, some plain, some jewelled. I swallowed down the lump in my throat. There were so many gowns I liked, but some mean little creature inside me asked why I should be contributing to her success while my fortunes were dwindling so. I left the shop empty-handed, while Janet gave me a sideways look and a small nod.

I worked my way through more of the men on Peregrine's growing list over the next two weeks, taught myself some tricks, and earned myself a decent amount of money. None of them were the select and wealthy clients Peregrine had implied. I learned to read them, and play up to their requirements. Some were content with straight sex, while others…

Take Mr P, as I shall call him. It started with a night out at the opera, and a meal. He was educated and amusing, but perverted. I accompanied him back to his rooms and he fell on me, tearing at my clothes, then forcing my body into uncomfortable positions, and binding me with lengths of rope. He coiled the rope around my breast, making them jut out, unnaturally engorged. He tied my ankles to my wrists behind me, so that my private parts were fully exposed to him. He slapped my breasts and, rolling me over, slapped my buttocks with a wooden paddle. I cried out in genuine pain, which made him empty his bladder over me, before taking me roughly from behind. Then he rolled me over again, forcing his rod into my mouth, plunging it in and out until his jets of sperm filled my mouth. I tried to spit it out, but he clamped my mouth shut with powerful hands until I was obliged to swallow his discharge. His business being spent, he untied me and slipped two pounds into my hand. I dressed, and left the house, making sure he didn't see me sobbing.

I wanted out of all this, more than ever, and told Peregrine so quite forcefully, but he waved the contract in front of me, smiling as he told me I'd committed myself to providing this service.

"I have been to considerable trouble to arrange these trysts to our mutual advantage, and really wouldn't want to use force to enforce the contract, so please let us have no more talk of dishonouring our agreement. Your supply of tonic depends on it. Besides, you enjoy exerting your power over the men you meet, don't you?"

"I wouldn't call being trussed up and abused 'exerting my power' exactly."

"There will always be the occasional exception, and even then, they are more to be pitied than begrudged."

There was a ruthless side to Peregrine that I hadn't seen before, so I agreed to continue, and two or three times a week I would meet clients. Some of them didn't want the 'extras', and it could be a pleasurable and sociable evening. But most were after sex and wanted to miss the initial niceties of a meal or a trip to the theatre. Most just wanted me to lie down while they squeezed my breasts like motor car horns before a few thrusts in and out of me ended in a few grunts and a hasty retreat. Some returned for a second evening, but most, it was obvious, were stricken with guilt, and would be scuttling away to their frosty wives to widen the gulf between them still further with yet another secret.

What's more, intercourse was getting painful with the number of encounters I was having and after one particularly difficult encounter with a very thick cock and its overenthusiastic owner, I examined myself with a mirror and saw a few ulcers around the entrance to my honeypot. They ulcers themselves weren't painful, they must have come from some small tears that the man had inflicted, but I might have to shut off my favours until they had healed. There was also a thick and smelly discharge coming from me. Besides, I was also suffering from a nasty nasal drip and ulceration from the now almost incessant inhalation of my tonic. Luckily my habit was paid for by my escort earnings, but I was drinking more than ever. It was getting hard to juggle normal life with my more nocturnal pursuits, and without Janet's presence any more the days became unstructured, so that I would lie in my bed, more often than not soiled with the stains of the previous night and, to be honest, the stains of many previous nights. I fed myself as best I could, but more frequently ate out at nearby cafés.

When I looked at my portrait, as I often did, I saw a proud woman, self-confident and beautiful. My mirror told another tale. Without a servant to wash and iron my clothes, or style my hair, or feed me, I had become dowdy and unkempt, and my age was starting to show. My belly was getting fatter than was fashionable, and my ribcage starting to show though sagging flesh. My eyes, ringed by dark shadows, were dull and world-weary. My body, my greatest asset, was fast becoming worthless.

I needed to pull myself together, to break loose from my cocaine and alcohol cravings. I desperately wanted to break free from Peregrine's hold over me. I could see a good future, and dreamt of helping create a thriving arts scene in the town. I could be the catalyst, the one who pulled together the huge talent in the town and showed it to the world. I called on Tristan to talk about it. We met at a coffee house, where I earnestly explained my vision. He was amenable to the idea, and thought it was a worthy ambition and agreed that, yes, it might pull the group back together and yes, the group should be more outward looking and yes, if I could interest some rich sponsors in the idea of a centre for the arts, he was sure that the group would be the nucleus that would attract the true talent to make the town a focus for progressive arts…

"For God's sake, Tris," I shouted, my voice loud enough to create a silence in the café. "Stop just saying the right words. Listen to me, will you? I want something good to come out of all this mess."

"What mess?"

I stared at him. He'd no idea. I obviously had some more shouting to do, so I paid the bill and we walked back to my little house.

I tried to tell him about the effect Charles' death had wrought on our group, and me in particular, and how desperately I wanted something meaningful to come out of it, that we might all be reunited in the common goal of a centre for the arts.

It was apparent that he wasn't really interested and was blowed if he was going to lift a finger to help anyone else's artistic endeavours. He could see it as a stage to display his talents on, that was all. I wasn't going to get anywhere with him, but as I tearfully drew our conversation to a close, he leant over and started to stroke my breasts through the sateen of my dress. I sat passively, letting him. As he continued, some faint spark kindled into a flame, and I found myself responding to him. As he unbuttoned my dress I sat there, not really caring any more, but shrugged my dress off to let him fondle my bared breasts. I don't think he'd noticed that they were not what they were. I started to run my hands mechanically over his back, until he stood up and removed his clothes, stroking his cock while I numbly stripped out of my clothes. We tumbled back on the sofa as he slobbered over my breasts while I pulled at his prick, which was surprisingly unimpressive given his otherwise leonine appearance, but it was quite effective, as I'd found out before. He shafted me like he played the piano, forcefully, with a distinct lack of finesse. After an interminable time of grunting and shoving, he pulled out, stood up and, grasping my hair so that my face was turned up to him, emptied his ejaculate over my face. He patted me on the head like an approving parent, dressed, muttered a few words about keeping up the good work, and left.

I was to attend another *soirée* at Margaret and Philip's house. A good chance, perhaps, to interest some possible patrons to the idea of building a centre for the arts in Brighton. I was rather afraid to go, aware that my appearance had changed for the worse. I found a gown that would suffice, and laid it out. I heated the water for a bath and steeped myself thankfully in it for some time. I towelled myself dry and sprayed my privates with eau de cologne to disguise the smell of the discharge, then applied makeup quite thickly, producing a passable result. As the hour approached, I felt my anxiety growing, but quashed it down with too much cocaine and a lot of wine. So much, in fact, that when the cab called to take me there, I found it quite difficult to walk in a straight line. The evening was in full swing when I arrived: Margaret came up and greeted me warmly,

"Dear Cordelia, it seems an age since I saw you! I trust your house move went well." She stepped back as she saw me at closed quarters. "Are you quite well, my dear? You look a little weary."

I tried to say I was fine and just adjusting to my new surroundings, but the words didn't come out right. She raised her eyebrows.

"Well, make sure you look after yourself. Do go in and enjoy yourself; we'll catch up later."

The same old faces were all there, and a string quartet was playing in the background. I took a glass of champagne and wandered over to join Tristan, who was talking with Lavinia. They greeted me and I tried to make some small talk, but fell against Tristan. Tristan, the bastard, who would never ever give a damn about anyone but himself, and I told him so, loudly and in no uncertain terms. They propelled me to the wall and propped me up, then moved quickly away. I called out to them, asking where the hell they thought they were going. It came out as more of a shout than I'd intended, and the whole room went quiet. Everyone was staring at me. Why shouldn't they? I was beautiful. I was Cordelia Edwards. I gave everyone a smile and a wave, then tried to make my way to the drinks table for another glass, holding myself upright with the dignity of a duchess, but tripped and fell onto the glasses and bottles instead. I found I couldn't get up until some hands helped me up and propelled me out into the hall. Izzy appeared in front of me.

"Izzy!" I cried. "You're here! Where have you been, my darling?"

"Shut up!" She sat me down on the stairs and watched me as I was sick. I have little memory of being painfully bundled into a cab, of Izzy undressing me and putting me to bed.

I can't describe the morning. I felt terrible physically, but more mortified at the way I had completely disgraced myself the previous night. I daren't show my face in polite society again. I cried and spent the day in bed.

The day after I sent a very apologetic letter to Margaret and Philip, saying that my recent move had affected me emotionally and I was in a low state. Then I walked round to Izzy to apologise. She was angry, understandably, and hurried me into her study,

"Now what the hell's going on?" she demanded.

"Nothing!" But my tears betrayed me. I broke down and told her everything: Peregrine, the posing, the films, my habit, my escort work, my ulcers and blisters, everything.

If I thought she'd understand and sympathise, I was wrong. She was furious. Izzy was never one for hiding her true feelings.

"You stupid, stupid woman! You whore! How could you have been sucked into this? D'you know what? I'm ashamed to call you my friend. I work night and day to make this world a better place and you come along, corrupting everything, especially yourself. Stop this insane cocaine habit and come back to the real world, otherwise you'll be dead in a few months."

"I don't know how to! You've no idea how much I need it."

"So you resort to prostitution to pay for it? I wish I'd never met you. I loved you for a while, but now I'm repulsed. Our friendship has ended. You are just a cold-hearted thrill seeker who's got what was coming to her." She was crying, too. "You've betrayed me. You've betrayed all of us. You fucking whore."

"I'm sorry, Izzy." Was all I could say. She pulled herself together.

"Too late for that," she said briskly. "Just spread your legs and let me have a look at the damage."

I showed myself to her. She grimaced and stood up.

"I'm no doctor, but I think those are chancres. We need to get Louisa to see you."

"Chancres?"

"Syphilis ulcers. And you also seem to have other blisters there. It looks a bloody mess."

"Oh hell. Not syphilis, please."

"I said, I'm no doctor. We'll see what Louisa has to say. Now leave me alone and go home."

So I did, utterly broken. It was the wrong thing to do, but I consoled myself with an excess of wine and cocaine.

Louisa examined me the next day, rather unsympathetically, I thought, on her cream cotton examination couch at the dispensary. She shone a bright light at my cunt and fingered it roughly with rubber gloves. As I dressed, she said, "Izzy was right. Those ulcers are gummata."

"Sorry?"

"Gummata. The classical lesions of primary syphilis. Painless ulcers with a punched-out appearance. If we don't treat it, it will progress to the later stages, with skin rashes, ulcers, fevers, ultimately paralysis, insanity and death. Do you have any problems in passing your water?"

"Yes, it has been painful."

"And a green discharge, I see."

"Yes."

"Well, I can only congratulate you. You have managed to pick up syphilis, gonorrhoea and the pox. Your sexual habits are reprehensible."

"Can they be cured?"

"Your habits? I doubt it."

"No, the fucking pox and everything!"

"The pox, no, but it only causes intermittent pain and is trivial. The gonorrhoea we can treat with Protargol, a type of silver compound which we can instil into your vagina and urethra."

I know, I've had it before."

"That doesn't surprise me at all. The syphilis we must treat with mercury. A pity, there is a novel treatment I've read about in the journals. A chemist has developed an arsenical compound which appears to be much more effective, but it won't be available for a year or two, so we must rely on the mercury tablets, although I must warn you, they do have side effects."

"Such as?"

"Dribbling, mainly, but vomiting, diarrhoea, neurological effects, failure of the kidneys…"

"Then I don't think I'll bother."

"You have little option. The syphilis will disfigure and kill you."

So, my treatment started. Every day for a week I attended the dispensary to have silver douches into my vagina and to take a mercury tablet. Izzy was good enough to accompany me but said very little. Dr Martindale was quite right: they did have side effects. I dribbled incessantly and the effect on my bowels was drastic. I also had trouble walking and would stagger and bump into things. Much of my hair fell out, too. It became unbearable. I had to eke out the last reserves of cocaine to stop the hunger, for I could not eat.

I received a reply from Margaret and Philip. They were shocked and disappointed by my drunkenness and behaviour, and did not feel they could in all conscience receive me back into their house and society, and so on… So that was that.

My resentment towards Peregine grew into hatred. He had used me as a mere pawn in his growing pornographic empire. I had deluded myself that I had power over the men who ogled me, while all the while I was just an object of titillation, a woman debasing herself for their transient pleasure and cast aside when done with. He'd deluded me with his soft words. Well, he wouldn't be using me any more, that was for certain.

I received a message from him, stating his displeasure that I had failed to turn up to my appointments with his clients for two weeks, and would I please call on him to discuss the matter with some urgency. I wrote a reply with difficulty as my hands did not do as my brain wanted. Even writing in big capitals it was almost illegible. My dribble muddied the words as I tried to write them. It was almost a week now since the treatment had finished, but the side effects had not diminished, in fact they were getting worse.

With great difficulty I went to see him the next morning. Before I went, I took a last look at the portrait, which now mocked me as it captured my false pride. I looked at myself in the mirror at the creature I had become: emaciated, with sparse filthy hair, sunken flesh and a dress beyond all recognition. I crawled backwards down the stairs as I had been doing in order not to fall into the kitchen, then back into the hall and into the street. People were staring and crossing the street to avoid me. I looked at the autumn sun on the sea although when I did, I lost my footing and fell. There was quite a crowd gathering, pointing, but afraid to come near. Well, let them stare, I was beyond caring. They followed me as I half walked, half crawled along the front to the studio and hammered on the door. Peregrine opened it and I almost fell through it. He stared and swore.

"God, what's happened to you? What's the meaning of this?"

I feigned politeness. "I must apologise for letting your clients down, but you see, they have rather let me down by giving me a variety of diseases which I would rather not have, and the consequent treatment has so far been worse than you could possibly imagine. I have come to ask again to be excused from my duties as a common whore."

"There is no need to ask. No one would want to come within a hundred yards of you. Naturally, you cannot continue to work for me. Now will you please leave? You're stinking the place out."

"I will, but first I want the money you owe me. I have to pay for my treatment. I think twenty pounds will suffice."

He tutted and sighed. "Of course. I will pay you now, then go. Our association is ended."

"It certainly is," I growled.

I wasn't going to need his money, but I did need him to turn his back on me. He did, to take the money out of his safe. I crept up behind him, and when he turned round again, he came face to face with me. I had taken out the knife from my sleeve that I had taken from my kitchen and with all the force I could muster, stabbed at him. I had meant to aim for his throat, but with my uncoordinated movements only succeeded in stabbing him in the eye. He screamed and dropped the money. Another stab and this time I concentrated hard and opened up his jugular vein. As he fell to the floor, the dark blood poured out of his neck in a torrent and the severed vessels and windpipe opened up, just as my father's had done. His screams started to fade as he weakened, only to begin again as I carved my way through his trousers and began to hack away at that magnificent penis. My tremor made it a much cruder job that I had done before, but I managed to force it a long way down his throat before he died.

I sat down calmly on the couch, now covered in blood, while a group of men, alarmed at the screams, poured in through the door.

Chapter 13

I thought my story might be one worth telling, and I thank Izzy for having the good grace to forgive me and write it down for me during her visits to me here in Holloway and via my letters to her. She is the most understanding of women. There is no moral to be had and no purpose other than to tell the tale, as truthfully I may. I have been here for four months, awaiting my trial and the inevitable verdict. It is a frosty February morning. My remaining hair has been shaved off, but at least the grey prison gowns are clean. I still cannot walk straight; they will have to support me as I approach the gallows, and I hope it will not be taken for fear. The key turns in the lock. The executioners have come for me. I beg them ten minutes to write this, and they grant it.

One last hitch up of the gown and I stroke my cunny, closing my eyes and thinking of Janet while I do. My fingers tease my clitoris and push into my passage while I remember the days we spent in my bed with the sun streaming in through the slatted blinds. I shudder and moan, and my vulva weeps the last tears I will ever shed. The door opens and I hear the priest intoning some nonsense, while I think of the slot machine on Brighton pier…

Postscript (1920)

By Isobel Fallon

I have assembled this manuscript from my personal visits to Cordy and from the descriptive and detailed letters she has sent. She has been honest, and I have transcribed it all as told to me or written. It has been a painful experience for me, if the truth were known.

She was hanged, as she knew was inevitable, for the murders of Peregrine Pollitt and also one Nicholas Fairburn (by modus operandi and her own confession), and buried in an unmarked grave within the walls of Holloway Gaol. To be honest, I think she welcomed her fate. I have begun to understand what demons and conflicts lay below the surface, but still find her actions hard to forgive. Her portrait hangs in the gallery, and is much admired. Only I can see the truths underneath the rich colours.

The Mouettes drifted apart. The sobering deaths of two of our members in tragic circumstances changed our youthful confidence for ever. As a follower of European events, I saw the troubling tensions growing in the Balkan states and saw the great cloud approaching that rendered all the group's artistic endeavours completely irrelevant as the vilest of all wars engulfed us.

Tristan was called up and shot as a deserter in 1915.

Lavinia enrolled as a nurse and tried to describe her experiences in poems, but couldn't. Words weren't enough. She married a soldier who beat her to death, his mind unhinged by what he'd been through.

Both Margaret and Philip developed dementia over the course of the war and were placed in a nursing home. I still visit them from time to time, although they do not know me. I think the shock of the war turned their minds.

Now, after the most meaningless slaughter the world has ever seen, the world is a dull grey, despite the superficial levity of the age. Perhaps the rights of women and the working classes have taken a step forward — we shall see — but at a dreadful cost. How quickly the children of the war forget, though. They dance and listen to American jazz and lead such self-indulgent lives, while the poor are still the poor and now I know, always will be.

Janet and I live happily together, and her business, is more than thriving. Her wealth allows me to indulge myself in writing second class novels. Idealism never lasts.